BEAUTIFUL PIECES  BOOK TWO

Erik's REDEMPTION

NYSSA KATHRYN

An NW Partners Book
Cover by Deranged Doctor Design
Developmentally and Copy Edited by Kelli Collins
Line Edited by Jessica Snyder
Proofread by Amanda Cuff and Jen Katemi
Cover Photography by Andrey Bahia at Wander Book Club

 Created with Vellum

The difference between delight and devastation...a single moment.

Until recently, Hannah Jacobs thought she was living. One look at her new neighbor, and she knows she was simply surviving. Going through her days hiding behind a mask, similar to the broken man next door. Together, they slowly realize they want more...happiness, love, a future. And for a fleeting moment, Hannah thought they were well on their way.

Until Erik began to backslide...

Angry. Damaged. Resigned. Erik Hunter didn't believe himself worthy of anyone's time or attention. Until Hannah. She became his light in the dark. His angel. Offering salvation where once there were only shattered pieces of a weary soul. But just when he thinks he can have it all, he learns something that threatens their fragile union.

Her will indomitable, Hannah is determined to preserve the life they're building. But Erik is equally resolute. He'll do anything to protect the woman he's coming to love—even from himself.

Erik and Hannah's love story continues where it left off in Erik's Salvation. I recommend starting with that story first, to fully enjoy the serial. Their story concludes in book three, Erik's Refuge.

ACKNOWLEDGMENTS

Thank you to my beautiful book team who edit and proofread my work, making sure it's the best quality possible – Kelli, Jessica, Amanda and Jen, you guys are amazing.

Thank you to my ARC team who read my words first and fill me with confidence to release my work into the world.

Thank you to my readers, you are the reason the next gets written.

And thank you to my husband and daughter. Will and Sophia, you are my joy. You are my heart. And you are the reason I can do what I love.

PROLOGUE

*E*veryone will break at some point. Their pieces will pull apart like little fragments of destruction. The tragedy will cause damage for the world to see and make one wonder if they'll ever be whole again.

But after the shatter comes a choice, and that choice will decide everything—set the pieces back together or remain broken.

Choose restoration. Because there's a beauty in survival and the strength that comes from it.

No scar is ugly. Because each one is a sign of those who choose life.

CHAPTER 1

"So he just left?"

Hannah swallowed as she wrapped her fingers around her lavender oat milk latte. This drink had become the highlight of her day. Heck, it had pretty much been the highlight of every day for the last month.

She took a breath before finally looking across the booth at her friends and answering Henry's question. "Yeah. At some point in the middle of last night, he left. Just like the night before. And just like the night before that. He comes to bed late and leaves before I wake up. He's avoiding me and I have no idea why."

Pain lanced across her chest, twisting her insides. The words hurt even more out loud than they did in her head. And there wasn't just pain, there was panic. Panic that she'd come to love Erik, *rely* on him, and maybe this was it. Maybe this was their relationship fizzling out.

Brigid reached across the table and covered her hand. "Hey. I can see what you're thinking. Stop. He loves you. And I'm not saying that because of the ridiculous amount of money he's spent on your car or your Apple watch or your type 1 devices. I say it because of the way he *looks* at you, like the very thought of being apart destroys something inside him."

"I want that to be true, but since my twenty-fourth birthday, I barely see him, and that's his doing. He's just been…off."

So for a month, she'd lived with a man, slept with a man, she hardly saw. A man who maybe even regretted committing to her.

Her chest squeezed.

"No. Don't do that."

Her gaze flew up at Henry's words. "Don't do what?" Were her friends mind readers?

"Assume he doesn't love you. That you're some kind of mistake. You're not." Henry leaned forward. "The man is obsessed with you."

"Then why did things change?"

Tears pricked at her eyes, and she desperately blinked them away. Crying didn't solve anything. She hadn't shed a single tear since things had shifted between her and Erik. This entire time, she'd kept the hope that things would go back to how they were.

"Han." Brigid's fingers tightened around her hand. "Talk to him."

"I've tried. He's so closed off and gives me these half answers. I don't know what to do anymore." She sucked in a deep, settling breath. She needed to calm down because stress always made her blood sugars go crazy. "Talk to me about something else. Take my mind off things. Henry, how's this new guy in your life, and when do we get to meet him?"

Henry had met someone in a bar a few weeks ago and hadn't been able to stop talking about him since.

A slow smile quirked Henry's mouth. "Well, I gave him a key to my town house."

Brigid reared back and gasped. "What? When?"

"Last night."

Hannah shook her head. "Wait, how long have you two been dating?"

"If we count it from the night we met, which we probably should, then fifteen days."

Hannah opened and closed her mouth. She didn't have words. Henry's relationships were the definition of slow burn. He'd once dumped a boyfriend because the poor guy had given him a key to his place after *six months* of dating.

"You must really like him," she finally said, and took a sip of her latte.

"I do."

An emotion she couldn't quite identify crossed Brigid's face. It came and went quickly. A small drop of the lips. A tugging together of the brows.

Hannah's fingers tightened around the mug, concern pulling at her chest. "That's great, Henry. And are you doing okay, Brigid?"

Her best friend's gaze swung to Hannah, and a smile that was both too wide and didn't reach her eyes stretched across her face. "Yes. The shop's been busy, and I've been redecorating my apartment. Life's good."

Was it though? Since everything that happened with James, Brigid's ex, there had been moments where Hannah caught deep sadness slipping into her friend's eyes, taking out all her shine. She was pretty sure Brigid thought no one saw...but Hannah did.

"Still loving the new glucose monitor and insulin pump?" Brigid asked, clearly trying to change the subject and get the attention off her.

Hannah touched the Dexcom on the back of her arm. Her pump sat on the right side of her stomach. "It makes my life easier. I don't have to test so much. There aren't as many lows and highs. And the Dexcom streams the data straight to my Apple watch, which is handy."

The watch was another gift Erik had insisted she accept. She tapped the screen, reading her sugar level in the bottom left-hand corner. The watch even vibrated when she was high or low. So, yeah, her insulin levels were easier to manage.

Henry frowned. "But…"

Of course, he knew there was a but. She lifted a shoulder. "He gave me the monitor and pump on my birthday, and…I don't know. Everything from then on feels…tainted." She sighed and checked the time on her watch. "I have to go. I have a two o'clock appointment at work."

She was about to stand when Henry reached across the table and wrapped his fingers around her wrist. "Hey. Remember what we said. He loves you. Don't do anything drastic."

Drastic as in…moving back into her place? It was something she'd been thinking about recently. Because maybe she'd moved in with him too quickly. Maybe that had scared him.

Argh. She had no idea what the problem was.

She plastered a smile to her face. "See you both later."

Henry rolled his eyes because, yeah, she'd made no promises, while Brigid gave her a small smile.

Outside the coffee shop, cold air brushed her cheeks. Tugging her jacket tighter, she headed down the street toward her office. Her fingers twitched to pull out her phone and text Erik. To check in on him. Push until he shifted back to the man who loved her easily. Laughed with her.

God, she loved him so much. Her heart *ached* when they were apart. But lately, her heart ached when they were together too. Because the way he looked at her…it was almost as if he was in pain.

She was halfway down the street when she felt it—eyes on her. The fine hairs on her arms stood on end, and she almost stopped. What was that?

Discreetly, she turned her head to glance around. A couple of people walked along the sidewalk. A few cars moved down the street, and some were parked in front of businesses. But there was no one she could see who was just looking at her.

She shook her head, barely suppressing a shudder. She'd gotten the same feeling more than once in the last couple weeks, and every time, it creeped her out.

It had to be because of everything that had happened with James, Marco, and Angelo, right? Maybe everything she'd endured a couple months ago had freaked her out to the point she couldn't even walk down the street without feeling scared.

Gritting her teeth, she moved faster.

She was just nearing the office when her gaze brushed over the Genesis G70. *Her* Genesis G70. Because that had been her Christmas present from Erik.

He'd claimed it was a safety thing. That she needed a reliable car that wouldn't break down. And yes, her red Honda was old. But honestly, the G70 was just so…flashy. It wasn't her. Since Erik had been acting strange, she just kind of wanted to drive her old car again. She still had it at her house, so she *could…*

She slipped into the office and was so in her own head that she walked straight into a big chest, almost falling backward. *Would* have fallen back if strong fingers didn't wrap around her upper arm and straighten her.

She looked up, straight into a set of bright green eyes. "Oh God, Leo, I'm sorry! I wasn't looking where I was going."

The new real estate agent gave her an easy smile, one perfect dimple showing. "It's okay. Although, I like to think I'm pretty noticeable."

She laughed. Leo had been hired to replace James, and he was a great addition to the office. Friendly. Charming. And if you asked Taylor, the other selling agent here, she'd tell you he was pretty easy to look at, with his sandy-blond hair and dimples.

And yeah, he wasn't bad to look at. He just wasn't her type.

"You are. If I hadn't been so far in my own head, I would have seen you." Heck, the man was at least six-two—there was no missing him.

"Everything okay?"

His voice was quiet and gentle. And a little part of her almost wanted to say no. To tell him exactly how not okay she was. But then she gave herself an internal shake. She barely knew the man. He did *not* need to know about the mess that was her relationship.

"Of course."

He continued to hold her gaze for another beat, almost like he was assessing whether he believed her. She wanted to squirm under the scrutiny.

Finally, he nodded, releasing her arm. "Good. Well, I'm off to a client meeting. I'm ready to put my charming, you-need-me-to-sell-your-house smile on."

She scoffed. "With those dimples, how would anyone turn you down?"

If possible, his smile widened. "I'm counting on it." He brushed past her, grazing her side as he stepped outside.

On her way down the hall, Hannah passed Taylor, who sighed. "Isn't he gorgeous?"

"I hear he's single."

Taylor scoffed as she walked toward the kitchen. "Yeah right."

Hannah laughed as she entered her office, then sat behind the desk.

Work was her escape lately. And fortunately, it had been busy. She'd had so many houses to sell, it was sucking up all her time. Weekdays. Weekends. Even evenings.

Usually, she took her work home with her—with the hope that she wouldn't have time to actually do it. That things between her and Erik would shift back to what they were, and they'd spend the evening together.

But that never happened. She'd usually return home to a note on the kitchen counter telling her that he was working a job. Or helping someone in the family. Or, the most common one, boxing.

Her Omnipod beeped at her, signaling it was almost out of

insulin. Not only that, but her Dexcom sensor had almost expired. They rarely needed changing at the same time. The pump lasted three days, whereas the Dexcom lasted ten.

She opened her second drawer and pulled out a new sensor and sticker. She'd found this great company called Lukas' Part Time Pancreas, which sold a bunch of colorful Dexcom stickers to place over transmitters. Today's sticker was an insulin vial with flowers. It brightened her day just a little every time she looked at the stickers.

Carefully, she peeled her old Dexcom off her arm, cleaned her transmitter, and pulled off the old sticker to replace it.

Using an alcohol wipe, she swabbed her other arm before taking the new Dexcom out of the packet and pulling off the stickers on the back. She pressed it to her arm and took off the safety piece. With a quick breath, she pressed the orange circle to click it into place.

The jolt of pain came and went quickly as she clicked in her transmitter. Her final step was putting a patch over the Dexcom to keep it more secure.

When she looked at her pump, she groaned. While she loved her new Dexcom, she'd found a lot of aspects of the pump harder to adjust to. First of all, it beeped at her...a lot. It was also bulky, and she always had to remember to take her PDM with her, which of course she often forgot, which in turn meant she had to inject. Then there were also the rashes she'd started getting from the adhesive.

The pump was good but also a lot to deal with.

She should change her pump now, but honestly, she was tired. So instead, she peeled it off. She'd just inject until she put on a new one.

With a sigh, she finally gave up and lifted her phone to text Erik.

Hannah: I'm going to stay and work late tonight. Don't wait up.

The second she hit send, she scrunched her nose. Usually, she added some fun emoji. Maybe a love heart or a smiley face. The text she'd just sent kind of felt...cold. But then, she didn't have it in her to send anything else.

She was setting the phone onto the desk when the response came through. Her heart beat faster, a nervous trickle skittering over her skin. Because even though he'd been distant, she still loved him. She still got excited at the mere sight of his name on the phone screen.

Erik: I'd prefer you didn't leave the office after dark. It's not safe.

Her belly dropped, a sadness she couldn't quell sweeping through her. He didn't want her home early because he wanted to see her. Maybe have dinner with her for the first time in forever. He just wanted to make sure that, physically, she was okay.

What about the other parts of her, like her heart? Was that safe?

Hannah: I'll be okay.

She hit send, then turned off her phone and dropped it into her bag. She set her elbows on the desk and her head in her hands.

Her heart didn't feel safe. She'd given it to Erik. Trusted him with its keeping. And that heart was already feeling the loss of him, even though he hadn't gone anywhere.

CHAPTER 2

*E*rik pumped his legs fast as he ran, the air soaring in and out of his chest while every fucking muscle in his body ached. But he didn't stop. If anything, the ache forced him to work harder. To run faster.

Sometimes, when he pushed himself close enough to the edge, he could almost forget what he'd done. What he'd taken from Hannah, and the heartache it had caused her.

And he could almost convince himself that they'd be okay.

So he ran as fast as his body allowed, like he could somehow outrun his reality and the ticking clock that followed him. Haunted him. Reminded him that eventually, he'd have to tell her.

He was so damn angry at the world. For giving him this beautiful woman, convincing him he could have it all, then ripping it out from under him. It almost felt like just as he'd reached for a fucking fraction of happiness after years of being alone, God laughed at him.

Maybe it was his fault for choosing to fall for her. But whenever that idea started to pulse at his temple, he was reminded that loving Hannah had never been a choice. The second he'd seen her, touched her, heard her sweet, lyrical voice, his heart had been chained to hers.

He ran so long that the small shadows of light began to fade and the moon cast a dim glow over the road in front of him. He'd been pushing his body to the limit almost every day lately. But it didn't help. Nothing helped.

When he finally returned to his house, his jaw ground at the absence of Hannah's car. He'd told her he didn't want her leaving the office late. She hadn't listened. But then, was that a surprise? He'd barely spoken to her lately, because he'd barely been *able* to talk to her, *look at her*, without feeling like every fucking rock in the world was sitting on his chest, crushing him. So why should she listen to his advice or heed his concern?

He pushed inside and moved up the stairs, tugging his phone from his pocket as he went.

Erik: Are you on your way home?

When he reached the bathroom connected to his bedroom, he turned the shower on so fucking hot that the air immediately thickened with steam. Then he stripped off his running shorts and stepped under the water.

The same question repeated in his head every single day... when was he going to tell her? When was he going to drop the bomb?

At some point, he had to. But the very thought of doing so, of setting those words free, made a band pull against his lungs. Stopped every breath to the point he almost keeled over.

He didn't spend long in the shower. When he turned off the water and grabbed his towel, he went straight for his phone. He cursed when he saw the blank screen, and his fingers twitched to text her again. To call her.

Instead, he pulled on sweats and a T-shirt, then went down the stairs to his office. He'd just sat behind his desk when his phone rang. But it wasn't Hannah's name on the screen, it was his sister's.

He let Andi's call ring out, feeling like the asshole he was for not talking to her. It wasn't just Hannah he'd been avoiding for the last month. It was his family as well. Because every time his world imploded, he did the same damn thing—closed himself off from the people who loved him most, afraid they'd see the cracks in his walls.

He opened his bottom drawer and pulled out the documents he'd printed a month ago. He'd read them so many times, he could recite the information word for word. Yet he still pulled them out, needing the repeated confirmation of what Hannah's foster brother, Nico, had done…and why Erik had killed him.

When his phone rang a second time, it wasn't Hannah or Andi. It was Chandler—a man who was both a friend and his eyes and ears for every job he went on.

He touched the cell to his ear. "Chandler."

"Hey. I sent over the notes for tonight's job."

He swallowed, eyeing his laptop. "Okay. Great. We're still set for midnight?"

"Yep." There was a small pause. "Hunter, I've been meaning to talk to you about something."

His gut clenched so damn tight it took a moment to form words. "I already know what you're gonna say."

"Good. So you know you're working too many jobs."

"I can handle it. I'm fine."

"Don't lie to me. What are you doing right now? Are you sitting at your desk, looking over the information I sent you on Nicolas Spalder for the hundredth damn time?"

He dropped the papers like they'd burned him.

"He was involved in a human trafficking ring," Chandler said slowly, as if it was the only way the words would make sense to Erik. "That was confirmed information. He was a scumbag, and the day he died, this world had one less threat to worry about."

"He was important to her. Fuck, he was her only family. And I *took* him from her."

"You also saved countless women from being sold like objects, Hunter."

He knew that. And it made sense in his head. So much fucking sense that if he had to kill the guy a second time, he would. But when he looked at Hannah, when he saw her fingertips run over the cloud charm on her wrist, heard the emotion in her voice when she spoke about her beloved brother, all of that sense fell out the window.

"Tell her," Chandler said quietly.

"If I do, she'll either believe me and it will damage her memory of a man she considered a brother. Or she won't believe me. And then what? What if she doesn't forgive me?"

"She will. If she loves you like she says she does, and if she's the good person you say she is, how could she not?"

Erik almost laughed. How could she not? There were so few people in her life who'd loved her. Protected her. And he'd taken one of those people away.

When he heard the click of the front door unlocking, he cursed under his breath. "I've got to go. I'll read over the notes you sent before I leave tonight."

The second he hung up, he grabbed the printed documents on Nico and shoved them into the bottom drawer. He'd just closed it when she appeared in the doorway. Just like every other time he looked at her, he felt like he'd been sucker punched.

Fuck, she was beautiful. Her soft features. Her long blond hair that cascaded over her shoulders like a goddamn waterfall. And those blue eyes...the shade of the sky in a storm.

She offered a small smile. "Hey."

"Hey."

He wanted to mention how much he'd missed her. How just the sight of her made his heart beat to a new rhythm. But "hey" seemed about all he could manage. Because every time he looked at her, he lost himself.

She tilted her head. "I wasn't sure if you'd be home."

Not a surprise. He hadn't been home much in the last month because he'd been putting everything into delaying telling her, even though it was inevitable. "I have a job later tonight."

The light dimmed from her eyes, and he wanted to take his words back.

She gave him a slow nod before stepping back. "Well, I had dinner at the office, so I might just shower and go to bed."

She didn't wait for him to respond. Her heels clicked against the wooden flooring, so damn loud in the otherwise quiet house.

He dropped his head into his hands and ran his fingers through his hair, pulling the strands at the roots.

With a short growl, he opened his laptop and clicked into the job notes Chandler had sent him. He tried to read them. Fuck, he tried so hard. It was only when he read over the same line five damn times that he slammed the laptop closed and rose to his feet.

He was moving before he could stop himself, up the stairs and toward her.

When his eyes fell on her across the room, his heart finally stopped pounding and the air slipped into his lungs with a bit more ease. She'd just stepped out of the shower and had a towel wrapped around her body, beads of water still running over her silky skin. When the towel dropped, his dick twitched.

So damn beautiful.

The sight of her glucose monitor on her arm put him at ease. Her health was easier for her to manage now, and that was like a weight off his shoulders.

Where was her pump though?

She slipped one of his shirts on. Seeing her in his clothes made every territorial part of him scream *mine*.

She lifted her Apple watch. "You know, some would consider it rude to stare."

Those people didn't understand that it wasn't always a choice.

Sometimes looking away was impossible. "I don't understand those people. I find it perfectly acceptable."

He expected a smile. Maybe a small laugh. Instead, she bit her bottom lip, looking at him with such open vulnerability his chest cracked open. He closed the space between them and slipped his fingers around her wrist, doing up the clasp of the watch before tapping the screen to read her glucose levels.

A hundred and twenty-six. Good. She was okay.

He caressed the inside of her wrist. "Did you have a good day?"

She nodded. "Yeah. Work's been busy, but I got away to have lunch with Henry and Brigid."

"That's good. You deserve a break." He shifted his gaze between her eyes, wanting to drown in them. No part of him felt capable of leaving her, but he had a job to do. "I'm going back down to do some work before I leave tonight."

Disappointment flashed in her blue eyes, gutting him. He lowered his head and kissed her temple. He'd just turned when she spoke.

"I've been thinking…I might move back to my place."

Panic slammed into his gut so hard and fast it felt like a physical blow.

"No." The word was a soft growl on his lips as he turned back toward her.

No fucking way was she leaving him. He couldn't lose her. But then, he had no idea how to keep her.

She swallowed and turned, lifting her moisturizer. "I wasn't asking for your permission, Erik. I think it would be good for us to have some space."

Space… The word tasted like acid in his mouth. He was moving before he could stop himself, his hands going to her hips as he stood behind her, lips to her ear. In a voice that hid none of his pain, he whispered, "Stay with me."

A loud breath shuddered from her lips. He touched a kiss to

her neck, feeling her pulse thump beneath his mouth. Then another.

"Erik…" she whispered.

His hands moved to her thighs, shifting up the material of the shirt. "I can't lose you."

She leaned back into him, gasping when one hand trailed all the way up her body and cupped her breast. He found her nipple and rolled it between his thumb and forefinger.

She moaned.

God, he loved every sound she made. "You're my entire world."

Her breaths started to quicken, her hand sliding up into his hair.

He kept his lips on her neck. Kept sucking and nipping. He grazed his thumb over her nipple. He was just sliding his other hand up the inside of her thigh when she grabbed his wrist.

"Erik…tell me this is forever first. Tell me that *you and me* are forever."

He stopped, his blood turning cold in his veins. He wanted to promise that. All he wanted was to spend his life with this woman. But would she feel the same when she knew his secret?

He moved his hands to grip her hips, his temple touching her head. "Hannah…"

"You can't."

The hurt that weaved through her tone gutted him.

Lie, Erik. Tell her that sweet fucking lie to save her the pain. Tell her there's nothing that could break you apart.

But he couldn't.

He stepped back. "I'm sorry. I have to go get ready for this job."

He didn't look up, because he didn't want to see what he knew was there. What he knew he'd caused. But he felt it. The heartache. The pain. And every step he took away from her felt like another piece of himself was being left behind.

CHAPTER 3

annah's fingers tapped the keys of her laptop. She was buried in paperwork today, but she didn't mind. She loved her job, and after struggling to get homes to sell for nearly a year, she felt fortunate to have so many now.

And maybe a part of her was also happy to have the distraction.

Tell me this is forever. Tell me you and me are forever.

The request should have been simple, right? Easy. Yet Erik hadn't been able to answer. And that silence, the withdrawal from her…God, it hurt.

She'd wanted to rave and yell. To throw something across the room.

"Hannah." Taylor came into her office, holding out an envelope. "I was the first in this morning. Someone had slid this under the door."

She looked down, frowning at her name scrawled across the front of a slim envelope.

"Probably someone else wanting you to sell their mega-mansion." Taylor nibbled her bottom lip, concern skittering

across her face. "I also wanted to check in on you. You've been...
quiet lately."

Hannah lowered the envelope to the desk before running her
fingers over her charm bracelet, first the cloud, then the angel.
"I'm fine."

God, she was a terrible liar.

Taylor gave a slow nod, clearly not believing her for a second.
"Okay, but if you're not, and you'd like to talk to someone about
it, I'm a great listener."

Taylor was a nurturer. She personified the word mother. But
she didn't need Hannah to dump her problems on her. "Thank
you. But I'm okay. How's Elliot?"

"He's perfect. And with those clients you passed off to me,
we're doing really well. It's a relief."

"Good. I'm glad I could help."

Everyone was enjoying the sudden abundance of stock. At
least some good had come from the bad that had been Angelo
Bonetti. Not to mention, the top realtor at a competing company
had lost his job once it was discovered he'd been working with
James to bad-mouth Hannah to steal her clients.

"You sure you're okay?" Taylor asked.

Hannah nodded, probably too quickly. "I'm great. But thanks
for checking in."

She shifted her attention back to her screen, forcing her mind to
focus on the work in front of her. A couple hours passed, and she was
rummaging around her desk for some information she'd printed off
when her fingers brushed over the envelope Taylor had given her.

She frowned. She'd completely forgotten all about it.

Turning it over, she noticed there was no return address.
Strange. And there was no stamp. Proof that, as Taylor said,
someone had obviously hand-delivered it. Quickly, she tore it
open, and a single piece of paper slipped out.

I know what you did, Hannah.

She sucked in a sharp breath.

What the hell? Who had written this? And why?

There was nothing overtly threatening about the words, but every part of her still rebelled against them. Against the way the envelope had been left at the office. The lack of signature. The single sentence.

"Hey, Hannah."

She jolted, the note slipping from her fingers as she looked up at Leo. "Hey."

"I'm heading over to Black Bean for lunch. Want to join me?"

She slipped the note back into the envelope and lowered it into her drawer. "No, that's okay. I've got so much to do."

One side of his mouth lifted. "Come on. You can't tell me you aren't hungry. I need to make sure my coworker isn't going to pass out on me from a low."

Right on cue, her watch vibrated. She didn't need to look down to know it was her Dexcom telling her she had to eat.

Leo raised a knowing brow. He had a brother with type 1, so he understood.

The corners of her lips tilted up. It was the first genuine smile all day. "Okay. Let's go get some food."

"So, tell me how you came to be such a popular real estate agent," Leo said as they walked down the street. "You have more houses listed than any agent I know."

She almost cringed at the question. If she told this man the truth—that a rich businessman had mistakenly sent a hit man after her and was now trying to right his wrongs by sending work her way—he'd probably think she was crazy. Hell, he might even run for the hills.

Leo knew that his job had become vacant because of James's drug issues. He also knew that, because of said issues, the man had stepped into the office with a gun and shot their boss, Reuben—almost shooting Hannah too. But that was all he knew.

She lifted a shoulder. "I guess people just know my name around here and trust me with their properties."

He looked at her as if he knew there was more to the story. "I'll pretend I believe you."

"What about you? How did you come to sell here in Redwood?"

"That is a very short and simple story. I live in Leavenworth, so only a five-minute drive from here. Saw the job ad. Decided I needed a change of scenery. Luckily, I charmed the pants off Reuben and he hired me."

Hannah laughed as they approached the entrance to Black Bean. And man, it felt good to laugh.

* * *

"ERIK HUNTER. Stop walking right the hell now."

Erik's body locked at the angry words. He turned to see his sister climbing out of her car. He cursed under his breath at the look on her face. It was one that told him she wasn't going to allow him to blow her off again.

Dammit, he'd almost made it to the coffee shop.

She stopped in front of him and shoved his shoulder. "What the hell is wrong with you?"

He opened his mouth, but apparently the question didn't require an answer, because she was talking again before he could get a word in.

"You come back to town after *eight years* of barely talking to your family, promise us you're a changed man, but now you're back to ignoring us?"

He wasn't sure he ever promised he was a changed man. "Andi—"

"You *told me* you wouldn't do this again. You *swore* that you were here to stay."

"I *am* here."

Her brows rose to her hairline. "Really? Then where have you been, Erik? Because you haven't been coming to Mom and Dad's for Sunday night dinner. You haven't been answering my calls or responding to my texts."

"I've been busy." The excuse sounded as weak out loud as it did in his head.

"No. You haven't been busy. Something's wrong. And when something's wrong, you shut yourself away from the world."

He wanted to argue with her, but it was true. Hiding was something he'd become infinitely familiar with. "Can we not do this here?" He noticed a couple of people covertly watching them and scanned the rest of the street.

"Where else can I do it? I can't get through to you, and I need to know that you're okay."

"I'm okay." The words came too damn quickly, and if the look on Andi's face was anything to go by, she knew it.

Something akin to fear darkened his sister's hazel eyes. It made Erik's gut knot. His sister never showed fear. She was a doctor and one of the bravest people he knew.

"I can't lose you." She stepped forward, her voice lowering as she touched his chest. "If you're not okay, I'm here to be whatever you need me to be. You're not alone. You've *never* been alone."

Her words dug their claws into his chest. They were true, but they also felt like a damn lie. Because all he'd felt was alone this last month.

"Thank you." It was all he could manage, and by Andi's short sigh, she didn't like it.

"Where are you going?" Her gaze skirted around him.

"To get a coffee."

"Great. I need caffeine. Let's go."

He opened his mouth to tell her he didn't want company, but her eyes narrowed on him as if she dared him to send her away.

So instead, he turned and headed toward Black Bean, not

surprised when Andi slipped her arm through his. "So...you remember that it's my thirtieth birthday party in a week, right?"

Shit. He'd forgotten. "Yeah."

Her eyes narrowed on him. "You're coming." It wasn't a question. "No. You don't have a choice," she said before he could respond. "So I'll see you there."

"How's Finley?" he asked, needing a change in subject.

Andi's best friend had gone on a Christmas work trip to Canada and been targeted by a stalker. The guy had tried to kill her, and if it hadn't been for the bodyguard their brother, Nate, had organized for her, a former SEAL friend of his, she might not have survived.

Andi's smile softened. "She's great—living with Nixon and so in love. She's coming to my party, so you can ask her yourself then."

"I'm glad things worked out. Have you heard from Nate?"

"Nope. He's too busy saving the world." She cast a quick glance up at Erik, and her expression softened. "You should call Mom. She's worried. So is Dad."

The muscles in his forearms bunched.

She tilted her head. "You know they won't ask any intrusive questions, if that's what you're worried about."

It wasn't. What he worried about was them seeing just how *not okay* he was. Because they would see it. They'd see right through his "I'm fine" mantra and fake smiles. "Maybe."

Her arm tightened on his. "Please think about it. They're not getting any younger, and they miss you."

Guilt slashed at his chest like a knife. He knew they weren't getting younger. That, in combination with his father's heart issues, meant he needed to do better.

"Hey," Andi said as if she heard every internal thought he had. "Don't do that. Just...visit them."

"When did you become so..."

"Wise?" She grinned. "I'm surprised you're only just seeing it. I've always been the smartest in the family."

He laughed and shook his head. "And the least humble."

"Eh. Humble's overrated. Besides, I prefer to refer to myself as confident."

They stepped inside Black Bean, and immediately Erik stopped, his muscles turning to stone at the scene in front of him.

Hannah, sitting at the long counter with some blond guy in a suit. His hand was on her forearm, and her head was thrown back as she laughed at something he said.

How long had it been since he'd seen her laugh like that? So free and uninhibited?

Erik was moving before he could stop himself. He vaguely heard his sister call him back, but he ignored her, seeing nothing but Hannah.

The second he reached her side, her gaze shot up, eyes widening and the smile slipping from her face. "Erik…what are you doing here?"

"Grabbing a coffee." He looked at the blond. At least he'd taken his hand off her.

Hannah wet her lips. "Oh, um, well, you've heard me mention Leo before. He's the new agent in our office. Leo, this is my… partner, Erik."

She stumbled over the word partner, and he hated that. He wanted everyone in the goddamn world to know she was his.

"Erik! I've heard so much about you. It's good to finally put a name to the face." The guy stood and held out his hand.

Erik didn't shake it immediately. It took an elbow to the ribs from Andi, who was now standing at his side, for him to finally hold out his own hand.

"And who's this beautiful lady?" Leo asked, looking at Andi.

Why the fuck was the guy calling his sister beautiful? Before he could respond, Andi held out her own hand. "Andi. The sister."

As Andi and Leo spoke, Hannah looked up at him. "Everything okay?" she asked quietly.

"Yeah. I didn't expect to see you here." A plate of fries and a half-eaten sandwich sat on the table. "Lunch break?"

She nodded.

He shouldn't be angry. All the guy had done was touch her arm and make her laugh. But when it came to Hannah, none of his emotions made sense.

"The job go okay last night?" she asked.

"Yeah, it went okay, Angel."

Then, because he couldn't stop himself, he lowered his head and kissed her. And every worry, every bit of panic and fear, just…left him.

CHAPTER 4

*E*rik lay on his stomach, finger on the trigger of his .338 sniper rifle as he looked through the scope. Cool evening air filled his lungs, the scattering of stars across the dark sky offering dull light, while the only noise was the quiet breath of his spotter behind him.

His spotter was responsible for observing the target and providing information about wind speed, distance, and anything else that might be useful. Erik would use that intel to make the necessary adjustments to hit the target.

The roof offered little in the way of protection, but he didn't need it. The apartment building was five floors, and they were on the rooftop. It was the dead of night. This would be an easy in-and-out job.

His heart didn't pump too fast in his chest as he waited for the command. His hands didn't shake. The lack of nerves wasn't just because of his training and previous experience as a Marine. It was because in this line of work, he had to be steady. He couldn't make a mistake. He had one chance to hit his target. But it was all he needed.

Tonight, a man who didn't deserve the air he breathed would die. A man who was not only part of a trafficking ring but one of the leaders in the organization. A man responsible for countless women being sold off to the highest bidders. Fucking scum of the Earth.

There wasn't an ounce of guilt in Erik that he was taking away this man's right to a fair trial. As far as he was concerned, predators like this didn't deserve one. He deserved to take his final breath, then never hurt anyone again.

A rustle of movement sounded behind him. His spotter had already searched for any immediate threats and identified any dead space. He'd also broken down the sector into smaller quadrants and identified reference points.

They were ready to go.

"Fire eye, go to the exit point of Redisence Bar," his spotter said quietly.

Erik positioned the crosshairs on the location, watching through the scope as the door opened and a man stepped out. "Contact."

The word had just left Erik's mouth when the man moved out of his view through the scope.

"From the exit point, go toward three o'clock approximately three mils," the spotter said.

Erik shifted the rifle, and the man came back into view. "Target acquired. Crew cut, suit."

The asshole was exactly who they were after. He matched all the photos Erik had studied. He was the man who needed to die tonight. Still...Erik waited for his spotter to confirm.

"That's your target. Check parallax and mil."

Erik adjusted his mil. "One point one-six."

There was a short pause while his spotter plugged the information in and searched for the ballistic calculation. That would tell Erik if there were any adjustments he needed to make to hit his target, given the distance.

"Check level," Spotter said after a short pause. "Hold over three point nine."

It was time.

Erik exhaled slowly, the outside world fading as he slackened his finger on the trigger. With his last bit of breath, he said, "Ready."

"Left point two."

The second Erik got the command of execution, he squeezed the trigger. The guy dropped.

"Perfect kill shot to the chest. Shooter, lock and clear."

That was exactly what Erik wanted to hear.

He was just taking his eye off the scope when his spotter cursed.

"A car just stopped in front of the target. People are getting out. We should get out of here."

Erik dismantled his weapon quickly before rising to his haunches and loading everything into his bag. He'd just risen to his feet and turned, expecting to see his spotter behind him.

But instead he saw...her.

The blood drained from his face, and a fear like he'd never felt before rushed through his veins like ice. "Hannah..."

"What did you do?" she whispered, voice full of pain. "He was my family!" Her hand went to her opposite wrist, running a finger over the cloud charm on her bracelet.

"Hannah, please..." He took a step toward her, but she shuffled back. And that distance between them killed something inside him. "He wasn't a good man."

"How do you know that? Because you read some information on a piece of paper? I knew him. I knew his heart. He was good. And you took him from me."

The tears that gathered in her eyes gutted him.

"I'll make it right." But even as the words left his mouth, he knew they were a lie. He couldn't go back and undo what he'd done. He couldn't bring a man back from the dead.

"You can't," she whispered, a single tear falling down her cheek.

She turned to walk away. The despair inside him turned to poison. He couldn't lose her. She was his world. The only person on this goddamn planet who made him feel whole and healed and alive.

He tried to follow her, to drop to his knees and beg for her forgiveness, but something grabbed his arms, fingers so strong that he couldn't move a single step.

"Hannah!" he yelled.

She didn't pause or turn. She just kept walking away, the distance between them becoming greater with each step.

He growled and tugged at the hands on his arms, the desperation a living, breathing beast inside him.

He couldn't let her leave. He couldn't lose her, dammit! He pulled harder, swearing he'd tear down the world around him to keep her.

He turned and attacked the figure touching him, sending them both to the ground as he wrapped his hands around their throat.

* * *

PAINED GROWLS CUT into Hannah's sleep, tugging her consciousness to the surface. Sleep tried to pull her back under, but the sounds grew louder, the mattress beneath her body shifting with movement.

She opened her eyes to darkness. It was the middle of the night.

At the sound of another growl, she reached for the bedside light and turned it on. Beside her, Erik was twitching, his head shifting from side to side, his hands fisted. And that look on his face…it was something between pain and utter terror.

God, what was going on in his head? It looked like he held the entire world on his shoulders, and right now, that world was crushing him.

She touched his arm. "Erik, wake up."

He didn't. If anything, the sounds tearing from his chest grew louder. The thrashing grew more violent.

She swallowed, desperation starting to stamp out every ounce of self-preservation inside her. She leaned over him and grabbed his upper arms, her voice louder this time as she yelled, "Erik! Wake up!"

Suddenly, his growl turned into a snarl, rage ripping across his face as he shoved her away. Air burst from her lungs when she hit the floor beside the bed, hard.

Before she could rise, he was on top of her, his fingers around her throat.

For a moment, fear made her body lock and her breath halt in her lungs.

He looked like a predator—and she was his prey.

The fear was spidering through her chest, icing her skin, when he blinked. That small action seemed to pull him out of whatever hell he'd been caged in. His expression shifted from anger to horror.

"Angel…" He yanked his hand from her skin like she'd burned him and pulled her to her feet, inspecting her body. "Did I—"

"I'm fine, Erik. You didn't hurt me."

He looked like he didn't believe her. Like everything she represented, he wanted to get away from.

She stepped closer, the need to comfort him drowning out every other emotion. "Erik…I'm okay. But I need to know that you're okay too. What happened just now? Where did you go?"

"I dreamt that I lost you." The words were spoken so quietly, she almost didn't hear.

She cupped his cheek, relieved when he didn't step away. "I'm right here, Erik."

"You're here." He lowered to the edge of the bed and pulled her to his lap. He held her so tightly, there was no space between them, his temple touching hers. "You're here," he repeated, as if trying to convince himself.

"Erik, in your dream, how did you lose me?"

"I did something…something that was unforgivable."

"But you know it wasn't real, right? I'm here and I'm yours. I'll *always* be yours."

The agony that flashed across his face was so distinct, she almost felt it.

She pressed her hands to his bare chest. "Erik…what's going

on between us?" She needed answers, even if it was just crumbs of truth that she could pull together to make a little bit of sense.

"I never fear anything." He touched a light kiss to her neck. "But when it comes to you, I fear *everything*." Another kiss, this time lower. "The thought of losing you…it's like losing the skin off my body. The air in my lungs." His hands slipped beneath the material of her shirt. "I need to touch you," he whispered. "Feel you."

Her hands went to the hem of her top and, with his help, she tugged it over her skin. "So touch me."

The words had barely left her lips when his mouth dropped to hers. The kiss was passion. It was fire and love and desire, all wrapped up together.

She grabbed his shoulders. God, she'd missed his kisses. His touch. His *love*.

His mouth slipped from hers and moved down her neck, then her chest. When his lips wrapped around one pebbled nipple, she gasped and arched her back, her fingers digging into his muscles.

The blaze inside her burned hotter, turning into a wildfire that sped through her limbs. Like her hips had a mind of their own, they ground against his cock, feeling every inch of him through the material of her panties and his briefs.

He switched to her other breast while his hands went to her hips, and he tore the lace off her body like it was nothing.

"Tell me you want this, Angel. Tell me you're mine."

She gasped again when his fingers brushed the apex of her thighs, and he swiped her clit. "I'm yours," she breathed.

"I need you more than I've needed anything or anyone in my life." His thumb pressed to her clit, moving in circles as his finger slid to her entrance. Her breathing stopped. He pushed inside, and it was an explosion of sensation and desire.

One of her hands shifted to his hair, tugging. "I feel all of that. You're inside my bones. My blood. You're a part of me, Erik."

He started a slow thrust of his finger, his thumb always working her clit, his teeth grazing her nipple.

She moaned, wanting more. Needing to feel him inside her. She reached for his briefs and slipped her hand inside, her fingers wrapping around his cock. He groaned as she shifted her hand from base to tip.

He released her nipple and kissed up her chest. "A part of me is so damn scared that I have something so important to me. That I need you so much." He took her mouth with his own, then lifted her hips and positioned himself at her entrance. "But it's too late now. I'm forever tethered to you." He slid inside.

She whimpered as her walls stretched around him. Oh God. Every time he was inside her, she felt like a missing part of her heart had been returned. Like everything was finally right in the world.

He lifted her hips and brought her back down, his tongue tangling with hers.

"I love you so damn much, Angel," he breathed against her lips.

"I've never loved anyone like I love you, Erik."

The words seemed to propel him to move her hips faster. To pump up into her with a new need. The desire in her lower abdomen built, the throb intensifying. There was almost a desperation to the way Erik touched her. Was he scared the dream would come true? That he'd lose her? Didn't he know that every breath she took was for him?

Tears pooled in her eyes, and she tightened her arms around him, like she could somehow lock them in this moment forever.

He cupped her breast, his thumb grazing over her nipple. And even though she tried to hold off, she couldn't. She broke. Her back arched, her head swung back, and she screamed Erik's name.

His mouth shifted to her neck. "You're so fucking beautiful, Angel."

He kept pumping, kept lifting her up and lowering her back onto him, prolonging her orgasm, until finally his world splintered along with hers. He grabbed the back of her neck and tugged her to him, their lips colliding in another passionate kiss.

And for one fleeting second, Hannah could almost convince herself that this moment could put back together whatever had fractured them this last month.

CHAPTER 5

*A*n incessant beeping pulled Hannah from her sleep as light hit the backs of her eyelids.

Good God, it was her pump. She needed to change it.

Blindly, she reached over and grabbed her PDM, squinting as she hit different keys to make the beeping stop. But she knew the only way to *really* stop it was by changing the damn thing.

Dropping the PDM back to the nightstand, she reached across the other side of the bed, expecting to find Erik...only for her fingers to brush over cold sheets.

Her eyes flashed open. He wasn't there. The bed was empty...*again.*

Her heart squeezed so hard in her chest it was a physical pain. Last night had felt like the wall between them had finally crumbled. Like Erik had finally returned to her, and maybe they could get back on track.

Only, if that were true, wouldn't he be here?

She swallowed, lifting her phone and spotting the text from Erik.

Erik: Hey. I had to get up early to help Dad with a few jobs. See you tonight. Stay safe.

He'd used the "I'm helping Dad" excuse a few times. Sometimes it was his mom. Occasionally his sister. Mostly he'd left the bed early to work out or do some prep for a job.

No part of her believed they were things that needed doing at the crack of dawn. He *chose* to get up and do them early because that was more appealing to him than waking up together. Holding each other. Talking.

What was going on between them? At some point, something had happened. Something had damaged them. She just wished she knew what.

With a long exhale, Hannah rose from the bed and went downstairs into the kitchen to change her insulin pump. When the world felt heavy around her, and she had to do anything for her diabetes, she suddenly hated every part of her type 1 diagnosis. She hated that her pancreas didn't work the way it was supposed to. That the disease was incurable. And she hated that she was required to do so many more things just to survive than most other people.

Yeah, today was definitely one of those days.

In the kitchen, she deactivated the pump using the PDM before pulling it off. Opening the second drawer, she then pulled out a new Omnipod. From the fridge, she took some insulin, then, using the pen, injected about a hundred and thirty units of insulin into the pod. The beep told her it was ready.

Hannah held the pod against the PDM so it could prime by circulating the insulin. When it was finished, she pulled the stickers off the back of the pod and pressed the pump to her right thigh, keeping it on the same side of her body as the monitor.

Lifting the PDM, she hit start, then scrunched her eyes as those damn clicks sounded. There were five before the pump pierced her skin. She flinched. She *always* flinched. It wasn't actually that painful—the countdown was worse than the pain—but it still bothered her.

Twenty minutes later, showered and dressed, she burned her toast and realized they were out of oat milk. Great.

With a huff, she pulled out the box of Frosted Flakes. Of course, without the oat milk, she had to eat them dry.

It was official…today sucked.

She quickly adjusted her pump before lifting a spoonful of dry cereal to her mouth. The kitchen window gave her the perfect view of her small house next door. She swallowed, thoughts of moving back flickering in her head once again. Some distance would help, right? It certainly couldn't make things worse.

She got halfway through the cereal before tipping the rest into the trash and slipping the bowl into the dishwasher. With a sigh, she lifted her bag and moved to the door. Her Honda key sat right next to the key for the G70.

Screw it.

She grabbed that one instead. The second she slid behind the wheel of her old car, a small semblance of peace returned. Not a lot, but some. And God, she needed that right now.

As she drove to work, her phone dinged. She turned her head to see the message was from the group chat between her, Henry, and Brigid. The group had become a lot less active in recent months. Henry was well and truly the most frequent participant.

She really needed to check on Brigid. They texted daily, but that wasn't enough. She needed to catch up with her best friend in person.

After parking at work, she took a few deep breaths, then headed inside. She was just pulling the office door open when Reuben stepped out.

She smiled at her boss. "Hey."

"Hannah, hi." His brows furrowed. "Are you okay?"

God, did she look as awful as she felt? "Yeah, just a rocky night's sleep. You off to a meeting?"

He held her gaze for a beat before answering. "Yeah, meeting a potential client. Give me a call if you need me."

"Will do."

He gave a nod, still looking like he didn't believe that she was okay, before walking down the street.

She blew out a breath and stepped inside. Since everything had gone down with James and Angelo, Reuben had been the best boss. But that wasn't always a good thing. It meant on days like today, when she tried to mask the fact that she was feeling fragile, it was impossible because he looked at her too closely.

As she dropped behind her desk, she pulled her phone from her bag to see the stream of messages from her friends.

Henry: What do you mean, you might not go to Andi's party?

Crap. She'd forgotten about that. Erik's sister was turning thirty, and it was her party this weekend.

Brigid: I haven't been feeling in a party mood. Plus, it's outside and it'll be cold.

Brigid was always in a party mood, and the weather would normally be the last thing to stop her. But after everything with James…who could blame her?

Henry: Then we'll get some alcohol into you, woman! You have to go. I'm bringing Owen so you can both finally meet him.

Hannah: He's right. You have to go because I have to go. And I need drinking and dancing friends.

Brigid: I'll see how I feel.

Worry for her friend rippled through Hannah. Brigid and Erik were two of the most important people in her life, and neither of them were acting like themselves. Neither of them would tell her why, either. Though in Brigid's case, she could easily guess.

A couple of months ago, Brigid's long-time boyfriend, the love of her life, went to jail for trying to kill Hannah.

Years. They had been dating for years, and Brigid had had no idea he was doing drugs, sabotaging Hannah's career, or was capable of attempted murder. That wasn't something her friend would get over any time soon and Hannah needed to be there for her during this tough time.

She placed her bag onto the floor and turned back to her screen, her mood sinking further when she saw a buyer was pulling out of a purchase just before the cooling off period had ended.

Really? Did today hate her that much?

With gritted teeth, she lifted the phone to call the homeowners. As she knew they would be, the client was upset, but Hannah did her best to assure the woman they'd do more opens and find another buyer.

When she hung up, she felt depleted. And it wasn't even nine thirty, dammit. She still had the entire day in front of her.

Tears gathered in her eyes, and she quickly opened her drawer to get a tissue, only what she found was the envelope Taylor had delivered to her office yesterday. She'd forgotten all about it.

Tentatively, she pulled it out and slipped the note from the envelope. Her gaze ran over the words again.

I know what you did, Hannah.

Her heart started to thump, the heaviness of everything going on in her world beating down on her. The sale falling through. Brigid's pain. The note. And Erik.

God, Erik…he'd given her so much hope last night. In the way he'd touched her. Kissed her. The things he'd said. Then this morning, it had all been ripped away, like none of it had happened.

A tear slid down her cheek.

"Hannah, I—" Leo stopped, brows pulling together as he looked at her.

Shit. She whisked away the tear. "Sorry, it's been a long morning."

She wasn't sure if she expected empty words of sympathy, or

for him to just nod before awkwardly leaving her office. He did neither of those things. Instead, he walked around the desk and squatted beside her.

His eyes were gentle as he pulled a tissue from his pocket and handed it to her. "I've had a bad morning too. My coffee was so hot I burnt my tongue and my cat, Gisele, scratched me when I was on my way out because I forgot to put food in her bowl."

Despite everything, Hannah laughed. "You have a cat named Gisele?"

"I do. She runs the household. When I mess up, she sure as hell tells me about it."

"I bet that's not often."

"No, I'm a pretty good cat dad. But it doesn't take a big mess up for her to express her displeasure." He cocked his head. "Can I do anything?"

For some reason, that simple question made her tears dry up. She loved that he didn't ask her if she was okay, because he could see she wasn't.

She opened her mouth to tell him no. That this was a mess only she could tunnel her way out of.

"What the hell's going on?"

Her heart jumped, her gaze shooting up to the doorway. Immediately, she rose to her feet. "Erik."

Leo was slower to rise. If he was affected by Erik's hard tone, he didn't show it. "Hi, Erik. I was just checking in on Hannah."

Erik's focus switched back to her, and he searched her body like he was looking for an injury. "Are you okay?"

She nodded slowly, the lie slipping easily from her lips. "I'm okay."

* * *

ERIK DIDN'T BELIEVE that for a second. Hannah's eyes were red-rimmed like she'd been crying, and there was a sadness about her, both in the hunch of her shoulders and the crease in her brows.

But why the fuck was this asshole on his knees in front of her?

When Leo turned and squeezed Hannah's arm, anger pulsed in Erik's temple.

"I'll see you later, Hannah. Call if you need anything."

When Leo passed him, Erik locked his body to stop himself from grabbing the man.

"Erik…" Her voice pulled him back to her. "What are you doing here?"

He crossed the room, pulling her Apple watch from his pocket, and lifted her wrist. "You left this at home." He turned her wrist over and secured the latch. When he was finished, he didn't turn it back over, instead caressing her smooth skin and allowing the touch to calm some of the storm inside him. "You also left the G70…I was worried."

An emotion he couldn't place flashed over her face. The hint of wetness on her cheek sent his concern into a spiral, and he was again reminded of what he'd walked in on.

He reached up and cupped her cheek. "You've been crying."

She swallowed. "It's been a long morning."

Because of him? Because he hadn't been there when she'd woken up? Fuck, he was hurting her without even trying now. "I'm sorry."

Tears gathered in her eyes. "I feel like I'm losing you."

"I'm yours, Angel, for as long as you'll have me." When a tear fell down her cheek, he lowered his head and kissed it away. "And even if one day *you* choose to leave, my heart will still belong to you."

"Never," she whispered, before resting her head on his chest, right over his heart. A heart that beat for her. Only for her.

He was holding her close when he noticed a handwritten note on her desk.

I know what you did, Hannah.

What the fuck was *that?*

"Who wrote that?" he asked before he could censor the anger in his tone.

She pulled away, following his gaze to her desk. "Um…I'm not sure. Someone left it for me."

He frowned. "And you don't know who?"

She shook her head.

"Can I take them?"

At her nod, he lifted the note and envelope from her desk and slipped them into his pocket.

She massaged her forehead. "I need to get back to work."

His gaze flashed back to her. "Why didn't you take the G70?"

"I don't know. I needed the comfort of something I'd paid for myself."

Her words cut a fucking hole into his chest. He leaned down and pressed his lips to hers. And, damn, the kiss was all that kept the air moving through his lungs. "Please drive the G70. I need to know you're in something reliable. If you don't like it, we can go get something else. It just needs to be safe."

She opened her mouth and almost looked like she was going to argue with him. But then she simply nodded. "Okay."

Thank God.

One more kiss, then he whispered against her lips, "I'll see you tonight."

She nodded but looked like she didn't quite believe him. And he didn't blame her. He'd barely been home. He wanted to kick his own ass.

As he left her office, he passed Leo's. The man was behind his desk, phone to his ear. When their gazes collided, there was a small tightening of his eyes before he gave Erik a small chin tilt.

Erik's jaw clenched as he stepped outside. He didn't like the guy. But then, maybe that was because he'd seen him get too damn close to his woman twice in two days.

The second he was outside, he hit a key on his phone before putting it to his ear.

"Hunter. To what do I owe this pleasure?"

"Chandler...I need you to do something for me."

His friend chuckled. "So what's new?"

"I need a note fingerprinted. I also want protective detail put on Hannah."

There was a small pause before Chandler responded. "Everything okay?"

The note could be nothing. But after the last couple months, he wasn't taking the fucking chance. "I'm not sure. And Chandler...the person is to remain hidden. Watch the office from a distance. Watch *her* from a distance. I don't want her to know he's there."

Because something inside him knew she'd refuse the protection. And that wasn't a fucking option.

CHAPTER 6

*H*annah heard the music before she climbed out of the car. It was loud and echoed through the quiet night from the back of the house.

The home was a heritage-style colonial with a beautiful sandstone façade, and it sat pretty much on its own, with no neighbors on either side.

Gorgeous.

"I see the doctor has good taste," Henry said, climbing out from behind the wheel.

Brigid opened the back door. Henry had basically wrangled all three of them together, telling them that if they weren't at his place by five p.m. with their shit for tonight, he'd hunt them down. He'd even asked his partner, Owen, to meet them at the party.

Because Henry had been feeling it too—the drift between them. The distance that Brigid, in particular, was putting up.

Arriving together was fine with Hannah. Erik had told her that he might be late, so coming with her friends was better than arriving alone. And she wanted to bring the three of them back together. Henry and Brigid were her family by choice.

Hannah slipped her fingers through Brigid's. "Ready to party?"

"Depends," her friend said with a small grin. "We gonna dance?"

Hannah's smile widened. Brigid seemed a little better tonight. Happier. Hannah had no idea what had instigated the change, but she was hopeful it was here to stay.

Henry came to the other side of Brigid and slipped his arm through hers. "And cocktails. Andi said there'd be lots of cocktails, including pisco sours, which I'm dying for."

Hannah frowned. "What's a pisco sour?"

Henry looked at her like she'd just asked what trees were. "Pisco…as in the grape brandy which, when added to bitters, syrup, and lime, is the best damn thing you'll ever drink."

Brigid wrinkled her nose. "Don't pisco sours have egg whites in them?"

Henry lifted a shoulder. "Yeah. Extra protein to keep me going."

Hannah laughed as they headed around the side of the house, passing a large lit-up lap pool with steam coming off the surface. When they reached the backyard, her jaw dropped.

Okay…when a Hunter wanted to throw a party, they went all out.

A huge dance floor centered the grassed yard, and behind it was a five-person band. Tables scattered from one end of the yard to the other, but it was the lights strung above that had the space feeling almost magical.

And of course, there were people everywhere. Gorgeous people, all wearing the most beautiful dresses and suits.

Brigid moved straight over to a heater. "Yes…warmth. I love it."

Hannah searched the area for Erik, her heart doing a sad little turn when she didn't see him. She shouldn't be surprised. And it wasn't like he'd miss tonight altogether. It was his sister's thirtieth birthday. At least, she was pretty sure he wouldn't. But then, she wasn't sure she really knew the man at all right now.

Andi popped out of the crowd, her gaze colliding with Hannah's. She beamed and headed toward them, first wrapping Henry in a hug, then Brigid, then Hannah. When she pulled back, she frowned. "Erik's not with you?"

He hadn't told her? She squirmed uncomfortably. "No. We decided to come separately. He'll probably be late."

What exactly he was doing to warrant being late, she wasn't sure. She hadn't asked. Maybe because a part of her had been scared that whatever he said, she wouldn't believe after all the reasons for his absences already.

Disappointment flashed over Andi's face, but she recovered quickly. "Well, we have a food table to the right. A dance floor. And of course, a bar with plenty of cocktails."

"Yes, please," Brigid said, eyes already on the bar.

They moved toward it and, without asking, Henry ordered them each a pisco sour.

"Henry," Brigid complained. "I wanted something sweet."

"Trust me. You'll love this."

When the three drinks were set on the counter, Henry handed one to Brigid and another to Hannah. She was usually a vodka soda drinker, and she always nursed her drinks because alcohol made her blood sugar drop, but tonight she didn't want to play it safe, and with her new glucose monitor and pump, all she had to remember to do was eat throughout the evening.

As they moved to a table, she took a small sip, expecting not to like it.

Interesting…it wasn't too bad. A bit sour. A bit bitter. But also sweet.

"Mm," Brigid groaned. "This *is* good."

Hannah nodded, looking up at Henry. "You can choose my cocktails from now on."

"I can't believe you guys ever doubted me. You should *know* that I know my shit." Henry was just taking a drink when his gaze lifted to someone over her and Brigid's heads. His eyes lit up. "Are you excited to finally meet the man who rocks my dreams?"

"Yes!" Brigid said a bit too loudly.

Hannah glanced over her shoulder to see a guy striding toward them, his eyes only for Henry. He had shaggy brown hair that reached his chin, tattoos poking out from under his white shirt and up his neck, and an eyebrow piercing. He was nothing like the kind of clean-cut blonds Henry usually dated.

When the guy reached their group, he leaned in and kissed Henry.

Brigid sighed. "Aw. Cute."

They separated, and Henry turned to face them. "Owen, these are my friends, Brigid and Hannah. Guys, this is Owen."

Owen reached out a hand, and Hannah slipped hers into his. "It's nice to meet you."

When it was Brigid's turn, instead of shaking his hand, she stepped forward and wrapped her arms around him. Hannah chuckled. Anyone would have thought the woman had been drinking *before* she'd arrived tonight.

"I love how happy you've made Henry," Brigid said before pulling back. "Thank you."

Humor danced in Owen's eyes. "He makes me happy too."

Henry's grin widened. "Come on, Owen. I'll get you a drink, then my friends can tell you every embarrassing story they have on me."

Hannah shook her head and was just turning when she spotted a familiar face in the crowd.

Leo? What was he doing here?

The second Leo's gaze hit hers, he cut through the crowd toward her. "Hey."

She cocked her head. "I wasn't expecting to see you here."

"Andi invited me when you and Erik were talking the other morning. I told her I didn't know many people in Redwood, and she took pity on me and asked me to come. Said everyone who was anyone would be here."

Hannah laughed. "Sounds like Andi."

Brigid cleared her throat, and Hannah turned to her friend. "Sorry. Leo, this is my best friend, Brigid. Brigid, this is Leo, the new realtor at work."

The smile slipped from Brigid's face, and Hannah's chest tightened as realization hit. Leo had taken James's job. She hadn't told Brigid who'd replaced him because her friend hadn't asked.

Leo didn't seem to notice the slip of the smile, or if he did, he didn't point it out. Instead, he reached out a hand. "It's nice to meet you, Brigid."

For a moment, Brigid was still, and Hannah wondered if her friend would avoid shaking with him. Then, she finally stuck out her hand. "You too, Leo."

The second Leo released her, Brigid took a big gulp of her cocktail, basically finishing it in one go. "I might go get another while Henry's over there."

Hannah's heart thumped as she watched her friend walk away.

"Did I do something?"

She turned back to Leo, shaking her head. "No. She just…she dated James for a long time."

"Oh. I see. So we probably won't be fast friends."

"It's been a tough time for her."

Leo nodded. "I can understand that. Erik's not here?"

"Not yet."

An almost disapproving look came over Leo's features, but it was gone as quickly as it came.

Hannah was just taking another sip of the pisco sour when Henry called to her, indicating they were heading to the dance floor.

She smiled up at Leo. "I'm going to go dance."

"Can I join you?"

She opened her mouth, wanting to say no just to protect Brigid, but her manners refused to allow her to be rude. "Sure."

* * *

ERIK HAD BARELY PULLED up at Andi's house when a tap sounded on the driver's-side window. He frowned, surprised to see his brother standing on the other side of the door. Andi hadn't even told him their brother was flying in for the party.

He opened the door and climbed out with a smile. "What, were you out here waiting for me?"

Nate lifted a brow. "I went for a walk. Saw your Corvette and thought, that's strange, I haven't seen my absentee brother at the party."

He shot a look at his watch. "I'm only twenty minutes late."

"Twenty minutes that Andi will kick your ass for."

Nate wasn't wrong. "I didn't know you were coming home for this." As a Navy SEAL, getting time off wasn't easy for his brother.

"We're between missions, so I took a couple days of leave to be here for my baby sister."

Erik shoved his hands into his pockets as they moved toward the party.

"So..." Erik's muscles tensed at the single word from Nate. "You gonna tell me why Hannah came with her friends and not you?"

"I told her I might be late."

"Doing what?"

"Working."

His brother looked at him too damn closely. "Is something going on between you two?"

He clenched his teeth. "We're going through something right now."

When his brother was silent, Erik turned to find Nate studying him.

"You wanna talk about it?" Nate asked.

He thought his brother knew him better than that. "No. Tell me how *you're* doing. How are your missions going?"

A muscle in Nate's jaw flexed. "Honestly, I don't know. My head hasn't been in it since we lost Jasper, and in my line of work, that's not good."

Erik understood that. He'd lost members of his own team, and it had fucking killed him. Still to this day, darkness tried to weave through his vision at the memory. "I'm sorry, Nate. Maybe it's time to get out."

Nate was only thirty-one, so he had a lot left in him. But when you were a Navy SEAL, not having your head in the game made it dangerous, not just for you but for your team.

"Maybe."

They stepped into Andi's backyard. The first person he saw was his mother. She was talking to Judith, a woman who worked at the grocery store, but the second her eyes fell on Erik, she excused herself, grabbed his father's arm, and moved toward him.

Shit. He'd thought he'd have at least a couple of minutes to settle in first.

His mother pulled him into a hug. "Erik. I almost thought you weren't coming when I saw Hannah arrive alone." She pulled back but kept hold of his arms. "Is everything okay?"

"Yeah. I'm okay. Sorry I'm late." Before she could push for an explanation, he turned to his father. "Hey, Dad."

His father clamped a hand on his shoulder. "Hi, son. You sure everything's all right?"

He swallowed. He hated lying to his parents, but even if he knew how to word the truth, this wasn't the place or the time. "Yeah. I'm fine."

The man who raised him studied him with eyes that saw too much.

"Erik!" He turned to see Andi marching toward him. "Why are you so late?"

Instead of answering her question, he pulled a small gift box from his back pocket. "Will this make you forgive me?"

Some of the anger dimmed from her eyes. Not all of it, but she still slipped the small box from his fingers. He hadn't wrapped it, but he'd asked the shop to place a bow on top. That counted, right?

She opened the box, and her eyes widened when they fell on the sapphire solitaire pendant. It was a deep blue, her favorite color.

"Erik…" she whispered. "It's too much."

"For you, nothing is too much." He leaned down and kissed her cheek. "Happy birthday, A."

She wrapped her arms around him. The hug was tight and warm and familiar. When they separated, his gaze moved around the party, searching for Hannah.

"She's on the dance floor," Andi said, obviously knowing exactly what Erik was doing.

"Thanks. I'll be back." He squeezed his sister's arm and moved forward. It wasn't until people on the periphery of the floor walked away that he finally saw her dancing in the center.

A muscle ticked in his jaw, and his body went hard at the sight of a familiar guy leaning in to talk into her ear.

Leo. Why was he even here? And why was he always so goddamn close to her?

Erik was moving before he could stop himself, his eyes frozen on Leo's lips near Hannah's ear. Suddenly, every fucking thing that had been annoying him this last month boiled over, breathing rage through his lungs and heating his blood.

He shoved the guy hard in the chest. "What the fuck are you doing?"

Audible gasps sounded around him. Hannah touched his arm. "Erik—"

"Every time I see you, you're too close to her."

The guy's brows pulled together. "I was just trying to talk to her over the music."

"Yeah? And the other day you were *just* comforting her while she cried, and the time before that you were *just* touching her arm in the coffee shop."

"Erik, stop it!" Hannah hissed as she tried to pull him away, but he didn't budge.

Leo remained so fucking calm that Erik's anger only heightened.

"I'm her *friend*, Erik. Friends comfort each other when they're sad. And they talk. That's it."

That wasn't fucking it. Erik stepped forward, but she was suddenly between them. "Stop it right now, Erik," she said in a low voice. "Walk away."

His hands fisted, but Hannah tugged his arm. Finally, he stepped away with her. She kept tugging until they stood in a quiet corner of the yard, then she spun on him. "What was that?"

"I didn't like him being so close to you."

"He wasn't touching me. He was just talking over the music. And everyone was there. Henry, Brigid, Henry's partner, Owen."

Erik scrubbed a hand over his face. She was right. "Hannah—"

"That wasn't okay."

"I know. I'm sorry."

He expected to receive more anger from her. He deserved it. Instead, she stepped closer and cupped his cheek. He felt that touch everywhere. The warmth. The softness. "Apology accepted. I'm more worried about why you overreacted. Are you okay?"

For once, he couldn't lie. It was like he'd reached his quota for the month. "No."

Her eyes turned sad. "Do you want to talk about it?"

"Not here. Not now."

He readied himself for the barrage of questions. For her to

push him for answers. But they never came. Instead, she slipped her arms around his waist and lay her head over his heart.

The embrace felt so fucking right, it was like medicine.

He wrapped his arms around her waist and hugged her back, needing everything this woman was willing to give him, while knowing he didn't deserve any of it.

CHAPTER 7

*H*annah watched Erik from across the garden. She stood at a tall bar table, mostly because she was all danced out. Erik was talking to his father, and their conversation looked…tense.

Was he telling him what he couldn't tell *her*? Was he giving his father any reason as to why he wasn't okay? Surely his parents noticed…

She'd wanted to push for answers earlier. The fact that he'd admitted he wasn't okay had been their first little breakthrough. But he was right. This wasn't the time and place.

She just had to have faith that the time would come when he would open up to her. That they would eventually find their way back to each other.

She lifted her water to her lips and sipped it as she watched the small group beside Erik and his dad—Nate, Andi, Finley, and a tall, intense-looking guy. With his arm around Finley, it was obvious they were a couple. Even without the arm around her, though, Hannah would probably have guessed that he was the bodyguard Finley had spent Christmas with in Canada. Andi had told Hannah bits and pieces about the whirlwind romance.

Their love looked easy, and she couldn't help but feel just a small jolt of jealousy about that. She didn't necessarily need *easy* in her relationship. She just wished things weren't so hard.

She took another sip of water. She'd switched after the two cocktails had spiked her glucose. She didn't mind switching. She wasn't a big drinker at the best of times. Brigid, on the other hand…

Her best friend was on the dance floor, eyes closed as she leaned back into Henry while they moved to the music. The woman had drunk far too much, and Hannah couldn't help but worry about that. Was she attempting to drown her sorrows? To dull the pain of losing James?

"Disgustingly cute, aren't they?"

She glanced up at Owen. She hadn't spoken to Henry's new partner much tonight, but from what she'd gauged, he seemed friendly and down to earth. "I think those two were destined to be best friends from the day they were born."

"It sure seems that way." He sipped his beer. "Henry told me you're a real estate agent."

"I am. Are you looking to buy?"

"Actually, I might be. I've been renting a small apartment since I got to town, but it means I'm also having to rent a garage for the bikes I'm fixing. I'd love a place with some land for my own garage."

"I've got a few I'm selling at the moment. You're welcome to come around to my office. I can show you what I have and you can decide if you want to look at anything."

He dipped his head. "That sounds good."

"Great. I'll call you Monday and we can set up a meeting time." And that would give her more time to get to know Henry's new partner. "Henry said you're a mechanic?"

"I am. I specialize in motorcycles."

"I'm guessing you have one or two of your own?"

"Three. I rode my favorite here tonight."

Wasn't a surprise. The man fit the biker stereotype. "Have you always been into bikes?"

"Yeah, it was a passion of my uncle's that kind of rubbed off."

"Hannah!"

She glanced up just before Brigid flung herself into her arms. The impact almost had Hannah falling back. She only avoided it thanks to Owen's quick hand on her shoulder, keeping her steady.

Brigid laid her head on Hannah's chest. "I love you, Han."

Hannah chuckled while Henry pulled Owen out to the dance floor. She rubbed her friend's back. "I think maybe you've had a couple too many to drink, Brig."

Brigid shook her head as she straightened and took the stool on the other side of the table. "Nope! I'm just getting started."

Hannah pushed her glass of water across the table. "Drink."

Brigid did but scrunched her nose the second the liquid hit her tongue. "Argh. It's water."

"Yeah. And you need to take another sip. Or better yet, finish the whole glass."

Brigid sighed, tipping back the glass and drinking before dropping her head into her hands.

Hannah frowned. "Hey. Are you okay?"

Without moving her hands, she shook her head. "No. I think I fucked up. Or I'm gonna fuck up. Maybe I'm in the middle of the fuckup, I don't know."

Something twisted inside Hannah. "That doesn't make any sense, Brigid."

"If you knew, it would."

"Okay, so tell me what you did, or are doing, or are about to do, and we can work out how to fix it."

Brigid was the most spontaneous person Hannah knew. Once, she'd woken up and decided she needed a vacation, so she'd closed her store for the week and driven down to California.

"The last month and a half has been so hard."

Hannah's heart suddenly felt unbearably heavy, and she reached out and stroked her hair. "I know. I'm so sorry, honey."

Brigid finally lifted her head, and there was a shimmer of tears in her eyes. "I've had this pain in my chest, right here." She pressed a hand over her heart. "Sometimes it hurts so bad that it feels like someone has dug their fingers inside me and is tearing my heart in two."

Hannah rose to her feet and moved around the small table to pull her friend into her arms. "You'll be okay," she whispered. "We'll get through this together."

God, she wanted to go back and murder James for doing this to Brigid. For accepting the woman's love for years, then suddenly stomping on her heart.

Brigid wrapped her arms around Hannah and cried, the tears wetting her chest. She wanted to cry along with her. Christ, it hurt seeing her in so much pain. Every part of her just wanted to fix things, but the only thing that fixed heartache was time.

She needed to do better for Brigid. Check in on her more. Help her to heal in any way she could.

She wasn't sure how long she held her friend, but it was only the ringing of her phone that finally had Brigid pulling away.

"You go take it," she said quietly, wiping the tears from her cheeks.

Hannah shook her head. "No. I'm not leaving you."

"I'm okay." She sniffed. "I might go to the bathroom and touch up my makeup."

"I'll come with you."

Brigid was shaking her head before Hannah had finished speaking. "No, it's okay. I could use a moment alone."

Hannah's heart hurt as she watched her friend move toward the house.

With a heavy sigh, she pulled her phone from her bag to see there was no caller ID. She pressed the phone to her ear. "Hello, Hannah Jacobs speaking."

Whatever the person said was lost in the sounds of the crowd around her. It was too loud. She blocked her other ear and moved toward the side of the house. "Hello? Can you hear me?"

The person responded, but all she heard was a muffled male voice.

Damn. It was still too loud. She jogged to the side of the house, rounding the building. "Hello? Can you hear me now?"

She was walking beside the long lap pool when the snap of a stick cracking sounded behind her. Before she could turn, a hard shove to the shoulder had her arms swinging wide and air rushing at her face.

The phone fell from her fingers, and a scream ripped from her chest moments before her body hit the water and she sank below the surface.

* * *

Erik nodded as his father explained the work they were doing on the guesthouse at the back of their property. It was extensive, and there was no part of Erik that thought his father should be working on it.

"You're getting contractors in though, aren't you? You're not trying to do any of the work yourself? Not with your arrythmia."

There was a small whitening of his father's knuckles on his glass. His dad hated that he couldn't do as much as he used to. "Don't worry, your mother has made sure we use contractors."

Good. That made him feel better. Because what Jennifer Hunter wanted, she got.

Erik's gaze returned to the spot where Hannah had been. Even though he wasn't with her, he'd had eyes on her all night. She'd been with Brigid at a table, then the two women had been hugging, but now she was gone.

Fuck, where'd she go? To the bathroom? He scanned the dance floor, spotting Henry but not Hannah.

He clenched his father's shoulder. "Sorry, Dad, I need to check on Hannah."

"You go, son."

Erik was moving toward the doors to the house when his mother touched his arm. "Darling, where are you off to?"

"I'm looking for Hannah. Have you seen her?"

His mother's brows rose. "Actually, yes. She was on the phone and walking around the side of the house."

"Thank you."

He'd just started moving in that direction when a scream sounded. It was faint below the music and the chatter of guests, but it was there.

When he heard the distant splash of water, his blood ran cold.

Hannah couldn't swim…

His heart jumped into his throat. Praying it wasn't her, Erik sprinted toward the side of the house, passing Andi and Nate, ignoring their questioning gazes.

He rounded the corner to see Hannah in the pool, her arms flailing, head bobbing in and out of the water.

He didn't think. He threw off his jacket and dove into the pool. The second she was within reaching distance, he wrapped his arms around her and pulled her to the surface. Immediately, her arms wrapped around his neck, her legs around his waist.

"Erik!" she sputtered, latching onto him so tightly, she almost choked him. Her breaths moved quickly, but she wasn't coughing. And at least the water was warm.

He cupped her cheek and studied her pale features. "Are you okay?"

She nodded quickly.

"You're safe, Angel. I've got you."

"Oh my God!" His sister's voice came from the side of the pool, and he turned to see both her and Nate standing there.

He swam to the steps and climbed out, Hannah still wrapped

around him. The second the cool night air touched her skin, she shivered.

Nate took off his jacket and draped it over her shoulders.

"Come into the house," Andi said quickly, leading them to the front rather than the back to avoid the crowd. "I'll get you both some towels and find some clothes for Hannah. I don't have any men's clothes. Sorry, Erik."

"I've got some stuff in my car," Nate said, jogging toward the front of the house.

Erik followed Andi inside and down a hall to her bedroom. She opened the door, and he carried Hannah inside.

Andi disappeared into the attached bathroom, returning a second later with towels. She gave them to Erik before rummaging through her drawers and pulling out some yoga pants and a sweater for Hannah.

"Is there anything else you need?"

Hannah shook her head. "Thank you."

"I'll leave you two to it." At the door, she stopped, eyes meeting Hannah's. "Are you okay?"

She nodded. It was too quick, and her skin was too pale. Anger pounded through Erik's veins.

Nate stepped in. "Here, I had these." He left the clothes on the bed.

The second the door closed behind his siblings, Erik peeled the jacket off Hannah's shoulders. Even though the pool water had been warm, her skin was chilled, probably a combination of the shock and the cool evening air.

He moved into the bathroom and turned on the shower. When he returned to Hannah, he gently slipped the straps off her shoulders and let the wet material of her dress fall to the floor. A shudder rocked her body, and he cursed under his breath.

Quickly, he pulled off his own clothes and lifted her into his arms. The second they stood under the stream of hot water,

Hannah sighed. He lowered her to her feet, and she rested her head on his chest.

For a moment, he let everything fade. The anger. The dread that had pitted his gut for weeks. He just released it all to hold her. Love her.

They stood under the water for so long that steam billowed around them. Still, he didn't move to get out, and neither did she. It was only the vibration of her watch from the bathroom countertop sounded that had him putting a bit of separation between them.

Was she low?

Without a word, he stepped out and grabbed both their towels, wrapping one around her shoulders first.

Quickly, they both dried, and he helped her into the spare clothes before urging her down to sit on the bed. He pulled on the jeans and T-shirt Nate had left him, then checked her watch. Yep. Low.

He moved to Andi's dresser drawers, opening the second one and digging to the bottom of her socks for the bag of sour worms.

Humor sparkled in Hannah's blue eyes when he returned to her. "How did you know they were there?"

He lowered to his haunches in front of her. "Andi loves candy. In particular, sour worms. When we were kids, if Mom bought any form of candy, she'd take it and hide it. It took me a few searches to realize she always hid it in the same place, but I never ratted her out or took it back."

"Why not?"

He lifted one shoulder with a slight grin as he pulled a worm from the bag. "Knowledge is power. I thought I might need to use it against her one day. As it happens, I didn't use it against her then, but I *am* using it now."

He touched a worm to Hannah's lips, and she opened for him, the candy disappearing inside her mouth.

He waited for her to swallow before cupping her cheek. "What happened?"

Her brows knitted together. "I was on the phone but couldn't hear whoever was on the line, so I moved around the corner to look for someplace quieter. And I think…"

Erik frowned when she stopped. "You think what, Angel?"

"I think someone pushed me."

CHAPTER 8

"**I** want a list of every guest who attended the party."

There was a beat of silence over the phone, and he could almost hear his sister thinking. It was early, and the morning sun reflected off his laptop screen in his office. Hannah was still asleep, but luckily, Andi was an early riser, party the night before or no party.

"Erik, I can give it to you, but I just can't imagine anyone I invited pushing her in."

"You think she's lying?"

"No." The answer came so quickly, he knew it was true. "I don't know *what* to think. Maybe someone came who wasn't invited? There were a lot of people, so there's every chance someone could have snuck in without me noticing. And it's not like I had security."

He growled. "Next time, I'm ordering security. We're also putting up cameras at your place."

A choked noise sounded over the phone. "Uh...no."

"Yes."

"Erik, I know this has shaken you and that you're angry."

Fuck yes, he was angry. Someone had *pushed* Hannah into the pool. Had they done it because they knew she couldn't swim?

He'd wanted to go back outside and question every goddamn guest there last night. Hell, he would have if Nate hadn't grabbed him before he could make a scene.

"But…" Andi continued, "I don't think this had anything to do with me. I'm okay. My home is okay. Nothing's missing. And I won't be having another party like that for a while, anyway. Probably another ten years."

Erik ran frustrated fingers through his hair. A part of him wanted everyone he loved to have as much security as possible. But Andi was right. The danger hadn't been directed at her. If she didn't want cameras at her home, that was her choice.

She sighed. "I don't have a full list because some people invited partners, and I invited a few different people here and there. As far as I know, there was really only one person in attendance who wasn't already closely connected to anyone…"

One name immediately came to mind. "Leo."

"Yeah. I invited him because I met him at the café that day, and he mentioned he didn't know anyone in town."

"I'll look into him. Can you just send me who else you remember?"

Andi sighed. "Sure. Is Hannah okay?"

"Yeah. We pretty much went to bed as soon as we got home last night. She woke up a couple of times because she kept going low, but she's okay."

"Good. I've still got her dress and your suit. I'll get them cleaned and bring them over. Can I bring you guys some food?"

His heart softened at his sister's words. "We're all right. But thank you."

"Okay. Call if you need anything."

"I will."

"Love you, big brother."

"Love you too."

The second the call ended, Erik dialed Chandler. It took him three rings to answer.

"You know, some of us like sleeping in every once in a while."

"I don't understand that."

Chandler chuckled. "Yeah, you have to like sleep for that. What do you need?"

"Why do you think I need anything?"

"Because I know you."

"Fine. I need you to look into a guy for me."

"Knew it." There were some rustling sounds. "Who?"

"I only have a first name. Leo. But he works at Reuben's Real Estate here in Redwood."

Chandler chuckled. "You never make my job easy, do you?"

"Where's the fun in that?"

Footsteps sounded outside the door, and a second later, Hannah stood there wearing just his T-shirt, which went down to her knees. His dick twitched while something hard and territorial burned in his chest.

"I've got to go, Chandler."

"You wake me up at the crack of dawn and there's no, 'How are you? What are you up to today?'"

The corners of Erik's lips pulled up. "You sound good to me, and you're probably working."

"Fuck, you're right. I need to get a life. I'll let you know if I find anything."

The call ended, and Hannah had all of Erik's attention. She crossed the room slowly, her hair tumbling over her shoulder like a waterfall, her features soft.

The second she was close, he rose and tugged her into his body. "Good morning, Angel. How are you feeling today?"

"Good. Thanks to you looking after me."

He shook his head. "I didn't do anything."

She laughed. "Yeah, you only pulled me from the water, got

me warm, and woke up with me every time I had a low last night."

A rumble sounded from his chest. She shouldn't have had to deal with any of that.

Her features smoothed. "I need to visit Brigid today."

He frowned. "Is she okay?"

"I don't know. I'm worried about her. She was drinking a lot last night and saying something about a mistake. This James stuff has hit her really hard."

"I'll drive you."

She opened her mouth like she was about to argue, then snapped it closed and nodded. When she rose to her toes, he didn't hesitate—he lowered his mouth and kissed her, letting her take away all his worries for a brief moment.

* * *

Hannah keyed in the code to the side door of Brigid's apartment building, Erik watching her closely. She didn't miss the fact that he was also watching other things. The street around them. The parking lot at their backs.

When they stepped inside, they took the staircase to the fourth floor, and Hannah knocked on Brigid's door. It was ten thirty. She'd tried not to come too early so her friend could sleep in, but she hadn't been able to hold off any longer.

When no one came to the door, she banged harder, then tugged her phone out and called Brigid. She thought it was going to go to voice mail, when Brigid finally answered.

"What?"

The corners of Hannah's lips twitched. "I'm at your door. Open up."

A groan sounded. "I can't. I'm in bed dying. My head hurts and I've thrown up way too many times."

"Open the door and I'll give you your favorite hangover food."

There was a small pause. "Bacon and egg bagel?"

"Yep. And a chocolate croissant."

The line went dead, and four seconds later, the door opened. Brigid stood on the other side, hair down and all over the place, the previous night's makeup still on her face and smudged, wearing only an oversized shirt.

"Where is it?"

Hannah turned and kissed Erik. "I'll see you later?"

"I'll be in the car doing some work. Call when you're done, and I'll come to the door."

She nodded. "You remember the code?"

"Yep."

She was still watching him walk away when the bag was snatched from her fingers. "Hey!"

Brigid was already heading back to her bedroom. Hannah closed and locked the door, then followed, entering just as Brigid flopped to the bed and took out the bagel.

Hannah perched on the side. "You know, I can get you a plate so you don't drop crumbs on the bed."

Brigid took a big bite of the bagel. "I need to change the sheets anyway."

Hannah looked around the bedroom, spotting Brigid's discarded dress from the previous night. Her clutch had also been dropped on the floor.

She cleared her throat. "Brigid. I'm sorry."

She stopped mid-chew and frowned. "For what?"

"I've had a lot going on and haven't been checking in on you nearly enough."

Brigid shook her head and opened her mouth, but before she could get a word out, Hannah continued.

"I know everything that happened with James hit you so hard." Pain cascaded through her friend's eyes. "I want to be here for you. For whatever you need."

"You're an amazing friend, Hannah. You don't need to feel like you've done anything wrong or you're not doing enough."

"I should be checking in more." She shuffled closer. "Last night, you mentioned a mistake that you were making, or are about to make."

Brigid's eyes widened, as if she'd forgotten all about that.

"Will you tell me about it?"

Her head dropped, and she picked at a bit of bacon on the bagel. "It's nothing."

"It's not nothing. It sounded very important, and I want to help you with it if I can."

She shook her head. "No. I'm okay. Really. I just…I need more time."

"Brigid—"

"I actually have to do some paperwork for the shop today. Would you mind making us some coffee while I shower?"

She was avoiding the subject. Hannah wanted to push until she found out exactly what her friend was hiding. She'd sounded so distraught last night. But she knew Brigid. And she knew pressing the matter would only get her back up. All Hannah could do was be there for her and trust that Brigid would tell her when she was ready.

Hannah reached over and squeezed her arm. "Of course."

CHAPTER 9

$\mathcal{A}$ beeping from Hannah's phone pulled her from her sleep. Not only that, but also a vibration from her watch.

She peeled her eyes open, tapping on the screen.

Crap. She was going low again. It wasn't a surprise. She'd barely eaten dinner.

With a sigh, she reached over to the bedside table lamp and flicked it on, then stilled when she saw the other side of the bed was empty.

Erik wasn't here again.

He'd been better this last week, going to bed with her. Holding her. She'd quickly gotten used to it. She looked at her watch again. Three in the morning.

Swallowing the disappointment, she climbed to her feet. She had candy in her bedside drawer, but when she ate that at night, it often kept her awake.

Slowly, she went downstairs and into the kitchen, where she prepared a bowl of Honey Bunches of Oats cereal, which she topped with oat milk. A smile tugged at her lips at the memory of the first time she'd seen oat milk in Erik's fridge. It had been a few days after Christmas, and she'd opened the door to see the carton sitting on a shelf.

For most, that wouldn't have been a big deal. But for them, it'd been huge. Erik hated oat milk. So the fact he'd bought it for her meant he wanted her here, in his home, with him.

She hadn't convinced him to bring her coffee pod machine over yet. Maybe one day.

She adjusted her pump and spooned some cereal into her mouth. Halfway through the bowl, she headed into the living room, her gaze brushing over the expansive fireplace. This house was all class and money—everything hers wasn't.

She was walking to the window when a noise pulled her attention to the right. Soft thuds.

What was that?

She spooned one more bite of cereal into her mouth before lowering the bowl to the coffee table and moving into the hall. The closer she drew to the basement door, the louder the sounds got. Thumps, some close together, others not.

Quietly, she opened the door to hear the thumps now combined with heavy breathing. She started down the stairs. She'd only been down here once, when Erik had offered to show her the space where he worked out, and it looked exactly the same. A pull-up bar to one side—he had another outside that he used when weather permitted—various weights scattered around the space, a jump rope hanging on a wall. There were a couple of machines that she would have no idea how to work. And in the center of the room, the heavy bag.

Erik stood with his back to her, fists raised and gloves on. He was shirtless and shoeless, only wearing low-hanging shorts as he danced in front of the bag. Small beads of sweat dripped from his skin, and there were earbuds in his ears.

When he hit the bag, the entire thing shook. The sound of each impact was loud in the otherwise quiet space. He hit it again and again, and she almost stepped back, intimidated by the force behind the hits.

The man was all power.

She inched closer, hearing the music blaring through his earbuds.

When he did a fast combination of hits, her breath stopped. He'd been a professional boxer for a while after getting out of the military, and after that, he'd done some cage fighting. She couldn't imagine someone being on the receiving end of those hits. The thought was terrifying. Surely, one punch and they'd be down and out.

What was causing him so much discontent in the middle of the night? Was it his past? The death of half his team on his last mission? The death of his wife and their unborn baby all those years ago? All of that affected him on such a deep level, and none of it was stuff he'd ever forget.

But still, this felt...different. New.

She took one more step forward as Erik's arms dropped, and he turned to the side. That's when his gaze collided with hers. His brows flickered, and he pulled off his gloves, then his earbuds.

"Hey. How long have you been down here?"

She swiped her finger across the charms on her bracelet. "Not long."

He glanced down at that bracelet, and she thought she saw a twist of pain in his eyes.

Strange. Why would her bracelet cause him pain? It had a cloud charm on it from Nico, and an angel charm from Erik. Did he regret giving it to her?

She dropped her hand. "Will you show me how to hit?"

"You want to know how to hit the bag?"

"Yes." She lifted a shoulder. "It might come in handy one day."

He paused for so long she thought he was going to say no. Then he turned and dropped his gloves into a box before pulling out another pair. The second he touched her wrist, her skin tingled.

"Knowing how to hit effectively is important. But there are other things that are important too."

"Like what?"

"The other night, when you woke to my hands around your neck…" She felt the guilt in his words as much as she heard it. "You can fight that by grabbing one of my fingers, just a single one, and pulling it in the opposite direction."

She nodded, even though the idea of having to fight off a person who was strangling her was horrifying.

"And if someone's on top of you, bring a knee up, or your hips —anything to create space so you can get away."

Instead of strapping her other hand straight away, he lifted her wrist and read her glucose reading. Obviously, he was okay with what he saw, because he slipped off her watch and did up the other glove.

Once the gloves were on, his hands smoothed up her arms, one hand continuing its journey to brush some hair from her face. "Ready?"

She nodded because sometimes her voice was another thing she lost when he touched her. The words in her throat literally got stuck.

He shifted to the side, and she stepped toward the bag. Immediately, she felt him behind her, his heat covering her back, his arms around her.

"Stand with your left foot forward, and visualize a line on the ground between your legs."

She nodded, trying to absorb the instructions. To not focus on the gravel of his voice.

He lifted her arms. "Hands by face, chin down, and elbows tucked. That's your boxing stance."

She nodded again.

"When you step forward, keep your knees loose, and step with your front foot first." His breath brushed her cheek. "Ready for a jab?"

"Yes."

"Your left hand is going to go straight out, and you'll turn your hips into the move." With his fingers wrapped around her forearm, he moved her fist forward so that it lightly touched the bag. "Exhale on the end."

"Exhale…got it."

"Try that on your own and in real time, then I'll show you the cross punch."

He stepped back and she wanted to protest. To turn around and demand he put his hands back on her. Instead, she forced a deep breath into her lungs, then threw a fist into the bag. It was like hitting a brick wall.

"I can't move it like you."

His deep chuckle slid into her veins, heating her blood. It had been so long since she'd heard him sound relaxed.

She swallowed and jabbed the bag again.

"That's good." When his heat returned to her, the rhythm of her heart changed, speeding up in her chest. His hands returned to her wrists. "For a cross punch, send your right fist straight forward, again turning your hips."

For a second time, he guided her fist to the bag. "Ready to try it on your own?"

Absolutely not. She nodded.

He stepped back, and she took one steadying breath before shooting her right fist forward. Again, the bag didn't move. Still, she reset herself and hit it again.

"Good. Now try a combination. Two jabs, then a cross punch."

This time, she didn't think about technique or the way the bag remained so still. She just…punched. Then she punched again. Suddenly, the moves were like breaths of fresh air. Like every frustration in her body was released in a single impact of fist against bag.

She did it again and again, feeling the same release each time. It was crazy that she was standing here, punching a bag in only a T-shirt and panties at three in the morning, and she *liked* it.

"How's it feel?"

Her lips twitched. "Good. I can see why you like this. But I think I need a bit more help. Can you put your hands on my hips and guide me?"

There was a small pause, and she could just about hear the man thinking.

Yeah, she was playing a game. But she didn't care. She wanted more of *this* Erik. The Erik who touched her without hesitation. The Erik who laughed freely.

He stepped to her back and touched her hips, and suddenly that sense of rightness, of peace, returned to her.

* * *

THE HEAT of Hannah's skin moved through the thin material of her shirt and straight into Erik.

He'd come down here because, yet again, he couldn't sleep. He'd been looking for refuge. He hadn't found it. But since Hannah had arrived, he could almost convince himself he had.

"Can you guide my hands again too?" Her soft voice cut through the quiet, twisting his insides.

He grazed his hands up her sides to her shoulders, then down her arms to her wrists. Carefully, he guided her jab and cross punch. When her ass pushed into him, he bit back a groan. He tried to ignore it as he led her through another combination hit. But her ass pressed back again...and this time she ground against him.

He stilled, and the words that came out of his mouth were short and sharp. "What are you doing, Angel?"

"I'm learning how to box. But I think I need you a bit closer so you can guide my entire body."

He stepped closer. Immediately, she wiggled her ass. His cock hardened. "Angel—"

"That's good. I feel like I can really get an idea of what to do with my body now." She leaned back into him.

He groaned. "You need to stop."

"Okay. Could you take these off for me?"

Erik frowned. That was too easy.

He unstrapped the gloves, but once they were off, she didn't walk away. Instead, she turned and grazed her fingers down his bare chest. "That's better. Now I can *really* feel you."

She leaned forward and pressed a light kiss to his chest, right over his heart. It was barely a brush, but he felt it like she'd marked him. Carved herself into his flesh.

His breath caught in his throat. She kissed him again.

"Angel, it's the middle of the night. I need to shower. And you need sleep."

She was shaking her head before he'd finished speaking. "No. The only thing either of us *need* to do is find *us* again."

He gripped her hips, not sure if he intended to push her away or pull her closer. He did neither. He just stood there, incapable of moving, feeling like a man in chains.

"I love you, Erik." Her breath whispered across his skin, her words turning his insides into a tattered mess. "I love your heart. Your goodness. And I love how safe I feel with you, body and soul."

Safe…she felt safe with him. But was she?

She cupped his cheek, pulling his thoughts back to her. "I can see your mind working. But Erik, there is nothing you could say that would make me doubt us. Do you understand? You're my person. In every scenario. In every version of every story that's ours, you are mine, and I am yours."

Then she tugged his head down and kissed him again, slipping her tongue between his lips and tasting him. It was instant fire. An explosion of need and desire inside him.

He lifted her against his body and turned, pressing her to the wall. The shirt gathered around her waist, the heat of her core pressing into his bare stomach.

"Erik…"

His name whispered from her lips, slipping into his heart.

This. This is what got him through his darkest days. The feel of her in his arms. The knowledge that she was still his. That she loved him.

In one swift move, he tugged her shirt over her head and dropped it to the floor before taking one pebbled nipple between his lips.

Hannah whimpered, her back arching, pushing her farther into his mouth. He flicked her bud back and forth, then sucked.

"Erik…now. I can't wait!"

He slipped a hand into her panties, grazing over her clit, loving the little jolt from her. So damn responsive. His thumb moved over her as he touched a finger to her entrance and pushed inside.

Fucking soaked.

"Erik, please!"

He growled, tearing her panties from her body before pulling out his cock and positioning it at her entrance. He intended to go slow. To stretch her walls carefully. But Hannah tightened her legs, yanking him closer, and he thrust inside her.

The ripple in his chest was something between heaven and agony. "Hannah…you kill me."

It was like they were made to fit so perfectly, nothing and no one else could ever compare.

Her gaze bored into his. "Remember, you and me. In every version…every story."

In this moment, she made him believe her. Believe that nothing and no one could tear them apart.

His mouth crashed to hers, and he kissed her deeply. His hips began to move, thrusting in and out. Every time he returned to her, it was like coming home. Returning to his heart.

He tangled his tongue with hers, slid his hand up her side to cup her breast. Her fingers dug into his shoulders, soft moans slipping from her throat as he swiped her nipple back and forth.

"You're so fucking perfect, Angel."

"For you," she whispered, her breath brushing over his lips. "Only for you."

His thrusts became harder. Faster. The sounds rippling from her throat louder. It was only when he reached down and circled her clit that her body tensed and broke, her walls clenching around him.

He continued to thrust. To taste her. Touch her. But too soon, his own body tightened, and he shattered, breaking into so many pieces his knees almost buckled.

He forced himself to remain upright. To keep her in his arms. When he finally stilled, it was only their chests that moved.

She kissed his lips again, but this kiss was different. It was soft. Almost a graze. Then she whispered, "Us. It's always us."

CHAPTER 10

*H*annah climbed out of the car and walked toward Reuben's Real Estate. She wanted to be happy. Last night had been everything. The way Erik had touched her. Needed her. But this morning when she woke, he'd been gone again. No note. No text.

Every time they took a step forward, it felt like they then took two steps back. Or at least, *Erik* took steps back.

She'd just touched the office door when her phone beeped with a text. Her heart thumped like it always did at the possibility she'd see Erik's name on the screen. That he'd write sweet words. Maybe ask her to spend the evening with him.

Hope sucked. It made her wish for things that often didn't eventuate.

She pulled out her phone and frowned when she saw an unknown number. She clicked into the text...and all the blood rushed from her head.

Unknown Number: You think I'm playing? I'm not. You're a murderer. And I'm gonna make sure you pay for the crime you tried to hide all those years ago.

The nausea came so hard and fast, she almost threw up then

and there. She barely forced the bile down her throat as she spun to look up and down the street. Who *was* this person? Were they watching her?

She read the text again, needing the words to rearrange into something different. Because this wasn't possible. *No one* knew what had happened all those years ago. No one but Nico, and he was gone. She hadn't even told Erik yet. She'd meant to, then he'd gotten distant and she just…hadn't.

Her heart raced so hard, she pressed a hand to her chest to keep it from beating out.

As she stepped into the foyer of the office, Owen rose from the couch.

Her breath caught, but this time for a different reason. "Owen! Oh my God, our meeting…that's this morning."

She'd been so distracted by everything else going on in her life, she'd completely forgotten. She shot a glance at her watch. Ten past nine…the meeting was scheduled for nine. She was late. She was *never* late.

He gave her an easy smile. "It's okay. You're here now."

"Still, I'm so sorry. Please, come to my office." She led him down the hall and into her office, indicating the chairs on the other side of the desk. "Have a seat. I'll just get organized."

She tapped on her watch, cursing at the slight glucose high. Not a surprise—stress always made her go high.

Thank God she'd already prepared a folder of information for Owen a few days ago. She pulled the folder from her cabinet but didn't immediately hand it to him. Instead, she forced her lips into a smile. "So, I know you want space for your bikes. What else are you looking for?"

He leaned back in his seat. "I don't need a lot of space inside the house because it's just me. As long as there's somewhere for me to sleep and cook. Although, if the right house happened to be big, I wouldn't rule it out. I'd find shit to put in the rooms." He grinned. "Optimally, I'd love a large garage to lock up my bikes.

But that's not absolutely necessary if there's space to have one built."

She nodded. "Great." She opened the folder and pulled out a couple properties that wouldn't work. The tremble in her fingers was obvious. She needed to calm down. But how could she? Someone knew what she'd done all those years ago. Not only that, they knew where she worked, had her phone number, and they were *threatening* her.

When a hand touched her forearm, her gaze shot up to see Owen leaning forward, concern on his face.

"Hey," he said quietly. "Are you okay? You're shaking."

She nodded, but the move felt jerky and wrong. "Yes. Sorry. I…my day's just gotten off to a rocky start."

How she was even functioning right now, she had no idea. Fear ran through her blood, so quickly and fiercely she could barely breathe.

"I understand bad mornings." Slowly, he pulled his hand away. "Is there anything I can do?"

"No. But thank you. And again, I'm sorry for being a bit of a mess."

"You don't need to apologize. Henry's told me you're the best."

She almost laughed. "Henry *would* say that. He's a good friend." She passed him the folder of printed properties. "These are all currently on the market, and they either have secure garages for your bikes or acreage to put in a garage. Some of the houses are maybe a bit larger than you want."

Owen nodded, still looking concerned as he slipped the folder from her fingers.

She had no idea how she got through the rest of their meeting. Somehow she said the right things, arranged a time to show him some properties, and gave him all the information he needed for potential financing options. When he finally left, she pulled her phone out and read the text again.

The ice that slipped over her skin was instant, the fear blackening the world around her.

Her immediate instinct was to pick up the phone and tell Erik, but she hesitated. She had an entire workday to get through.

Tonight. She'd tell him tonight.

A part of her knew he'd understand. Of course he would. She'd acted out of self-defense. But she'd never told another soul about that day, or how much it had changed her. Telling him would be like exposing the most vulnerable part of herself.

When her phone beeped, she flinched and almost didn't want to look down in case it was the unknown number again. She forced herself to click on the screen.

Not an unknown number.

Erik: Hey, sorry, I need to go on a last-minute work trip tonight. I'll be back in a few days.

Another step back for them…

The weight on her chest was suddenly too much.

Without thinking, Hannah lifted her purse and left the office. Brigid's lingerie shop wasn't far. She wasn't sure what words might slip out of her mouth when she got there. Would she tell her what she'd done so long ago? Would she tell her about the text? She didn't know, but she needed her best friend.

She walked quickly, the tapping of her heels on the sidewalk loud. She felt it the entire way there—eyes on her. Was it because she was freaked out after the text? Or was there actually someone watching her at this very moment?

Her mind flicked back to whomever had pushed her into the water at Andi's party. They'd never found out who it was. There were no cameras, and no one was around when Erik had found her.

She sped up her steps, and when she finally reached Brigid's store, she all but fell inside.

The front desk was empty. Frowning, she walked further into

the store. The entire *place* was empty. She paused…and a quiet voice came from the back storage room.

She crept closer, slowly pushing the door open to see Brigid standing with her back to her.

"Yes, I understand," Brigid said quickly. "I just need to know when the money will hit my account."

Money?

"Really? It can't be sooner?" Brigid turned, her eyes widening when they caught Hannah's. "Yes, that's fine. Thank you. I've got to go." She hung up and stepped toward Hannah. "Hey. Sorry, that was…" She shook her head. "It doesn't matter. Is everything okay?"

"Not really."

Brigid's eyes softened. "Oh, Han…"

Her friend opened her arms, and without a word, Hannah walked into them, immediately letting the silent tears fall.

CHAPTER 11

 *E*rik's jaw was tight as he drove home. The job in Vermont had taken a week. Too fucking long. It was the middle of the night, and all he wanted to do was see Hannah. Touch her. Know she was safe.

After the incident at Andi's house, he hated being away from her. He still didn't know what had happened that night, and he wanted to kick his own ass for telling Chandler she didn't need protection at the party. He'd thought she'd be safe with his family.

As it was, Chandler had found nothing incriminating about Leo. The guy had grown up in Pheonix, gone to private schools, worked at a few different realty offices. He'd moved to Leavenworth two years ago.

He turned down his driveway, breathing a sigh of relief when he saw Hannah's G70 in the garage. He grabbed his bag from the back seat and headed inside.

He took one step into his bedroom before the bag hit the floor. The bed was empty.

Not only that, but it was still made, like Hannah had never gotten in.

What the fuck?

"Hannah?" he called as he moved into the connected bathroom. Empty.

Room by room, he searched the house, calling out to her. By the time he reached the kitchen, he was ready to lose his fucking mind. Panic had taken root inside him, spreading through his limbs.

He'd texted her throughout his trip, and she'd always texted back that she was okay. Their last communication had been the previous evening. Had something happened between then and now?

Fuck. Where was she?

He pulled out his phone and tried her number. When she didn't answer, he texted her.

Erik: Hannah. Where are you?

He didn't wait for a response, instead, calling Chandler. His friend answered on the fourth ring.

"Hunter, I was sleeping, man—"

"Where is she?"

"What?"

"Hannah. Where the fuck is she? Your guy should have been watching her. She should be safe, but she's not in my house." Every word was a hard fucking line, but the panic was eating at him.

"Calm down. I'm gonna call my guy. I'll get back to you."

The second Chandler hung up, Erik ran his fingers through his hair, almost pulling out the damn strands. He couldn't breathe. Couldn't see. He was barely remaining on his feet. Every minute that passed felt like ten.

When Chandler's name finally flashed on the screen again, Erik answered before the first full ring. "Where is she?"

"Calm down, she's okay," Chandler said slowly. "She's been sleeping at her house."

Erik's entire body locked. *Her* house?" Shit. Why hadn't he thought of that?

Because he'd been so panicked, he'd lost his goddamn mind.

"Yeah. Since the first night you left for the job."

The relief was instant, and it hit him so hard it felt like a physical blow. She was okay. She was safe. But just as quickly, his gut clenched.

She'd moved out of his house…

"You all right?" Chandler asked.

No. He was far from all right. "I'm fine. Thanks for finding out."

He hung up, grabbed his key to her house, and went straight outside. When he reached her door, he let himself in, locked the dead bolt, then walked down the hall. He *hated* that she'd been staying here. There wasn't enough security in her house.

When he reached her room, the air rushed out of his lungs. She was curled into a ball, half under the covers, wearing his T-shirt.

His. This woman was his.

For a moment, he didn't move. He needed to take her in. Then, without blinking, he tugged off his sweatshirt and jeans. When he was down to his briefs, he slid into the bed behind her and pulled her against him. The peace was so instant, it cut through every other emotion.

"Erik…" Hannah breathed his name, as if she knew his touch without opening her eyes.

He kissed her neck. "Yeah, Angel. It's me. You're safe."

* * *

THE QUIET SOUND of movement in the room pricked at Hannah's subconscious. The rustle of clothing. Hushed breathing.

Slowly, she peeled her eyes open to see Erik's back toward her as he pulled on his jeans. His muscles flexed which each movement.

She half remembered him climbing into bed with her last night. The warmth had penetrated her sleep, the strength of his arms around her middle like a protective circle. The second he'd touched her, her restless sleep had calmed, and she'd sunk into him.

But he was leaving already? The sun wasn't even up.

Her gaze shifted to the bedside clock to see it wasn't even six.

He'd just pulled his shirt over his head and stepped toward the door when she spoke.

"Really?" she said, the word full of hurt. "We haven't seen each other in a week, and you're leaving before I even wake up?"

He froze. It was a full three seconds before he turned, his expression unreadable.

She swallowed. God, she hated how closed off he'd become. If anything, that hurt more than the physical distance he'd put between them.

She sat up slowly. "You weren't even going to give me a kiss goodbye?"

"I didn't want to wake you."

Her brows flickered. Shouldn't he *want* to wake her? Shouldn't he want to see her smile and hear her voice, particu larly after days of being apart?

She climbed out of bed, something hard and uncomfortable coiling in her belly. The Erik in front of her reminded her too much of the man she'd met all those months ago. That man had been a stranger…and this man felt like one too.

"Tell me what's wrong, Erik. *Now.* I don't want to hear bullshit about you being fine. About *us* being fine. We're not. We're drifting apart. And I want you to tell me *why.*"

A muscle in his cheek ticked, but he remained silent.

She frowned. "Why can't you do it?"

"Because…then I lose you."

She paused. "Is *this* you keeping me? Leaving before I wake up? Barely speaking to me? Barely able to *look* at me?"

"This is me having no damn clue what I'm doing but scared to lose the only good thing in my life!"

She stepped toward him. "Then let me help you. Let me promise you that, whatever it is, it'll be okay. *We'll* be okay."

"But what if it isn't? What if the thing I'm keeping from you is the one thing that could shatter us completely? What if it's so bad that you'll wish you'd never met me? Would you still want to know?"

Her breath caught, fear tangling inside her chest. For a moment, she let that fear stall her.

Then she blinked and straightened. Whatever it was, they could work through it. They had to. "Yes. I would want to know. Because that at least gives us a chance."

Another beat of silence, and God, she wanted to scream.

At what point did she stop pushing?

"Erik...I don't know if I can keep fighting for us if I'm the only one wielding a sword." Her voice cracked.

Finally, a flicker of emotion on his face—pain. "Hannah..." That was all he said...her name. In a voice that held so much regret, her heart nearly broke.

That's when she knew for certain—he wasn't going to tell her. He just expected her to live in this new normal of censored words and fractured love.

"I can't do this anymore, Erik," she whispered, the words as broken as she felt. "I can't love you so hard, only to get so little back. You need to choose—be honest with me, tell me what's going on...or walk away."

She watched him, *begged him* with her eyes to say something, anything, that would give her a chance to fix them. Words that would give her some clue into what was going on.

But he didn't. He remained so perfectly still, so quiet, that the silence turned into this rock that sat between them, keeping them apart.

He'd chosen...but he hadn't chosen *her*.

"Leave." Emotion clogged her voice, tears she couldn't stop rolling down her cheeks.

"Hannah—"

"I gave you *everything* I had, and you can't even give me one truth that could save us. Get out. *Now.*"

Even in that moment, even when she thought she'd completely given up, a part of her still hoped, *prayed*, that he'd try to save them. That he'd say *something* that would bring them back together.

When he didn't, when he ran fingers through his hair, his face pained, then walked away, she felt like the floor was ripped from beneath her feet. Like the fire that had blazed between them, once so bright, was just extinguished with a single puff.

The click of her front door opening and closing felt like a bullet to the chest. Her knees gave out and she fell to the floor. Her chest heaved, the air barely making it to her lungs, and her heart felt like it was bleeding. *She* felt like she was bleeding. Like Erik had taken a sword, sliced her heart in two, and left her to bleed out.

⚔ ⚔ ⚔

ERIK'S FIST pounded the bag. With every hit, he found a new level of rage. A new fury to fuel him.

He wasn't in his basement. He'd had to get out of his house, put some distance between them. She was all he could think about. So he'd just started driving until he'd reached his parents' house. He'd known his father wouldn't be home. On Wednesday, he left early to go fishing. His mother was likely home but asleep. The house was so big, she probably wouldn't hear him though.

The old heavy bag was still in the basement. The bag he knew his brother used when he came home. The bag his father used to use.

Her sad eyes flashed in his mind, and he hit harder.

I gave you everything I had, and you can't even give me one single truth that could possibly save us.

Her words played over in his head again and again. He was a coward. But the truth wouldn't save them—it would only hurt her. Because she'd have to choose—believe Erik and lose the image she'd had of her foster brother; or choose her foster brother and believe Erik had killed him in cold blood.

Sweat dripped from his skin as he jabbed the bag, his chest burning with exertion. Every minute bled into the next and none of them were enough.

When the door to the basement opened, he didn't turn. It was like something inside him couldn't stop. Because when he stopped, he'd be thrust back into reality. A reality that hurt too goddamn much to return to.

"Erik?" His mother's soft voice clicked into his brain.

Jab, cross punch.

"Honey, are you okay?"

Her voice was close…too close. He wanted to shout at her to turn around and leave him alone. That he wasn't safe to be around right now. But fuck, was there ever a safe time to be around him? He'd lost so many people from his life. *He* was the common denominator. He was like a poison.

"Erik, stop and look at me."

It was when she touched him that his arms finally dropped, but only because he didn't want to swing an elbow back and hit her.

He didn't turn though. Instead, he leaned his head forward onto the bag and just breathed, the ragged air loud as it choked through his lungs.

A soft hand touched his back. "Baby, talk to me."

He scrunched his eyes closed, something about his mother's voice thrusting him back to when he was a kid. Making the hurt inside him ripple and fray.

"What's wrong?" she whispered.

One deep, shuddering breath…then the words fell from his chest. "I'm not sure I'm gonna survive this, Mom."

She smoothed her hand over his aching flesh. "Tell me the problem, and I'll tell you how we can fix it."

He was shaking his head before she'd finished speaking. "You can't fix this one."

"Try." One whispered word that held so much weight.

He straightened and pulled off his gloves. The second he dropped them into the box, his mother pulled him over to the weight bench. She didn't push him to speak. She didn't pester him with questions. She just waited, as if she knew he needed time.

"I did something," he said quietly. "And it's going to ruin us."

His mother took a moment to consider his words. "Us, being you and Hannah."

He nodded, and in that nod, he felt the weight of its devastation. "I've tried telling her so many times, and she's basically been begging me. But whenever the words crawl up my throat, I just can't get them out. Because I know as soon as they reach her ears…they'll ruin her, and I'll lose us. Fuck, I've probably lost her anyway. So now I need to figure out how to survive that. How to survive living without her."

His mother wrapped an arm around his shoulders. "Baby, you've been through so much pain in your life. You've lost more than any one person should ever lose. And I understand why you've always run from that pain. But what we run from always finds us." She leaned her head closer. "It's time to stop running and tell her what she needs to know. Then *fight*."

He *had* been running, for so long. He'd been running so fucking far and fast that he'd lost all sense of direction.

His breathing hitched at the thought of confessing to Hannah. His mother pulled him into her arms, and he let the weight of what he had to do swamp him. Gut him. Drown him.

Hannah's feet sank into the wet ground as she made her way from her house to Erik's. She'd seen his Corvette leave an hour ago, and she'd spent her time since then packing a bag.

Her heart rattled in her chest at the thought of leaving her home, but she didn't let herself collapse to the floor a second time. She was stronger than that. She had to be.

With steady fingers, she dug the key from her pocket and pushed it into the lock of Erik's front door. She'd been in here a few times over the last week to grab bits and pieces, but this felt different. Because today *was* different. She wasn't grabbing a few things here and there…she was taking everything. Erasing all traces of her life from his house.

Her breaths shortened as she stepped inside and keyed the code into the alarm, but she forced the air into her lungs to keep moving.

The soft thud of the door closing was loud behind her, and every step she took up the stairs felt like it required all of her energy. When she reached the bedroom, her gaze ran over his bed…a bed they'd shared. It had been a place of safety for a while. Then he'd started disappearing on her, and suddenly it had shifted into something else. Into the place that represented loneliness, where she merely waited for the man who so rarely returned to her.

Tears pressed at her eyes, but she blinked them away to lift the empty box she'd brought with her and opened the first drawer. Item by item, she removed herself from this house. Her remaining clothes. Her toiletries. Erik had made a lot of space for her here. He'd *wanted* her…at least for a while.

God, she'd give anything to know what had happened. Why wouldn't he tell her? She'd *begged* him!

When a tear fell, she swiped it away before pulling her phone from her pocket and calling Brigid. She'd called her best friend at least three times this morning, but she wasn't answering. This time was no different. The call went to voice mail, and Hannah hung up. Then she sent a quick text.

Hannah: Brigid…I need you.

She could call Henry, but in her gut, she knew she needed Brigid. The friend who knew exactly what she was going through, because she was going through something similar.

Argh. She hated crying. Her entire life, crying had felt like a weakness, and she hated feeling weak.

Quickly, she grabbed her diabetes supplies from the bedside table.

Her gaze moved over the space one last time before she turned and all but ran down the stairs. She grabbed her insulin from the fridge and turned to the door. Getting out was all she could think to do, before her heart broke completely. Before every carefully constructed protective wall came crashing down.

She'd experienced loss in her life, so many shades of it, but nothing like this. This felt worse, like she was losing her center.

She lowered the box to the floor and had just wrapped her

hand around the doorknob when panic rippled inside her. Panic at not knowing whether this was it, her last time in his home. She took a moment to stop and breathe. Immediately, she found herself touching her bracelet, but it wasn't Nico's cloud she was touching…it was Erik's angel.

God, the angel charm…she couldn't keep it if they weren't together. It would be a constant reminder of *them*. It would hurt at every touch. Every glance.

Slowly, she turned and moved into his office. She unlatched the angel charm and set it on his desk. Releasing it was so much harder than it should have been.

Another tear trickled down her cheek, but this time she didn't wipe it away.

The second the angel fell from her fingers, she felt bare, like she'd just set a part of her heart onto his desk and now had to walk away without it.

Her breath shuddered and her fingers shook. She stepped around the desk, her gaze brushing over the surface…when something caught her attention.

A piece of paper, poking out of a manila folder. The sliver she could see contained only a small fraction of a photo, but she didn't need to see the entire thing to know who it was.

Her heart stuttered. *What the hell?*

Slowly, she reached down and lifted the folder before opening it up.

The photo of Nico sat on the top right corner of the page, and beside it, his full name—Nicolas Spalder.

Her eyes ran over the text. Was it a bio? It had his date of birth. His description. His schools. She turned to the next page to find photos of him that looked to have been taken just before he'd died. Crossing a road. Inside various shops.

The blood ran cold in her veins. What the hell was this? Had someone been watching him before he was killed?

She flicked to the third page...a printout of an email addressed to Erik, from Chandler.

When she read the contents, her vision hazed, darkness closing in around her as a low buzz started in her ears.

The only thing to penetrate the buzz was the sound of the front door opening.

She looked up to see Erik standing in the doorway to his office. His gaze lowered to the folder in her hands, then shifted back up to her. There was no emotion on his face. None.

"What is this?" she whispered, not even sure her words crossed the distance.

He took a step toward her, but that damn silence remained.

The fear in her chest shifted to anger. "This is *not* a time for silence, Erik! You tell me what this is right now!"

A part of her knew, but God, she wanted to be wrong. She needed the man in front of her, the man she *loved*, to tell her that what she held in her hands was a lie. That her world still made sense.

"He was part of a well-established sex trafficking ring." Erik's words hit like blows to her abdomen, each landing harder than the last. "He was a recruiter, which meant he found the women, lured them in, then those women were kidnapped and sold."

"No." She shook her head, stumbling back a step. "You're lying."

"I'm not. People were tasked with taking out the leaders in the organization. He was one of those leaders."

No...she didn't believe it. Any of it! She knew Nico! She knew his heart. He'd made some bad choices, but he was a *protector*. He wouldn't have hurt women like that. Someone, somewhere, had to have made a mistake, and Nico had paid the price.

"The intel you received was wrong," she whispered.

"It's never wrong."

Five breaths... She sucked in five full breaths before she gained the courage to ask. "You said people were tasked with killing the leaders of the trafficking ring. Who, specifically, killed Nico?"

For the first time, his carefully constructed mask slipped—and she saw everything. The pain. The regret...and the answer to her question.

"You," she whispered, her voice so quiet it barely touched air. "*You* killed him."

His hazel eyes bled into hers, yet still he refused to speak.

"You need to say it!" she shouted. "I need to hear the words!" Because otherwise, they wouldn't be true. She needed his confession released into the world to make it real.

"I killed Nico."

* * *

THE SECOND HIS words were out, he wished he could take them back. Wished he could twist them into something different. Something that didn't hurt her. Hurt them.

The look on her face, the sheer ruin, reminded him of exactly why he'd been fighting this moment for so long. Because he broke her. Every wonderful thing she was, he'd taken from her. Her light. Her peace.

"Hannah—" He stepped forward in case she fell, but she held up a hand, shaking her head as she inched around the desk.

"Don't come near me!"

Her words slashed across his flesh like a knife.

"Take the folder," he pleaded. "Read it. It's all the information I have on him. It's everything that gave me justification to do what I did."

She shook her head vigorously, tears falling down her cheeks, the devastation flowing out of her. "I told you! He wouldn't do any of that! There are no words on any pieces of paper that could ever change my mind."

"Take it," he whispered. "*Please.*" The last word was so low and guttural it portrayed every bit of desperation he couldn't keep inside. He didn't want to taint her foster brother's memory. She loved him. He was family to her. But he needed to do everything fucking possible to get her to consider returning to him.

"I need to go. I need…" Her voice broke. "I don't even know! I just need to *breathe*!"

He clenched his hands into fists to stop himself from reaching for her. Wiping away her tears and begging her to stay. "Take all the time you need, Angel. I'll be here. And I'll always love you."

Her face started to crumple, but she just kept it together, slipping out of the room, then out of his house.

The second she was gone, the silence buzzed in his ears, deafening him. All he wanted was Hannah back. To touch her. Love her.

The air burned in his lungs as he moved to his desk. He lifted the folder she hadn't taken and threw it against the wall. Without a scrap of self-restraint, he swung his arm across the desk, sending every fucking thing flying.

He wanted to scream. To rage. But nothing would help. The hole in his chest would continue to widen, the pain so fucking deep he wanted to dig a hand into his chest and physically stop it.

He turned and shouted a curse, his voice echoing off the walls.

Then he saw it…the angel charm. It sat on the floor, shining amongst all the papers he'd just knocked off. Staring at him. Mocking him.

Slowly, he crouched and wrapped his fingers around it.

Gone. She was gone. And she'd left his heart here.

With a shout that ripped through the room, he turned and slammed his fist through the wall. The sharp edges cut into his knuckles, scraping across his skin, but it wasn't enough. He wanted to burn. To bleed. To feel anything but this ache in this chest. This annihilation of everything he was.

Why? Why had he left himself open to this kind of hurt when

he knew better? Why had he let himself love so deeply and uninhibitedly?

He turned and leaned his back against the wall before dropping to the floor. When he lowered his head into his hands, he felt every bit of the pain as his world imploded around him.

CHAPTER 13

Tears fell down Hannah's cheeks in a constant flow as she drove. She didn't know where she was going, just that she needed to get away. No matter how often she scrubbed the tears away, no matter how many times she begged herself to stop, she couldn't.

Erik had *killed* Nico...the closest thing Hannah had ever had to a brother. To family.

A choked sob escaped her throat as memories of the day she'd learned about his death came back to her.

Hannah frowned at the sight of Becca's name on the screen. Why was Nico's girlfriend calling her? The woman never called. Sure, Hannah had spoken to her from time to time when she drove down to visit Nico, but they were relative strangers.

She hesitated, a dread she didn't understand spidering through her belly. For a moment, she considered not answering. Then she shook her head. She was being silly.

One more ring and she lifted the cell to her ear. "Hey, Becca. Is everything okay?"

There was a small pause before Becca spoke. In that pause, all

Hannah heard was heavy breathing. "Hannah...something happened last night."

Hannah blinked, willing the memory away. The pain and grief that had followed.

In that moment, she'd broken. Thought she'd never be whole again. She'd thought that was the worst kind of pain she could experience, but this right now...it was so much worse. She was broken all over again, only this time, she didn't know if she could ever put the pieces back together.

She swallowed, reminding herself to breathe. To fill her lungs as she pulled to the curb outside of Brigid's shop.

Quickly, she rubbed her eyes, sucked in a few deep breaths as she looked at herself in the mirror. She looked exactly as she felt...like a mess. But this was Brigid, her best friend. She wouldn't care what Hannah looked like.

On the sidewalk, her knees trembled and her head ached, but she forced herself forward. When she reached the shop, she pushed on the handle—but it didn't give way.

What the hell? Why was the door locked?

She looked up and saw what she'd missed the first time...a closed sign. And inside the shop, all the lights were off.

When Brigid failed to answer her calls, Hannah had just assumed she was too busy working. It was only midmorning, after all. So why was the door locked? Brigid never closed her shop this early.

This couldn't be happening. Not now. Desperation and devastation raced through her body, threatening to snap her bones. She pushed down on the handle again and again, as if she could somehow unlock the door by sheer will.

Sobs built in her chest, tears once again flowing down her cheeks.

"Hannah?"

She vaguely heard the sound of her name behind her. It was like white noise as she started banging on the glass, calling

Brigid's name. She needed her best friend! She was crying loudly now, the grief so intense she had no idea how to deal with it.

Erik had *killed* Nico! Her only family was *gone* because of the man she loved. How was she supposed to live with that knowledge?

Her sobs grew louder still.

Hands gripped her upper arms.

She spun, gasping.

Leo lifted his hands and stepped back. "Whoa! I only grabbed you because I was scared you were going to hurt yourself."

Hurt herself? How could she possibly hurt any more than she already was?

She pressed a hand to her chest, as if that could somehow stem the pain, and when a blast of dizziness hit her, Leo stepped forward and grasped her arms again.

"Hey—Hannah. Talk to me. What's going on?"

"I can't...breathe." Another sob broke free, and it was all too much. The weight on her shoulders felt so heavy, her knees caved, and she would have fallen to the ground if Leo hadn't pulled her into his arms.

"I've got you," he whispered into her ear. "It'll be okay."

* * *

"TELL me you have eyes on her and she's okay?" Erik growled into the phone.

He felt hollow. Empty.

His one driving force, the one thing keeping him focused, was the deep need to know that Hannah was safe.

"She went to her friend's store, but it was closed," Chandler said quietly.

There was a pause, and in that pause, Erik's heart began to thud violently against his ribs. "Tell me."

"She was upset. Banging on the glass and pulling at the handle."

Erik ran shaky fingers through his hair. All he wanted to do was go to her. Be with her. But she didn't want him. Might never want him again.

"A guy she works with found her, and he drove her to her friend Henry's house," Chandler continued. "That's where she is right now."

A guy she worked with…Leo? Erik would normally hate that, but right now, all he felt was gratitude that someone had been there to help her. "So she's safe?"

"She's okay, Erik."

The air rushed from his chest in a long stream. "Thanks. Tell your guy to keep eyes on her."

"You know it's already done." There was a small pause. "Are *you* okay?"

The question almost made him laugh, even though that was the last fucking thing he wanted to do. "No. I'm not even close to okay."

He was tattered and torn, and there was this ache inside him so deep that it was the only thing he could feel.

"Anything I can do?"

He shook his head even though the guy couldn't see him. "Just make sure she's safe. I'll check in again soon."

He hung up and let his cell fall, the sound of it hitting the desk loud in the otherwise quiet room. He dropped his head into his hands.

Gone. She was gone. And there was nothing he could do about it.

Her expression as she'd walked away from him played over in his head again and again. He'd done that. He'd put that look on her face. It was exactly why he hadn't wanted to tell her what he'd done. Because he'd known it would kill her.

She'd already lost so much, having her parents die when she

was so young, then her foster mother. Nico had been her one constant.

He pressed his palms harder to his eyes, everything inside him swirling like a deadly storm.

When his phone buzzed, indicating someone had pulled up at the house, he didn't look down. He couldn't. He had nothing left in him. At the click of his front door unlocking, he knew who it was, anyway. There were only two people with keys to his home —Hannah and his sister.

"What are you doing here, Andi?" He didn't look up as he spoke.

The soft thud of footsteps moved across the room. Then her warm hand was on his back. "Mom asked me to check on you. She seemed pretty worried."

He looked up to see his sister beside him, watching him closely. "If you're going to ask me if I'm okay—"

"I'm not. I can see you're definitely not okay." She tilted her head. "Talk to me, Erik. Tell me what's going on."

"I did something I can't take back."

"What?"

He'd never explicitly told his sister what he did for work. His job was classified. But in this moment, he didn't give a fuck about anything. Certainly not the secrets he was supposed to keep for the government.

"I kill people, Andi. Bad people. Scum of the Earth who the US government can't get through the justice system."

She nodded slowly. If she was surprised, she didn't show it. "I always suspected as much."

"A few years ago, I killed a man who was important to Hannah."

Andi's chest rose on a deep inhale, understanding darkening her hazel eyes. "And you just told her."

The memory of the color leaving her face...the way she'd walked out on him...it sliced new cuts across his flesh.

He was up before he could stop himself and moving across the room.

"Erik, wait!"

Andi grabbed his arm and he spun, anger coating his words. "She left me, Andi! I am *nothing* without her!"

His sister shook her head. "That's not true."

"She came into my life and changed me. Made me feel like I was okay for the first time in years. Now I have to live in a world where I know she exists, but she isn't mine!" Every word ran into the next, pained and angry.

She stepped closer, wrapping fingers around his arm and pressing her other palm to his chest. "You've already had your world collapse more than once. Each time you got knocked down, you had to choose—stay down or get back up." Her hand moved up to his cheek. "Erik, you got up. Every time. Because you knew that nothing comes from staying down." Her voice lowered. "So *get up.*"

He shook his head. "This is different."

"You're right. It *is* different—because Hannah's not dead. She's here, alive, and you need to fight for her. Be the person she needs you to be."

His breath was a shudder in his lungs. "You didn't see the look on her face. I took something from her that can never be replaced."

"You killed a man because he hurt people." Andi tilted her head. "You're not a bad person. She knows that. Right now, she's in shock. The shock will lessen. And when it does, you need to be ready."

Ready? He felt a stone's throw away from his entire world collapsing.

Would Hannah at least talk to him once the shock had worn off?

Would she return to him? Was that even in the realm of possibilities?

The slight hope was the only thing keeping him from putting another hole in his wall.

Andi wrapped her arms around his waist and held him. Slowly, his arms went around his sister, needing both her words and her touch. Needing someone to tell him, promise him, that everything would be okay.

CHAPTER 14

*H*annah didn't have many photos of herself and Nico. At fourteen, they'd gone into different foster homes and hadn't spent nearly enough time together after that. But the times she *had* seen him, she'd cherished.

She paused at a photo on her phone. It was one of the very last times she'd seen Nico. They'd gone to Red Rock Canyon together, and they'd had the best time.

She rolled to her side, the mattress groaning beneath her body.

She'd been at Henry's for a week, and each day had blurred into the next, like one hazy gray mess. She'd gone to the office a few times, but Taylor and Leo had helped her out a lot with things like showings and calls to clients.

Today, she was going back to her place. She didn't want to—Henry's home kind of felt like a protective bubble. But there was a limit to how long she could stay. At some point, she needed to return to her place…to reality. And that day had come.

A knock sounded at the door, and she jolted, the phone almost slipping from her fingers. A second later, Henry stepped in. The man had been her everything this last week. He'd taken care of her, made sure her diabetes was well managed and that she was eating healthy foods. He was the only reason she was doing even slightly okay right now.

Brigid had also been there for her. She'd apologized profusely about not being at the shop and visited almost every night. Although Hannah wondered about her reasons for closing the shop and not answering her calls that morning—something about not having her phone on her and having to rush home briefly—she was too mired in her grief to press.

"Hey," Henry said quietly, pulling the door closed after him before sitting on the edge of the bed. "How are you doing today?"

She lifted a shoulder. "Honestly, I don't know."

Henry didn't know the exact details of Erik's job, so she hadn't been able to share what he'd done. No matter how upset she was, she couldn't betray him like that. But she *had* revealed that it had something to do with Nico's death. That Erik's job had given him intel into Nico's past that she just couldn't believe. And she ultimately told both Henry and Brigid what that intel said about the man she'd considered a brother.

"I've had an entire week to think about what Erik told me, but still none of it feels real." She ran her finger over the cloud charm on her bracelet. "A week ago, I was so certain Erik was wrong about what Nico did. *So sure* that he'd received incorrect information. But little things have been pricking at my mind these last few days…"

Henry cocked his head. "Like what?"

"For one, Nico's apartment. He went from foster care to living in a penthouse apartment in Bellevue. And whenever I asked what he was doing for work…he never really answered my question. Just gave me half answers about setting up a business."

Henry frowned. "Yeah, that's suspicious as hell."

"There were also changes in him before he died. He didn't seem to want me coming around as much. He also seemed to be keeping parts of his life secret. Still…I just can't imagine him recruiting women to be exploited so horribly." Her gaze fell to the cloud charm.

"Is Erik still contacting you?"

She nodded. "He's been texting me every day, asking if I'm okay. I haven't been able to bring myself to respond because, honestly, I don't know what to do or think. But he still messages."

"Do you love him?"

Her gaze rose. "It's not that simple."

"Yes, it is. Do you love him?"

"Henry—"

"Answer the dang question, Hannah."

"Yes. You know I do." Her love for him was so deeply ingrained that part of her felt like it was missing without him.

"Then *love* him. Don't turn one tragedy into two."

A tear rolled down her cheek. She was so sick of crying, but this last week had taken everything out of her. "But if I forgive him, it feels like I'm betraying Nico."

"You're not. You're choosing to live and love."

She swallowed. "My head knows that. But my heart's so unbelievably conflicted."

"Luckily, the heart often comes around." He leaned forward and kissed her head. "You still leaving today?"

She nodded. "Bags are all packed. After work, I'll go straight home."

Reuben had been really great. She'd told him she was going through some personal issues, and her boss, Taylor, and Leo had all banded together to help wherever they could. God, she was grateful to work with such good people.

"Remember, you've always got a room here if you need it." He nodded toward the door. "And Owen's out there making you breakfast."

Owen hadn't been around much during the last week, opting to give her privacy and alone time with her friends, but the couple times he'd come over, he'd taken just as good care of her as Henry. "I don't deserve you *or* him."

"No one deserves me, but I sprinkle my Henry magic anyway."

She chuckled. Only Henry could make her laugh at a time like this.

He smoothed some hair from her face. "Before I go, I want you to know that my official stance on this is that I think you should talk to him."

"I'm scared." The two honest words dropped from her lips before she could stop them.

"Of course you are. It's normal to feel fear when things are this important. Fear protects us. But don't let it stop you from doing what you need to do."

Her features softened. "I wouldn't have survived this week without you, Henry."

"You would have. You're stronger than you think." He tugged her into his chest. "I love you, Han. You're family. You know that, right?"

She relaxed against his strong chest, so incredibly grateful for him. "I love you too, Henry."

After he left, Hannah climbed out of bed. Her pump had expired a few days ago and her new one was at home, so she'd just been injecting since then.

It wasn't until she stood under the stream of water in the shower that the nerves started to rattle her belly. Nerves at the prospect of seeing Erik when she moved back home. Even if it was just through her window, it would hit her hard.

Once out of the shower, she pulled on a skirt and blouse for work. She didn't attempt makeup and her hair remained down.

The second she stepped outside the bedroom, she was bombarded by the most delicious smell of bacon and bagels. She'd barely had an appetite over the last week, but right now… yeah, she could eat.

She walked into the kitchen to see two plates sitting on the island, cutlery beside them, along with glasses of orange juice.

Her lips twitched at the sight of Owen in front of the stove, wielding a spatula. He turned and gave her a smile. "Hey." He indicated to the island. "Have a seat."

"One of these for me?"

"Yep. Henry gave me strict instructions to feed you before you leave for work, and you don't go against that man."

She sat at the island. "You don't have to feed me. Honestly, I could live off cereal and be perfectly happy."

"Well, in this house, you get more than cereal. You get real sustenance." He took two bagel halves from the toaster and set them on her plate before scooping up some bacon.

"Bacon's real sustenance?"

"Hell yeah. It's protein! And we have some eggs for *more* protein." Once an egg was on her plate, he turned and set the pan down. "All accompanied by bagels for carbs."

What she did to deserve this, she wasn't sure, but she wasn't questioning it. Before touching the juice, she opened her purse and grabbed a pen, injecting insulin before getting up and slotting it into the sharps disposal container that Henry kept on his kitchen counter for her.

Lowering back to the stool, she sipped the juice and groaned. Even that tasted amazing. Had he freshly squeezed the oranges? "You know, I've hardly been able to eat anything for a week, but this food suddenly makes me ravenous."

"Well, that's because I made it, and I'm kick-ass in the kitchen." He grabbed the butter from the fridge and set it in front of her.

She opened her mouth to thank him, but her phone dinged, and the second her gaze fell on the cell, she couldn't drag it away.

Erik.

There was a slight shake in her fingers as she unlocked the screen.

Erik: I hope you're doing okay this morning, Angel. I'm still missing you and thinking about you every day.

Her heart thrashed in her chest, her fingers itching to respond.

"Hey."

She glanced up at Owen's voice.

He tilted his head. "Everything okay?"

She nodded, even though very little in her life felt okay. "Yep. Are you gonna eat with me?"

"Fuck yeah, I am." He loaded up the second plate and sat beside her.

She finished all she could, but after the text, her appetite wasn't what it had been before. Owen filled a lot of the silence throughout the meal, asking questions about her work and her longtime friendship with Henry. She was terrible company, her thoughts always on Erik instead of their conversation, but Owen didn't seem to notice. Or if he did, he was too polite to draw attention to it.

By the time she reached work, she'd gone back and forth on responding to Erik so many times that a tension headache had formed behind her eyes. The decision was agonizing.

She massaged her temple as she stepped into the office, almost immediately running into Taylor.

"Hey, it's good to see you!" The smile slipped from Taylor's lips when her gaze fell on Hannah. "You're not looking great, Han. Are you okay?"

She nodded, the pain pressing at her skull. "Yeah, I've just got a headache."

"Do you need to go home? I'm sure Reuben wouldn't mind—"

"No. I'm okay." She couldn't go home. She had too much work to do, and she couldn't keep asking everyone to cover for her.

She forced another smile to her lips as she walked past Taylor and into her office. Once she was behind her desk, she turned on her computer and started responding to emails, but every second that passed made the thudding of her skull worsen, to the point she almost lowered her head to the desk and closed her eyes.

She lasted another half hour before it became too much.

God, what was wrong with her? Did she have the flu all of a sudden? Maybe the week of stress had finally caught up with her and her body had gotten sick?

She hated doing it, but she lifted her bag and left her office. She was tempted to leave a message on Reuben's desk for when he got in, but she quickly pushed that idea aside. She needed to get home because this headache felt like it would be turning into a migraine.

When she reached her car, she didn't immediately slide in, instead taking a moment to close her eyes and massage her temple again. After a few deep breaths, she got into the car.

The drive to her place was a slow blur, part of her realizing midtrip that she shouldn't even be driving right now, but she was so desperate to get to a bed and rest that she didn't pause to call someone for help.

When she finally got home, she barely managed to get inside before her body tried to give up on her.

She knew she needed to check her sugar levels. She needed to figure out why there was a shake in her fingers and an ache in her head. The symptoms almost matched when she had a sugar high, only worse.

The second she reached the couch, she dropped, because the bedroom was too far, and once she was down, there was no getting back up. All she could do was pray that she'd open her eyes later and have the energy to look after herself.

<h1 style="text-align:center">CHAPTER 15</h1>

*E*rik pounded a nail into the gutter. The thing didn't really need fixing, but he was trying to stay busy. That was all he'd been doing for the last week. Because staying busy was the only way he knew to keep himself from going to her. Begging her to forgive him.

He was trying to give her space. Time to get her head around what he'd done. He just had to hope like hell that, eventually, she'd return to him.

He'd pestered the shit out of Chandler to give him a job, something to do, but for once, there wasn't any work.

You're my person. In every scenario. In every version of every story that's ours, you are mine, and I am yours.

Those were the words she'd spoken to him. And he was holding on to them with two hands like a fucking lifeline. Every time he remembered the look on her face when she'd walked out on him, he tugged those words back and kept them close.

He climbed down the ladder and shifted it to the next section of gutter at the corner of the house.

He hated that Hannah hadn't returned to her home for the last week. An entire seven days of not seeing her. Not hearing her voice. He was living for those updates from Chandler. The confirmation that she was okay. He'd pushed for information every day. Chandler hadn't been able to give him much because she'd spent all of that time either inside Henry's house or in her office.

He tugged his phone from his pocket, checking the screen for what had to be the hundredth damn time.

No text from Hannah.

The muscles in his forearms tightened. He'd messaged her every day. Checking in. Reminding her that he'd like to talk and that he loved her. Because even though he could give her space physically, emotionally, he needed to make contact.

He was just about to shove his phone back into his pocket when it rang, Chandler's name flashing on the screen. Before he could answer it, the sound of a car engine in the driveway next door caught his attention. When he saw Hannah's old Honda, his heart stopped.

She was home.

When she stepped out of the car, the sight of her slammed into him.

It took him about three seconds to recover and notice the deep lines etched between her brows. The way her skin was too pale. And how she bumped into the doorframe as she stepped inside her house.

Something was wrong. Was she hurt?

He answered the call before it could stop ringing. "What's wrong with her?"

"That's why I'm calling," Chandler said. "The guy I've got on her today said she left work in a rush. She was holding her head before she got into her car and wasn't steady on her feet. He stuck closer to her than usual on the drive to her place because he was worried she'd get into an accident. She drove really slowly and swerved a couple times."

His skin chilled. Was she sick? Fuck, she shouldn't be home alone with her diabetes.

"Thanks for calling, Chandler." He hung up before his friend had a chance to respond, then he made his way across to her house.

A voice in his head said he should call someone else to check on her. That seeing him might make everything worse. But fuck, he couldn't stop himself. He needed to see with his own eyes that she was okay.

When he reached her door, all he wanted to do was walk straight in, but he forced himself to stop and knock. His fist hit the wood too hard. When there was no answer, he knocked again, this time harder. Every second that passed felt like ten.

No answer.

Fuck it. He turned the knob and stepped inside.

* * *

THE KNOCKING on the door pounded into Hannah's skull like a small hammer hitting at her head from the inside.

She scrunched her eyes closed, begging it to stop. It did, but only for a second, then it started up again, this time louder.

She groaned deep in her throat, wanting to cover her ears with her hands, but God, she felt weak. When the knocking stopped for a second time, the air rushed out of her. Then there was the soft click of the door opening, followed by footsteps.

The scent that tinged the air made emotion clog her throat. It was a scent she'd recognize anywhere. Crisp pine and deeply masculine.

"Angel, talk to me. What's going on?"

Erik's words seeped into her skin, calming some of the panic that had been unraveling in her belly from the pain. When his warm hand touched her cheek, she wanted to lean into it, borrow some of his warmth and strength.

She forced her eyes open, cringing at the light that shone into her eyes. "Need you to check my blood sugars."

She'd just closed her eyes again when strong fingers lifted her wrist and pulled up her sleeve. He cursed. "You're not wearing your watch." There was the distant sound of him rummaging through her bag. "Your phone isn't here."

It wasn't? Had she left it at work?

She knew the second he left her. Not because of footsteps or the rustle of movement, but because she *felt* the loss. Immediately, she wanted to tug him back, but she could barely move. God, why was she so tired? And not just tired. Achy and thirsty. And when she'd opened her eyes, her vision was blurred.

Those were the classic symptoms of high blood sugar, but she'd injected before breakfast. Why would she be high?

His voice sounded again, but it was distant. It took her a moment to realize he was on the phone. She heard words like "sick" and "sugars." She was half-asleep when she felt warmth surround her hand, then a prick. When he lowered her hand again, his touch only left her for a moment before arms slipped around her and air rushed around her body.

A mattress dipped under her weight. She wasn't sure if she fell asleep or not, but the next time she was cognizant, there was a second voice. It took her a moment to recognize it as Andi.

"Did you check her sugars?"

"She's high at four hundred and ten," Erik said. "I couldn't find the pump on her body. I don't think she's wearing one."

"Okay. We need to administer a correction in the form of an additional dose of insulin to bring her blood sugar back to normal. Then we'll wait a bit and recheck. Her level of exhaustion isn't in proportion with a high, though. So I'm thinking she has a virus that's pushing her levels up. We need to keep checking and watching her."

The words started to blur, and all she wanted to do was sleep.

Warm hands took hers, then there was a prick on her side.

"Sorry, Angel." Erik's soft words filtered into her head, soothing her. "We're going to make sure you're okay."

"Check her levels again in about an hour," Andi said.

"You don't think she needs a hospital?"

"All they'll do is give her insulin and fluids like we're doing now. She would only need to go in if her numbers got into the six hundreds—that will mean she's in diabetic ketoacidosis."

Hannah stopped listening as the headache pulled her under.

God, she hadn't had a headache like this in so long. It was an all-consuming pain, like a migraine. Even with her eyes closed, the light in the room hurt. She shifted her head, trying to ease the pain.

Suddenly, the light disappeared. There was the shuffle of movement around her, then that hand on her cheek again. So warm and familiar.

"I'm just gonna sit over there, Angel. Sleep. I'll check your levels in an hour."

Panic swelled in her chest that she was going to lose him again. That the darkness that had been a constant companion over the last week was going to return.

The warmth disappeared from her cheek, and immediately she reached out, trembling fingers wrapping around his wrist. "Don't leave me!"

The strong beat of his pulse thrummed beneath her fingertips. He was so still and quiet, she almost wondered if she hadn't said the words aloud.

"Please…" she whispered. "Hold me. I need you."

The pulse beneath her fingertips beat faster. When his wrist disappeared, fear crawled up her throat. But then there was the rustle of clothing, followed by the bed dipping behind her.

The second he touched her, the second he held her against him, relief filled her. Finally, she allowed sleep to tug her under, because in Erik, she found safety.

CHAPTER 16

*H*annah's heart beat hard in her chest as she climbed through the bedroom window. Cool air brushed across her skin, the night quiet around her, apart from a few dogs down the street and some cars from the highway a mile away.

The second her feet hit the carpeted floor, a chill swept over her skin...at the sight of her old bedroom. At the memory of what had taken place here the last time she'd slept in the single bed.

A nausea she couldn't stop rumbled in her belly, clawing at her throat, threatening to break free. She forced it down. She forced all memory and emotion to remain caged inside her and silent.

She had to be strong, at least until she found the bracelet. It had fallen off at some point that awful night, and she felt naked without it. Bare.

She just had to remind herself that there was nothing to be afraid of. Clarence was in jail, all the foster kids had been removed, and Robyn was probably passed out in the living room, an empty bottle of whiskey no doubt near her head. The woman rarely made it past six.

Quickly, she set her backpack on the floor, then hesitated. She rummaged through the bag before her fingers slid over the cool handle of the gun.

She shouldn't need it, but having it close felt safe. She sat it on the bedside table and shuffled through the still crumpled sheets. It had been a week since the incident, yet nothing looked touched.

She pulled the bed apart looking for the bracelet. Where was it? It had been her mother's—the only thing she owned from her. She had to find it!

When it wasn't on the bed, panic tugged at her. Every second that ticked by had her belly feeling sicker. All she wanted to do was get out of this hellhole of a house.

She lowered to the floor, searching the carpet with her hands. The dread was just spidering through her limbs when she reached farther under the bed, her fingertip brushing on something small and hard.

Hope lit inside her. She reached just a bit farther, wrapping her fingers around the jewelry, then pulling it out. The second she saw it, tears pressed to her eyes. This last week had been a nightmare. The attack. The police. The questions. But having this bracelet back in her possession...she almost felt okay again.

She rose and carefully slipped the jewelry around her wrist before doing up the clasp. A hint of moonlight reflected off the bracelet.

She had it back. Everything would be okay.

She took a step toward the window, cringing when her foot hit the bedside table. The furniture rocked, and she lunged for the lamp, but she was too slow. It tumbled to its side. It didn't break, but the thud was still loud in the quiet night.

Her heart thumped. It was fine. Robyn rarely woke after she passed out.

Hannah had just lifted the gun to slip it back into her bag when heavy footsteps sounded in the hall—footsteps that were too loud to be Robyn's. Steps she'd recognize anywhere.

Fear stole her breath. She eyed the window but knew it was too late.

The door flew open, and there, standing in the entrance, was her very own monster. A man who'd dragged her through hell. A man who'd tried to do despicable things to her.

He frowned, his gaze brushing over her face, then her body. A slow smile curved his mouth, but there was nothing friendly about it. "Hello, Hannah. This is a nice surprise."

That voice...so familiar. And so utterly terrifying.

She wanted to open her mouth to tell him to get away from her. To step back. But she couldn't speak or move. It was like she was frozen to the spot, terror rendering her motionless.

He inched forward. "You've made my life quite difficult with your...accusations."

Finally, she stumbled back, but her foot caught on a piece of clothing. She barely righted herself. She aimed the gun at his chest, fingers shaking. "You're supposed to be in jail." And the gun in her hand was just supposed to be a precaution. Something she had to feel safe but shouldn't have to use.

"Bail." He took another step forward. "Cost me a pretty penny too. Had to put my fucking house up as collateral. Something else you'll need to pay for."

She swallowed the nausea at his proximity. Tried to push away the terror that wanted to freeze her mind and body.

"I don't want any trouble. I just came for my bracelet." God, why hadn't she shoved it into her pocket and climbed back out the window faster?

He laughed. "You ain't taking that bracelet, girlie. Consider it compensation for my troubles."

"I am." Suddenly, the tremble in her voice was gone. Because no one was taking this bracelet from her. It was her one connection to her parents. A connection she couldn't give up. Wouldn't.

He stepped closer again.

"Stop moving or I shoot!"

He laughed. "You won't shoot me. You're too much of a good girl. It's why I liked you, you know. Usually I get these no-good foster kids with a shitload of baggage and attitude. Not you. You were like a diamond in the rough. All pretty and clean and polite."

"They should've never let you be a foster parent." He'd probably done to countless other girls the same thing he'd done to her.

His stained teeth became visible as he grinned, evidence of years of drug and alcohol abuse. "They shouldn't have. But they did."

He undid his belt, and she felt the blood drain from her face.

"Now how about that payment, girlie..."

The second the belt was in his hands, he lunged forward.

In that moment, it was as if the world slowed. As if every nightmare she'd ever lived and dreamed rolled into one terrifying reality.

The second he touched her arm, she reacted, screaming and shooting in a life-altering fraction of a second.

He dropped to the floor with a thud, blood blooming on his chest. Her panic shifted into something else. Something equally terrifying, but so different.

Oh God...what had she done?

She'd killed him. A man was dead because of her.

Her hands trembled so badly that she almost dropped her phone twice. She dialed nine-one-one...but before hitting call, she hesitated.

What if they didn't believe her? She was a foster kid. People rarely believed her. Even when she'd told the police what Clarence had done, that he'd climbed into her bed and tried to rape her, some officers had looked at her as if she was telling a story for attention.

Now, she'd broken into his house and shot him in the chest with a gun she shouldn't have.

Her chest began to heave, terror shaking her limbs.

She deleted the three numbers, and instead called the one man who'd always saved her. The one man who was family by choice.

He answered on the first ring. "Cloud, are you okay?"

She choked at the sound of his voice. "Nico...I need you..."

Hannah's eyes popped open, her heart beating so fast in her chest that it was almost painful. The moonlight cast a dim glow over her bedroom, and apart from soft breathing, everything was quiet.

She glanced around the room and found Erik in a chair. His head was down, chin on his chest and eyes closed.

How long had he been sleeping like that? The last she remembered, he was holding her.

She reached for her phone on the bedside table. Six a.m. He was usually awake and up by now.

She frowned…her phone. Erik had told her he couldn't find it. Maybe someone had delivered it to the house.

Because she wasn't wearing her watch, she used her phone to check her sugar levels. They were good. She'd felt terrible when she passed out. Her sugars had been high, and she'd been so sick. Her head still hurt, but nothing like last night.

"Hannah."

Erik was looking straight at her.

* * *

WHEN HANNAH LOOKED AT HIM, the air rushed from his chest in a long stream, and for the first time since he'd found her looking so sick, he could breathe again.

"How long have you been sleeping there?" she asked quietly.

He glanced at his watch. Fuck. It was six in the morning. He never slept this late. But then, he'd barely slept last night. "Two hours."

"You were awake until four?"

"I've been keeping a close eye on your glucose levels." He'd also been texting Andi all night, making sure that everything he was doing was right. He'd been so damn worried about screwing up. The only thing that stopped him from taking her to the hospital was the fact her sugars had steadily gone down and she'd been in a deep sleep.

Her brows flickered. "I remember you feeding me."

"I managed to get some soup into you after your levels came down. Andi said it looked like a glucose spike from a quick-onset virus." Thank God she was okay.

Slowly, he rose from the chair. He wanted to go to her. Touch her. Cup her cheek. But he had no fucking idea what *she* wanted.

He shoved his hands into his pockets to keep from reaching out. "How are you feeling?"

"Okay. My head feels a bit heavy and foggy, but that's normal after a high." She ran her fingers over the sheet. "I'm sorry you didn't get much sleep."

He almost laughed. He'd barely slept in the last week—the difference tonight was he'd at least been close to her. "I'm okay, Angel."

Emotion flickered in her ice-blue eyes. "How have you been?"

Did she want the truth? That it had been the hardest damn week of his life? That even keeping busy hadn't distracted him from the pain? "I'm struggling to learn how to live without you."

Her eyes widened. Maybe she'd been expecting him to lie. But he couldn't. Not now. Not when his secret was out in the open.

"Erik…"

"You don't have to say anything. I know you're trying to come to terms with what I did."

"My head's a mess," she said. "I miss you so much, but Nico meant everything to me, and I just…I can't see him doing what you said he did. That just doesn't make sense in my brain. And when I think about what you did to *him*…"

At the pain in her voice, he forced himself to remain where he was. To not cross the room and catch the tear that fell down her cheek with the pad of his thumb.

"That was one of the reasons I didn't want to tell you," Erik said. "I didn't want to take away the man he was to you. And I didn't want to make you choose."

Although a part of him, such a big part, had hoped she'd choose *him*.

"I don't know what to do," she whispered.

He couldn't stop himself any longer. He crossed the room and sat on the bed, then tugged her close, hoping like hell she didn't push him away.

She grabbed at his sides and cried against his shirt, soaking the material. He hated her tears. Each one fell like a blade to his chest.

"Nico was all I had for so long," she said, words muffled. "We grew up in the same foster home for so many years, and then when our foster mother died, he was still my family. I was put in awful homes, and he was always there to run to when I needed safety and comfort. Then that night…"

When she paused, he asked, "What night?"

"I…I did something. Something awful. It could have cost me everything. But Nico saved me. He was all I had, and he swept in and made it all go away."

Erik wanted to push, to know exactly what had happened. A week ago, he would have, but things between them had changed, and he needed to work his way back into her trust. Become her safety net once again.

"I'm glad you had someone looking out for you," he said quietly, stroking a hand down her back.

She looked up at him, heartache in her eyes. And that heartache gutted him. "I love you, Erik. I love you so much. But I wasn't lying when I said I'm a mess. I feel like my head and my heart are at war. I just need some time."

Time…the word felt heavy and wrong. He wanted to rebel against it. But he couldn't. Because the deeper part of him wanted to give her the world if she asked. If she wanted time, he'd give her time. Then he'd hope like hell she returned to him.

"I'll give you whatever time you need, Angel," he whispered, eyes forever on her. "And I'll wait for you."

CHAPTER 17

"You think you can drink ten shots and still walk in a straight line?" Henry scoffed. "Brig, I saw you eat five watered-down Jell-O shots at my twenty-fifth birthday party, and you could barely stand."

Brigid pressed a hand to her chest as if insulted. "That is so untrue, and I'm offended that you have such a warped recollection of that night. I had *seven* Jell-O shots, and I was so good after, I went home and made nachos and smashed an entire box of Pop-Tarts."

Hannah wrinkled her nose. "Nachos and Pop-Tarts after Jell-O shots?" She felt sick just thinking about that combination being in her belly.

"It was delicious. I was looking forward to my post-party meal that entire night."

"Yeah, because you needed food to mop up the five shots that got you wasted," Henry said, receiving a whack on the shoulder from Brigid.

Hannah chuckled. It felt good to be out at Tatum's Bar. This was their favorite spot to get a drink, and they hadn't been there in months. It was even better to see Brigid smiling, and Henry was his usual self, pushing Brigid's buttons and making them laugh every chance he got. Owen hadn't been able to make it tonight, which was fine. Honestly, it was nice just having some time with her two best friends.

She sipped her vodka soda. She'd been cradling it all night. Even though five days had passed since she'd been sick, the incident was enough to rock her. Since then, she'd been doing everything she could to take care of her blood sugars.

"Hannah, give us some good news," Henry said when he and Brigid were finally finished arguing. "Are you and Erik back together?"

The beats of her heart stumbled over each other at the mere mention of his name. She'd told her friends about what he'd done for her while she was sick. The way he'd cared for her. Called Andi and made sure her sugars were in range. Even how he'd slept on the chair in her room.

"We're not together, but we're not…"

"Avoiding each other," Brigid finished softly when Hannah couldn't.

"Yeah." She knew what Erik did wasn't his fault. He was doing his job. But a part of her still felt like letting him back in was betraying Nico.

Brigid set a hand on hers. "You still love him though."

You didn't just fall out of love with a person because you learned new information. The love she felt for him was so deeply ingrained, it was a part of her. "I do."

"Then be patient." Brigid smiled. "In time, you'll know exactly what you're meant to be."

She gave her friend a soft smile. "Thank you. How are *you* doing?"

There was a flicker of shadow in her friend's eyes. It came and went so quickly, Hannah almost missed it. "I'm good. Just… learning to live on my own."

She hated that Brigid wasn't okay. She understood it, but

she *hated* it, especially when so much of what happened with James had revolved around Hannah. Since leaving Henry's, she'd been making a point to check in on her friend every day with either a text, a call, or a visit to the store, but it never felt like enough.

It was Hannah's turn to cover Brigid's hand with her own. "If you want some company, I'm always happy to come stay with you."

She shook her head. "No, that's okay. I need to get used to it at some point." She sipped her cocktail.

"Hey, Han…isn't that Leo?"

Hannah followed Henry's gaze to see Leo on the other side of the bar. The corners of her lips tugged up, and when their gazes met, Hannah waved. The man had been nothing short of amazing during the last month. He'd helped Hannah time after time with her workload, with emotional support when he could, all while asking for nothing in return.

He crossed the room to their table, and she cocked her head. "Hey. What are you doing here?" She nibbled her lip, hating that Brigid was suddenly tense beside her. She inched closer to her friend.

"I've heard you mention this place a dozen times or so. Thought I'd see what the fuss is about."

Henry grinned. "The fuss is that the drinks are amazing, it doesn't smell like beer and sweat, and it's not so loud that you can't have a conversation. You're here alone?" he asked.

Leo lifted a shoulder. "Yeah. No better way to make friends than to show up somewhere alone."

Hannah's phone vibrated, and whatever Henry said next was lost on her when she saw Erik's name flash on the screen. Her skin tingled as she opened the text.

Erik: Hey. Just noticed your Honda's gone. Hope you're okay. X

He'd been checking in a lot more than usual over the last week. Texting. Bringing over meals, but not asking to stay to eat with her. Never expecting more from her than she was ready to give.

Everything about him made her want to take him back. His tenderness. His concern. No one had ever needed her to be okay as much as he did.

Her fingers hovered over the keys, unsure how to respond.

A shoulder bumped hers, and she looked at Brigid to see a soft smile on her friend's face. "I'm glad you're talking to him again. I was really worried for a while there. I want you to be happy."

"Thank you. I want *you* to be happy too."

Brigid's smile faltered, and she opened her mouth to say something, but Henry spoke first.

"Hannah, you didn't."

Her gaze shot up. "I didn't what?"

"You dedicated a *second* shelf in your work cabinet to cereal?"

Hannah gasped, her gaze whipping to Leo. "You told on me?"

His eyes widened, and he held up his hands. "I didn't know it was a secret."

Henry threw up his own hands. "That's it! It's time for a cereal intervention. Come Monday, I'm going to your office and taking anything I deem to be excess."

Hannah groaned, while Leo and Brigid laughed.

Over the next hour, her friends made her smile and laugh more times than she could count. It was nearing ten by the time exhaustion started to pull at her limbs. Not only that, but her poor feet hurt after a long day in heels, and her lack of alcohol did nothing to dull the pain.

She said a quick goodbye to her friends, thankful that Brigid seemed a bit more relaxed in Leo's company, then headed for the exit and stepped outside. The cool evening breeze brushed over her skin, causing the fine hairs on her arms to stand on end.

But that wasn't the only thing that had her skin cooling.

It was that same feeling she'd been getting so often lately... that someone was watching her.

And the eyes on her didn't feel *good*. The feeling reminded her of when she was a teenager and had been placed in some unsafe homes. She'd get the same uncomfortable pit in her belly.

She forced a deep breath into her lungs, then covertly scanned the area. But all she saw were people moving to and from their cars and into the bar. No one was watching her. In fact, no one was paying her one bit of attention.

Once she reached her car, she quickly unlocked the doors and slipped behind the wheel, then immediately locked them again, hating the tremble in her fingers.

You're fine, Hannah. No one's watching you. You're safe.

She hadn't received any more texts from that number. No more notes left at work, telling her they knew what she'd done. She hadn't figured out who was responsible, of course. There'd been too much going on, and a part of her—the naïve part—was hoping she could just forget about it and the person would disappear.

Ha. When did trouble ever just disappear?

She shook her head, quickly starting her car and leaving the bar.

She was halfway home when a loud popping noise sounded from the engine, and smoke began to billow from under the hood.

What the hell? Her car had been so reliable since it had been fixed by Erik's mechanic friend all those months ago. But then, that quick fix didn't stop it from being old as hell.

Slowly, she pulled over to the side of the road and grabbed her phone. For a moment, her finger hovered over Henry's name, but she hesitated. He'd been feeling no pain when she left the bar. He was probably too drunk to pick her up, and even if he wasn't, she didn't want to pull him away from his night.

Brigid had definitely drunk too much, and she didn't want to call Leo. The man had done enough for her lately.

She worried her bottom lip as she scrolled up to Erik's name, her pulse picking up speed. Was it terrible if she called him just because she needed something?

She waited one more breath before clicking on his name and closing her eyes. She didn't have to wait long—he picked up on the second ring.

"Hannah? Are you okay?"

She swallowed, a part of her hating that his immediate instinct was that she wasn't. But then, he was right. "My Honda broke down, and I was wondering if you were free to pick me up? If you're not, that's okay, I'll—"

"Where are you?"

Her gaze shifted to the dark road. "Halfway down Penley Street."

There was a small pause, and she could just picture the frustration on his face. Because this was exactly why he'd bought her a new car. "I'll be there in five minutes."

A relieved breath rushed from her chest.

"And, Hannah…lock your doors."

The second the call ended, she double-checked that her doors were still locked before leaning her head back. A sense of calm settled inside her chest. A calm at hearing Erik's voice. At knowing he was coming and she'd be able to see him. Be close to him.

She was just closing her eyes when high beams behind her car had her squinting. What the hell? She looked in the rearview to see a car was moving slowly toward her, the lights so bright they were blinding.

Why were they driving with their high beams on?

When they finally passed, she tried to push down the unease in her belly. She slowed her breathing and lifted her phone, trying to calm herself by flicking through social media.

It was just three minutes later when another car passed, this time from the other direction, and yet again they were driving slowly with high beams on.

Her breath caught. Was it the same car? Were they watching her? Doing drive-bys to check if she was alone?

They eventually passed, but a nervous shake had started to weave its way through her limbs.

When more lights shone from a distance behind her, the unease gnawed at her skin. But as the car grew closer, she realized the lights weren't so bright and, instead of passing, they parked behind her.

The nerves continued to eat away at her until the lights turned off and she saw Erik climb out from behind the wheel.

With a long sigh, she scrubbed her hands over her face. *It's fine. You're fine, Hannah.* She grabbed her purse and opened the door just as he reached it.

"Hey," he said quietly, his hand going to her arm as he helped her out. His gaze ran over her face. "Are you okay?"

She nodded quickly. "Yeah, I just…I'm glad you're here."

Concern flickered over his face. "I'm glad you called, Angel." His thumb caressed her arm. "You got everything you need?"

She nodded as she closed and locked her door. He rested his hand at the small of her back as he guided her toward his car, his eyes constantly looking down the street and around the area. The second she was sitting, and his hand was no longer on her, she wanted to tug it back.

As he slid behind the wheel and pulled onto the road, she craved what they used to have. When he'd set a hand on her thigh like it was the easiest thing in the world. Right now, his knuckles were white on the wheel.

"How are your blood sugars?" he asked.

She tapped her watch, flicking to her Dexcom stream. "Good. I'll grab a snack when I get home."

He reached over and opened the glove box, and she couldn't stop the grin. He'd started stashing food in there months ago but had clearly topped up in the last few weeks. Hell, he even had small single-serve boxes of cereal.

She pulled out a bag of chips, offering him one, but he shook his head. He looked tense.

"I'm sorry I disturbed your night," she offered quietly.

"You didn't. I always want you to call if you need me."

The rhythm of her heart picked up again.

He shot her a glance. "Were you at Tatum's with Henry and Brigid?"

Her lips twitched. He knew her so well. "Yeah. Leo showed up and had a drink with us too."

She regretted her words immediately. They'd just fallen from her lips without thinking. The muscles in his arms flexed, and his jaw grew harder. She'd told him so many times they were just friends and coworkers, but there was something about the guy Erik didn't like.

When he reached their street, he pulled down her drive instead of his.

"I'll walk you in."

She didn't have a chance to say he didn't need to do that, because he was already out. And the second she was standing, his hand on her back again, she couldn't have told him no if she wanted to. His touch felt too good.

Her hands were unsteady as she unlocked the door and stepped inside. She dropped her bag onto the side table and turned, looking up, way up, into Erik's beautiful hazel eyes. "Thank you for saving me tonight."

"You never have to thank me for that. It's my job."

"I've missed you." The words slipped out before she could stop them, the little truth tumbling from her heart.

"There are no words for what I've been feeling without you by my side." He stepped closer, the warmth of his body radiating into her.

He dipped his head, and for a moment, she thought he might kiss her, but instead his lips brushed her ear. "You're my heart.

My soul. My breath. And when you're away from me, I have nothing."

His words stole every breath she tried to suck into her chest. Every feeling other than her ache for him.

She reached up and cupped his face. "Erik…"

A slow kiss touched her cheek. Then another. Every touch of lips to skin made another piece of her heart slot back into place.

He lifted his head and pressed his forehead to hers. "I love you, Angel. I'll always love you. Even if you push me away. Even if you hate me. My love for you will burn until the day I die."

"I could never hate you. That would be like hating a part of myself."

The good part. The part that gave her breath and life.

Slowly, his head lowered, and the moment their lips touched, she was lost.

The kiss wasn't rushed or desperate. It was slow and familiar…it was love.

When her lips parted, he slipped his tongue inside, and she tasted him. Home. The kiss felt like home. It touched her heart. Her soul. Soaked into the little crevices of her chest that had hollowed at their separation.

The kiss was healing, and at this moment, she felt okay for the first time in weeks.

When their mouths separated, it was too soon. She needed more. More of the comfort. The love. More of him.

He touched his forehead to hers again and whispered, "I'll give you a million breaths and a million heartbeats apart if that's what you need. But know that I will be here, waiting for you. Waiting for us. Always."

"Son, I can do that."

"Dad, there is no way I'm letting you up on this ladder. I'll fix your gutters. I just did mine anyway." Erik kept his voice light because he knew it was killing his dad not being able to do it himself. He'd always been a hands-on, able-bodied man, but since his heart attack, he'd been doing a lot less. Very few people walked away from a heart attack unscathed, his father included.

Erik had received the call from their mother an hour ago, asking him to come over to fix the gutters because his father was already on the ladder doing it himself. Erik had sure as hell rushed over to make his stubborn-ass father get down.

"Fine," his dad grumbled from the bottom of the ladder. "But if you're not going to let me help fix my own gutters, at least tell me how you're doing."

He paused, the question surprising him. It shouldn't have. He'd barely been talking to his parents since everything had gone down with Hannah.

"Everything's actually okay, Dad." A hell of a lot better after kissing Hannah a few nights ago. Since then, whenever he'd caught glimpses of her, she smiled at him. Waved. And each time, he swore he saw the same emotion in her eyes that tumbled through his chest. The longing. The need. The *love*.

It gave him hope.

Once the gutter was secure, he climbed down.

"That's good," his father said, voice softening. "Your mother and I have been worried about you for the last few weeks. You haven't been coming to Sunday dinners. You've barely answered our calls."

His back teeth ground together, and he wanted to kick his own ass. He'd become so damn good at hiding from those who loved him when times were tough. He needed to stop doing that. "I'm sorry. Things between Hannah and I have been…complicated."

Complicated…that was a fucking understatement.

His father's brows slashed together. "But things are okay now?"

He ran his fingers through his hair. "They're getting better."

The older man studied him for what felt like endless seconds. "Can I give you some advice?"

Erik almost laughed. Even if he said no, he was sure his father would dish it out anyway. "Of course."

"Love doesn't need to be perfect, it just needs to exist. Every love is flawed in some way. Show me a perfect relationship, and I'll show you a lie."

"That's good. Because our love is far from perfect." He didn't want perfect though. He just wanted her. He looked over his father's shoulder, watching as the leaves in the trees moved with the wind. "I broke what we had. But I hope to put it back together."

"Love doesn't break, son," his father said softly. "It shifts and changes. It grows. And if we're lucky, we grow with it."

Damn, he loved his dad. He was the best person Erik knew,

and if he could be half the man his father was, then he'd be doing pretty damn well.

When his phone dinged from his pocket, he pulled it out to see a text from his mom. "Mom just got home and asked me to help bring in the groceries."

"You go help her." His father nodded toward the back of the yard. "I'll get those extra nails we need from the toolshed."

Before his father could turn, Erik gripped his arm. "Hey, thanks. You've always given the best advice, and that hasn't changed."

"My family is my world, Erik. *You* are my world. And I will always be here when you need me."

Emotion clogged Erik's throat, making it hard to breathe. He pulled his father in for a hug before stepping back and moving around the house to the garage.

His mother stood by the trunk, holding six bags of groceries in two hands. He was pretty sure one was hanging off a pinkie.

He slipped the bags from her fingers. "I see nothing's changed. You're still trying to turn three trips from the car to the kitchen into one."

She grinned at him as she lifted the last two bags from the trunk. "Darling, it's called efficiency. One painful trip is better than multiple light ones. Besides, it's a good arm workout."

He chuckled and shook his head as he headed into the house. "Maybe. Or maybe it's the perfect way to strain a muscle."

"Pfft. I've been doing this my whole life and never strained anything." They set the bags onto the counter. "How are the gutters going?"

He lifted a shoulder. "Almost done. I can see it's killing Dad to let me do it instead of him."

Concern flickered in his mother's eyes. "You haven't been letting him go up there, though, have you?"

"No." He frowned. "Is everything okay? I know he's been a bit shaky since the heart attack. But is there something else?"

She opened her mouth, but before any words came out, there was a shout from outside, then a thud.

Erik's stomach dropped, bile churning in his gut as he took off running through the back door. What he saw made his blood run cold.

His father on the ground, beside the ladder, arm at an odd angle and crimson blood staining the asphalt beneath his head.

* * *

HANNAH CLOSED her eyes as she leaned into the stretch. Butterfly was her favorite part of yoga class. Her arms were straight on either side, her knees bent with heels touching. And there was a folded towel beneath her back.

It was relaxing, and it also signified they were at the end of the class and she'd made it.

Well, *usually* it was her favorite part of class. Today, Brigid had decided to join her, and the woman had been talking in a whispered voice the entire time. Hannah had shushed her at least a dozen times, and they'd received a lot of angry looks.

Thank God they were almost done.

She wasn't a huge yoga person, but every so often, when she wanted to move her body in a form that wasn't running, this was her go-to.

She took in a long breath of air before releasing it.

"I'm not saying I think he should break up with the man, just that he can find someone less…scruffy."

Hannah's eyes popped open. Good God, would her friend be quiet for just one minute? She turned her head to the person on her other side to see the woman glaring at them. Hannah gave her an apologetic smile.

When the teacher finally ended the class, Hannah sat up and turned to Brigid. "I am never letting you come to a yoga class with me again."

Brigid pouted. "Why? Because you like Owen and I don't?"

"No. Because I don't like angry glares being directed my way. And yoga is *me* time. It's where I go inward and get both a workout and some meditation at the end."

"I didn't stop you from doing any of that."

She cocked her head, not sure whether Brigid was lying to herself, or she really was that clueless. With a sigh, Hannah pulled on her shoes. "Are you going to work now?"

"Yep. Time to sell some sexy lingerie. Business has been booming lately. Which is a relief because I need the money."

Hannah frowned, the phone conversation she'd overheard of her friend talking about money coming back to her. "Is everything okay?" The shop had always brought in a fairly consistent income. Had something changed?

Brigid paused, her brows tugging together. "Um, yeah. It's fine. I'm just used to having two incomes and now need to manage on my own. It's an adjustment."

Hannah watched her closely. Brigid's tell when she was lying was that her eyes darted around while she touched her face. Right now, she was doing both of those things.

"Brigid—"

"You're not going into work today, are you?" Her words cut through Hannah's.

Hannah wanted to push, but she knew *exactly* what it was like to struggle with money and not want to talk about it. "No," she said. "After two days of opens, I'm taking a day off. Although I'll probably do paperwork at home."

Home… Would she catch a glimpse of Erik again? Something light fluttered in her belly. She'd been living for those glimpses lately. Every time her eyes fell on him, it was like she forgot how to breathe.

He owned a part of her. And even though what he'd done had fractured them, they hadn't broken. She had a feeling nothing and no one could kill the love she felt for him.

"Look who it is," Brigid said brightly.

Hannah was just rising to her feet as Andi stepped through the door into the yoga studio.

Erik's sister smiled when she saw them and walked over. "Hey, ladies. I haven't seen you guys here before."

Hannah chuckled. "I'm a very irregular yoga goer. And Brigid…"

How should she describe Brigid?

Her friend lifted a shoulder. "I'm a 'once every so often when I need some best friend time' yoga goer."

Hannah laughed. At least she knew her place. She turned back to Andi. "Do you come often?"

Andi nodded. "Twice a week. I alternate between yoga and Pilates. It's what I do for my soul."

Before Hannah could reply, Andi's phone rang.

She frowned when she looked at the screen. "It's Erik."

Hannah's pulse sped into a gallop at the mere mention of his name. God, she was so hopelessly in love with the guy.

"Strange that he's calling," Andi said quietly, almost to herself. "Usually, it's me chasing *his* ass down."

Hannah expected Andi to step to the side to answer. Instead, she lifted the cell to her ear. "And to what do I owe this pleasant surprise?"

The color suddenly drained from Andi's face.

Oh God, had something happened? Was Erik okay? Was his family okay?

Hannah inched closer, concern and panic welling in her belly.

"Okay, I'll be right there." Andi hung up, fingers shaking.

"What is it?" Hannah asked, touching the woman's arm, wanting to comfort her.

"It's my dad…he's been rushed to the ER."

The world around Erik was a swirl of grays and blacks. Air moved around him as people rushed through the hospital waiting room. There were the sounds of beeping and footsteps and voices. But it all blurred in light of the fact his father was in a damn hospital.

His mother sniffed beside him. She'd cried a lot of tears, and he'd tried to be her comfort, but they both knew the only thing that would help was a doctor's confirmation that his father was going to be okay.

He gripped his mother's hand. "Hey. He's going to be fine."

"I shouldn't have asked you to help with the groceries. I knew your father was in one of his moods where he wanted to be useful. He's been in them so often lately, and no matter how much I tell him he needs to rest, he doesn't."

"This isn't your fault."

She nodded, but as she did, another tear rolled down her cheek. Fuck, he hated seeing her in pain. It made his own worse. It twisted everything into something that hurt far too much.

He tugged his mother into his chest and held her as silent tears wet his shirt. He'd rarely seen her cry. Once when he left for the military, and once when they'd lost a family pet. But that was it. She was the strongest woman he knew.

He was still holding her when a familiar face stepped through the hospital doors. Andi moved toward him, her eyes red-rimmed. He was so focused on his sister, he almost missed the person behind her.

Hannah.

"Andi's here, Mom."

His mother pulled away just as Andi reached them. His sister tugged them both into a hug at the same time, holding them for long seconds before stepping back. "What happened? It wasn't another—"

"It wasn't a heart attack," Erik finished before she could. "He was on a ladder."

"No!" Andi gasped. "He has an arrhythmia. He gets fatigued and dizzy."

That was exactly what had happened.

His mother nodded. "He fell and hit his head on the concrete. His arm was also at a weird angle. We're not sure if there are more injuries."

Andi pulled her mother into another hug. Erik moved back, finally giving Hannah all of his attention.

She stepped straight into him and cupped his cheek. "I'm so sorry."

Her whispered words slipped inside him, dulling some of the ache. "You're here. How are you here?"

"I ran into Andi after a yoga class. She got your call while I was with her."

And she came. Thank God. He needed her. He'd been so close to calling her, begging her to come. But they weren't together. Technically, they weren't anything. So he'd stopped himself. Put his phone away, telling himself he needed to be okay without her.

But he wasn't. He'd never be okay without her.

Her arms slipped around his waist, and she lay her head

against his chest. The grays and blacks began to shift back to color. The air settled around him, and the voices in his head quieted. Because Hannah didn't just make him feel okay...she made him feel strong, like he could handle another blow to his world without shattering.

"Dr. Hunter. Hunter family."

Erik raised his head to see a doctor entering the waiting area. Hannah stepped back, but her fingers slipped through his, continuing to hold him together.

"Dr. Bode," Andi said softly, stepping forward. "Is he okay?"

"His heart is fine. He hit his head hard, though, and has quite a significant concussion, which is something we need to keep an eye on for a few days. He also had two breaks in his arm—one in his elbow, and another in his forearm. We've had to do some surgery to bring his bones back to where they're supposed to be."

The darkness hedged Erik's vision again. Hannah shifted closer, her fingers tightening around his, her other hand wrapping around his forearm.

"Can we see him?" his mother asked.

"Yes. He's not awake from the anesthesia yet, but you can go in when you're ready. I'll show you to his room."

The doctor turned and started to walk. Erik began to follow but stopped when Hannah tried to untangle their fingers.

"I'll wait here," she said. "It's probably just family."

"You *are* family, dear," his mother said before he could.

Her lips parted.

"Please," Erik whispered. "Come."

She nibbled her bottom lip before nodding quickly. "Okay."

Every step Erik took toward his father's room made the ball in his gut feel heavier. Seeing his father bleeding on the ground had scared the hell out of him. Seeing him in a hospital bed would be even harder.

His mother and sister entered first, but he hesitated outside the room. His legs had just stopped working.

A soft hand touched his chest. Hannah stepped closer. "Seeing the people we love in pain is hard. But Dr. Bode said he'll be okay," she reminded him quietly.

"But what if *I'm* not?"

There was no judgment in her eyes. "That's okay too."

Was it? Wasn't he supposed to be strong for his family? If his father was down, he should be the one holding them on his damn shoulders. But the truth was, he didn't know if he could handle any more loss in his life.

He thought Hannah might push him. Instead, she leaned into his shoulder, looking like she'd wait for him all day. As if standing exactly where they were for as long as he needed was okay. He let her touch soothe him. Speak to him. Tell him without words that his pace was the only pace that mattered.

Finally, he tightened his fingers around hers and stepped into the room. The sight of his strong father, the man who'd raised him, so still in the bed, almost brought him to his knees. But again, he focused on Hannah's touch. Her warmth. And he pushed himself to move forward. To stand on the side of the bed.

His father had a cast on his arm and a bandage on his head. But he was alive. And *that* was what Erik needed to focus on.

* * *

HANNAH TRAILED a finger down a vein on the back of Erik's hand. The air was so thick and heavy around her it was almost hard to breathe. Her heart hurt at the pain and uncertainty on everyone's faces. All she wanted to do was make it better. But there was nothing that would make things better except Michael waking up.

As Andi stepped out to take a call, Hannah's own phone beeped with a text. She pulled it out to see her best friend's name.

Brigid: I've been trying to hold off messaging because I didn't want to disturb you guys, but how's Michael? Is he okay?

Hannah: Concussion and a few breaks in his arm. He fell off a ladder. Hopefully, he'll wake up soon.

Hannah was crossing every finger and toe because this family needed to see his eyes and hear his voice to reassure themselves he was all right. Hell, *she* needed the same.

Brigid: I'll keep everyone in my thoughts. Let me know if you need anything.

A small smile touched Hannah's lips. She was again reminded of how grateful she was to have her best friend.

When Erik's phone rang, he tugged it out, and she saw Rachel's name flash on the screen. He canceled the call and slid the cell back into his pocket. Rachel was his oldest friend from the military. She checked in on him every so often.

Hannah was about to push her own phone back into her pocket when another text came through. She expected it to be from Brigid. Or possibly Henry, because she was sure Brigid would have told him what had happened.

It was neither of them.

Unknown number: No one truly gets away with murder. No one.

Her skin chilled, her breath catching in her throat.

She hadn't heard from this person in weeks, and with everything else she'd had going on, a part of her had almost forgotten…almost.

Her fingers began to shake, and for a moment, the walls around her felt like they were closing in.

"Hey."

She clicked out of the text and looked up to see Erik frowning at her, concern on his features.

"You okay?" he asked.

"Yes." The word came too quickly. But she couldn't tell him what was going on when he had so much else to deal with. There was no part of her that was willing to drop this on him now.

He watched her closely, his brows slashed together. Before he could say anything, the door opened and Andi walked back in.

"I just got off the phone with Nate. He's requesting emergency leave." She came to stand behind her mother. "No change?"

Jennifer was just shaking her head when a low groan sounded from the bed. Everyone straightened, and she heard Erik's sharp inhale. There was a second small groan as Michael's head turned, his face scrunched in pain or confusion, and finally, he opened his eyes.

"Oh, darling, you're awake!" Jennifer said, leaning over the bed and taking her husband's hand.

"What happened?" he asked slowly.

"You climbed the ladder that Erik and I told you not to climb," Jennifer said, tears glistening in her eyes. "You fell, hit your head, and broke your arm in a couple of places."

Pain laced his features. And something else. Regret, maybe? "I'm sorry. I…"

He stopped, like the words were too hard to speak.

Andi leaned down and pressed a kiss to her father's head. "Dad. We love you. And we need you to look after yourself."

"I know. I've just found this heart thing harder to deal with than I thought."

The conversation felt intimate. As Erik moved closer to the bed, Hannah quietly crept out of the room. So many emotions roiled inside her. Relief that Michael was awake, and it looked like he'd be okay. But also something else…

Her gaze flicked to her phone. Someone knew what she'd done all those years ago. Someone who was using it against her and continuing to harass her. Did they have evidence? Had the body finally been found?

Fear crawled up her throat, choking her. She didn't even know what Nico had done with the body.

Erik stepped out of the room, concern on his features. "Tell me what's wrong."

God, now she was being less of a help and more of a

hindrance. "I didn't bring my PDM, and I need to eat something. I might run home and do all that."

He frowned and lifted her watch, reading the number from her Dexcom. "I'll come with you."

"No." She shook her head. "You stay with your family."

"Hannah—"

She cupped his cheek. "I'm so glad your father is okay, but your family still needs you. After I've eaten something, I'll message and check in."

He studied her so intently she wanted to squirm. He tugged her closer. "You promise?"

"Yes." Her voice softened. "I promise."

Pure need filled his eyes. He lowered his head and touched his lips to hers. The kiss was soft. Healing. And when they separated, his mouth went to her ear, his breath brushing her cheek as he whispered, "Thank you for coming, Angel."

"I'll always come for you." *Always.*

They remained in an embrace for a few more seconds. She had to force herself to step back. To walk down the hall. She could still feel his breath on her cheek as she stepped outside and walked toward her car at the back of the lot.

She was almost there when she saw that something had been left under her windshield wipers. At first, she thought it was just a piece of paper, maybe an advertisement for something.

But as she grew closer, the glint on the front told her it was a photo. An old one. The edges looked frayed, and the photo was wrinkled. A few more steps, and the man in the photo became clear.

Her heart stopped, her feet halting beside the car.

Clarence Burns.

It took her several seconds to work up the courage to lift the photo. Her fingers trembled as she turned it over and read the messy writing.

You killed him. And I will make sure that's a crime you pay for.

Erik leaned his head back against the car headrest. The day had felt so fucking long and hard that the minutes had bled into each other.

He shouldn't have left his father out there with that ladder. Yes, his dad was a fully grown man and could make his own decisions, but Erik had *known* he was itching to prove he was still able to do things.

The only point in the day when he'd felt just a fraction of okay was when Hannah had come. When she'd slipped her fingers through his and her warmth had seeped into him. When her scent had filled his senses, drowning out the smells of bleach and antiseptic. She'd said she'd message him when she got home. He'd waited for it, and the second her text had come, his entire body had relaxed just a bit.

One more deep breath, and finally he slipped out of the car. His house was cold and quiet as he stepped inside. Usually, he didn't mind the quiet. Hell, normally he welcomed it. But today he wanted noise.

He walked up the stairs, not bothering to turn on any lights, and went straight to his bedroom. A bedroom that felt too damn empty without Hannah.

In the bathroom, he stripped quickly before stepping into the shower. He pressed his hands to the tiled wall, hung his head, and just breathed. Even that felt hard.

After what had happened to his team and Vicky, he'd numbed himself. Forced himself to stop feeling. But at some point in the last year, he'd let it all in again. And right now, he felt everything.

He stayed under the water long enough for steam to billow around the room. For the heat to redden his skin and the burn to lose its edge. Finally, he turned off the water and grabbed a towel.

He'd just entered the bedroom when he saw her. She stood in the doorway, blonde hair spilling over her shoulders, eyes soft and chained to him. *Always* chained to him.

She looked like a damn angel. *His* angel.

"Hannah…"

She crossed the room slowly, her eyes never straying from his, chest moving in slow rises and falls. When she was right in front of him, her hands rose as if she was going to touch him, but then they dropped again. "I saw you pull in. I wanted to come over and check on you. Are you okay?"

For a split second, he considered lying. To anyone else, he would have. But after everything they'd gone through recently, he wanted to give her all his truths, no matter how ugly. "No."

She took a small step closer. "What can I do?"

His hands went to her hips. Just touching her went a long way toward healing him. "You're here. That's already everything."

Her small hands grazed up his ribs, her head leaning forward. His breath stopped as one perfectly placed kiss touched his chest.

"Hannah." His fingers tightened on her hips. "What are we doing?"

He wasn't talking about just in this moment, and she knew it. He needed to know if she was his again. To know if he could believe in them. Because if he thought he had her back, but he really didn't...he wasn't sure he'd survive that.

She pressed another kiss to his chest. "I'm standing in a house that doesn't belong to me, kissing you, because beneath this skin is a heart that's connected to mine. That touches mine. And every so often, even the beats feel like they align to mine."

"Everything I own is yours, Angel. My home. My heart. My damn soul. I have never belonged to another person like I belong to you. My heart beats because you exist. Only you."

She looked up, tears glistening in her eyes. "I love you. And I've realized that my love for you is stronger than anything either of us has ever done. I don't know if that makes me a bad person, or a selfish one. But I need you more than I need to be *away* from you. You're right here." She touched a hand to her own heart.

The ache inside him shifted to something better. Lighter. And every pain, every scar and break, almost felt worth it...because they had brought him right here, to Hannah.

He lowered his temple to hers. "You're all I feel. All I see. You're my world. And when you're gone, it's all darkness."

"Kiss me." She rose to her toes, and he dipped his head. The kiss was soft, her lips sweet. And in that kiss, he found redemption. He found peace and hope for a future that had felt so damn bleak only weeks ago.

He lifted her, pulling her against him. She fit around him so perfectly. Like God had planned for them to fit exactly as they should.

With one hand, he tugged her sweater over her head before turning and lowering her to the bed. His mouth never left hers as his hands went to the button of her jeans. Once the zipper was undone, he shoved the jeans down her legs, where she toed them off.

He kissed her cheek, then her neck, his hands slipping behind her back and unlatching her bra. The second her breasts were free, he took one pebbled nipple between his lips and sucked.

The cry that fell from her lips filled his head. Kissing this woman, touching her in any way, blasted little bursts of hope into him.

He shifted to her other breast, wanting to make her feel everything. To have everything. Hell, he wanted to give this woman the fucking world.

He swirled his tongue around her peak, nipping and sucking. When he slipped a hand into her panties, he stroked her clit and she arched, her fingers gliding into his hair and tugging him up.

Then he was tasting her again. Drowning in her.

"Now," she whispered. "I need you now."

Four words that gutted him.

He rose and slipped her panties down her thighs. When they returned to each other, his hand went to her cheek, eyes on her. "I love you, Angel."

"Forever."

He slid into her, that one whispered word becoming his everything.

Forever.

* * *

HANNAH GROANED deep in her throat as Erik filled her, her walls stretching for him.

God, she'd missed him. His strength. His familiar scent of crisp pine. She'd missed the way he looked at her, like she was *it*, she was his everything, and he'd tear down any enemy who tried to step between them.

His mouth trailed down to her neck, and he latched on as his hips lifted and drove back into her. She groaned, digging her fingers into his shoulders, trying to hold herself in place. He did it again and again. Every time he returned to her, it was like a piece of herself slotting back into place.

She started to lift her hips to meet him thrust for thrust.

When his hand slipped up her side and cupped her breast, she whimpered. He found her nipple with the pad of his thumb and grazed back and forth.

She moaned, the sounds being torn from her throat rivaling the slaps of his body thrusting against her.

"Fuck, you destroy me," Erik whispered. He lifted her leg higher and thrust at a new angle, hitting a different point inside her.

"Erik…" She wasn't sure if she was asking for something or just desperate for more of him. Nothing made sense in this moment but him and what he made her feel.

His mouth moved back to her ear, nipping the lobe before whispering, "Come for me, Angel."

He reached down and stroked her clit, and that was all it took to lose control. For her body to break into a million pieces, trusting Erik to put her back together.

Erik kept thrusting, his thumb continuing to roll her clit until his own body tensed and shuddered, and he broke with her. And God, it was everything seeing such a powerful man being brought to his knees, seeing and feeling him give her all he had.

She held him as they both descended into stillness, as the whispers of the night became the only sounds in the room.

When he finally lifted his head and looked at her, she saw it all. Every pain. Every fracture. Every emotion, good and bad, that had touched him in the last couple of months.

He didn't shield her from anything.

"Thank you," he whispered.

"For what?"

"Returning to me."

Her heart skipped a beat. "I'll always return to you, Erik. It doesn't feel like a choice anymore."

He lowered his face to her neck. She cupped his head with her hands and held him, memorizing this new version of them.

CHAPTER 21

annah's back rose and fell slowly beneath his hand, her cheek pressed to his chest. It was long past the time he would usually get up, but he couldn't move. Lying here, holding her...it was peace.

Yesterday had been a day to remember for all the wrong reasons...until last night. Until her touch. Her words. Her promise of forever.

A soft moan slipped from her lips, and a second later, her head turned, a lock of hair falling over her cheek. Gently, he reached down and slipped it back behind her ear.

Slowly, her beautiful blue eyes opened, and she looked up at him.

Every time her eyes locked with his, it felt like a sucker punch to the gut. She stole every scrap of air from his lungs.

"Hey." Her voice was soft, her breath brushing over his skin.

"Good morning, Angel." He cupped her cheek. "You sleep okay?"

The corners of her mouth lifted. "Better than I have in a long time."

Him too. "Good." His thumb grazed her cheek. "I'd ask how

your blood sugars are, but I didn't see a monitor on you last night."

She cringed. "My old monitor ran out yesterday, and the new ones haven't arrived yet."

A soft growl slipped from his chest. "Why didn't you tell me? I would have ordered you more."

"You know why." She drew a circle on his chest. "But even if we were in a good place, that's not your responsibility."

He could have laughed at the absurdity in that statement. "You are *always* my responsibility, good place or not."

The look she gave him said she didn't agree.

He turned them over, caging her to the bed. "Do you still mean everything you said last night?"

There was a small catch in her breath. It caused fear to spread over his skin like wildfire and burn into his chest.

Was she having second thoughts about them?

She reached up and cupped his cheek. "I meant everything. Not just last night, but before then. You're my person. It's not a choice, because we don't choose who we love. Our heart just links to another. And my heart linked to yours."

The air stalled in his throat, and he lowered his forehead, touching it to hers. "You have no idea what those words do to me."

He kissed her...a long, slow kiss. Tasting her. Loving her. When their lips separated, it was too soon.

He lowered to her side, his gaze catching on her wrist. Without thinking, he reached down and traced the cloud charm. "I'm sorry he's not in your life anymore."

He wasn't sorry that the man was dead, but he was sorry about the pain his death caused her.

She swallowed, watching as his finger moved over the charm. "I still don't know if I believe he did what you were told. He fell in with some bad crowds in his teens, but at heart, he was always a good person. Well...at least that was the side of himself he showed *me*." She wet her lips. "But they obviously had evidence, and you were just doing your job."

"It must have been hard being told he was gone."

Pain raced over her features. "It was the hardest moment of my life. I was only two when I lost my mom and dad, so I don't remember those losses. But Nico had been my family for years. His death was something I thought I would never recover from."

Damn, he hated hearing that. "Did you have to identify the body?"

Her eyes became wet, but she blinked away the tears. "No. There was no part of me that wanted to see Nico like that. I found out about his death because his girlfriend called me. When I saw her at the funeral, she said his body was burned beyond recognition when his place burned down, so I don't think anyone identified him visually."

Erik froze, his gut coiling. "Burned?"

Hannah either didn't notice his reaction or was too far in her own head. "We shouldn't talk about this. I need to test my blood sugars, take my insulin, and get ready. I have an open house today, and you need to check in on your dad."

She went to rise, but he grabbed her arm. "Angel—I didn't burn Nico's place. I used a sniper rifle and shot him on the street."

* * *

"The home is beautiful, but we're just a bit concerned that it's too much space for us."

Hannah offered a distracted smile to the woman and her husband. They were in their mid-fifties, both with a few grays weaving through their hair. "You're welcome to think about it, and in the meantime, I do have some smaller homes on the market I can show you."

The man nodded. "That would be great."

"Perfect. I've got your contact details, so I'll give you a call tomorrow to set up some viewings."

The woman grinned. "Wonderful. We look forward to hearing from you."

Hannah watched the couple walk down the path, then get into their black Toyota. It wasn't until they drove away that she finally dropped the smile. Her cheeks ached from the effort it took to act normal.

Her mind had been reeling all day, thoughts of Nico and the circumstances of his death racing through her head.

Erik had told her that a car had stopped and he'd had to flee the area, so Nico's death had never been confirmed, but if not Erik…who had killed him?

She stepped back into the house and set her sign-in iPad on the hall table. The open had gone for a few hours and was very busy. But then, a lot of her opens had been busy lately. It was so different from the position she'd been in just months ago.

Despite everything she'd gone through, at least she now knew the reason she'd had so few homes to sell was because that competing agent had been bad-mouthing her—with her coworker's help. Thank God the former had been fired.

Some people would walk over anyone to get a leg up. She hated that about the business.

She moved up the stairs, going from room to room to switch off the lights. She'd just slipped into the last bedroom when something sounded downstairs. She paused and listened. Had someone else arrived? It wouldn't be the first time people had come right at the end of an open house.

She went back down the stairs, but there was no one there. Strange. Maybe it was a neighbor?

She turned off the kitchen and living room lights, as well as the overhead in the downstairs bedroom, before moving to the alarm. Quickly, she punched in the five-digit code before slipping outside and pulling the door closed, hearing the lock click into place. Her phone dinged, and she smiled as she walked down the steps.

Erik: Leaving the hospital soon. Dad's damn stubborn, already pushing for the doctors to sign his release paper. Put me at ease and tell me I'm seeing you tonight.

She was about to respond when the home alarm went off.

She spun, her heart racing at the abrupt sound. Shit, that was *loud.*

She ran back up the steps, rushing to unlock the doors and key in the code again. The second the piercing noise quieted, she blew out a breath.

Had she done something wrong? Had she put in the wrong code?

Tapping into her phone screen, she pulled up her notes, including the alarm instructions from the owner. Nope. Everything appeared right. With a frown, she keyed in the code again, this time slower.

She waited a moment, and when the alarm didn't shriek at her, she turned and headed out of the house again.

She'd made it exactly the same distance, halfway down the path, when the alarm went off a second time.

This time, something cold slithered over her skin. For a second, she was tempted to just go back to her car, but the alarm was piercing, and she didn't want to upset the neighbors.

It was fine. She'd go back in, turn it off, then call the owners.

With quick steps, she jogged back to the door. After unlocking it yet again, she stepped back inside and moved straight to the alarm pad, where she typed in the five numbers.

The house silenced.

She was about to call the owner when the iPad caught her attention. It still sat on the hall table where she'd put it. Crap! She'd almost left it behind. Guess the faulty alarm was a good thing. She lifted the tablet and was about to turn it off—

But stopped when she noticed the last recorded name on the check-in list.

Ice slipped into her veins, nausea coiling in her belly. For a moment, she didn't move. She didn't breathe. Because that name was so familiar and utterly terrifying. A ghost from her past.

Clarence Burns.

A rustle sounded behind her.

She didn't have time to turn before a hand shoved her against the wall. She struggled as a body pressed into her back—then something sharp touched her side and she just stopped. Stopped fighting. Stopped breathing.

"I'm gonna make you hurt for what you did to him." She barely heard the whispered words over the buzzing between her ears. The fear fogging her head.

She opened her mouth to say something, but no words came out. Then the knife pressed harder, her side stinging as her world started to darken.

Suddenly, pounding footsteps sounded from the walkway outside.

The person behind her cursed, the knife disappearing before her head was slammed hard against the wall.

Pain blasted through her skull as she fell to the floor.

Footsteps raced down the hall—then a new set of steps. She tried to see the person running into the house, chasing after whoever had grabbed her, but she couldn't. Because remaining conscious took all her energy.

"I told you, I don't need a pacemaker. I've been handling the arrhythmia fine with medication."

Erik's hands fisted at his dad's words. His father had always been a rational man, but today it was like he had no damn sense.

"The doctor said it would help," his mother said gently, touching his hands. She'd been doing a good job at remaining calm. It was the only reason Erik had been staying the hell out of the conversation.

"Jennifer, I'd just like to go home."

"Me too. And we will, as soon as they've organized the procedure for this pacemaker." His mother rose, squeezing his hand. "I'm going to get some coffee, and I think you could use some rest. I'll be back."

She leaned down and kissed her husband before walking over and kissing Erik's cheek. She was probably escaping to get some space so she didn't explode on her husband.

Once she was gone, Erik lifted a brow at his father. "Why are you making this so much more difficult than it needs to be?"

His father sighed as he leaned back against the pillows

propped behind his head. "Because, son…getting older is harder than I ever thought. Your body gives up on you before your mind, and in a way, it feels like your body's betraying you."

Some of Erik's frustration left him. "I'm sorry. But fighting everyone on the pacemaker isn't going to change anything."

"My body knows that. My brain just needs some time to catch up." His brows slashed together. "I'm sorry."

"You don't have to be sorry, just accept the medical aid."

"No." His dad looked straight at him. "I'm sorry about climbing that ladder. That I put you through that and you had to find me on the ground looking the way I did."

A vein in Erik's temple throbbed at the reminder of what he'd seen. At the fear that had seized every limb of his body. "Just tell me you're not gonna do it again."

"I won't do it again."

"Good. And take the damn pacemaker."

His father's lips twitched. "You know I'll end up with the *damn pacemaker*. When does your mother ever *not* win a fight?"

Erik chuckled. "Happy wife, happy life. That was something you taught me."

"That's right. It's been true since the day I married her." He paused, eyes softening. "It was nice to see Hannah here yesterday."

Erik wet his lips, feeling the familiar uptick of his pulse at the mere mention of her. "She was with Andi when she received my call."

A knowing smile stretched his father's lips. "But she came for *you*."

She did. And fuck, he was grateful for that.

"That's why you're different today."

Erik's brows rose. "Different how?"

"Well, for one, you're not scowling."

"You're in a hospital bed, Dad. Of course I'm not scowling."

"Ah, but even when you try to keep whatever you're feeling inside you, there's still a hint of it on your face. Trust me, the family's been looking at that scowl for over a month."

Had they? It was probably true. "Things are better today."

Relief spilled over his father's face, so distinct Erik could almost feel it. "Good."

His mother had just returned when Erik's phone rang. Nate. He stepped into the hall and answered the call. "Hey."

"You at the hospital?"

"I am. You get some time off?"

"Yep. And I'm here. Which room's he in?"

Damn, that was quick. "Eighteen."

Less than a minute later, Nate was stepping out of the elevator down the hall. There was a hard look on his brother's face. When he stopped in front of him, Erik gripped his brother's shoulder. "He's okay. A concussion and some broken bones."

"Why would he have climbed the damn ladder?"

"Because he's stubborn."

Nate laughed, but there wasn't a lot of humor behind it. "The most stubborn man I know." He took a breath before stepping into the room. Erik started to follow, but his phone rang again, this time Chandler's name flashing on the screen.

Had he found any information about Nico? Erik had called him the second Hannah left the house this morning. "What did you find?"

"You're not gonna like this."

Erik's muscles tensed. "Tell me."

"I couldn't find any hospital records for the day you shot him, but I found something else...his death certificate. Hannah was right. Cause of death was burned to death."

Fuck. "What's the recorded date of death?"

The mission was on May tenth. He'd read over his job report so many times in the last month, he knew it by heart.

"It's May thirtieth."

The air rushed from his chest. "Someone got him to a hospital that night. They saved him."

"What does this mean?" Chandler asked, frustration in his voice. "Did someone save him, only to kill him later? Maybe the trafficking ring needed him alive because he had something they wanted? Or hell, maybe he was saved by a friend, only to have an enemy torch his place later?"

"Maybe." Erik's temple throbbed. "Or maybe he escaped and is still alive. The person was burned beyond recognition. No one identified the body."

Chandler cursed. "We need more information. We need—" He stopped when a beeping sounded over the line. There was a brief pause. "The guy I have on Hannah's calling me."

* * *

HANNAH CRINGED as the paramedic prodded at the bump on her temple.

"It just appears to be bruised," he said, finally stepping away. "You said you didn't lose consciousness?"

She shook her head. "I felt dizzy, but that's it."

He grabbed a light and checked her eyes. "Well, I'd say it was a lucky escape. No signs of concussion. I'll get you some ice and painkillers."

She nodded as the paramedic disappeared, her gaze falling on the guy who was talking to the police officers. Who was he? And where had he come from? He didn't look like anyone she recognized. He was big, both in height and breadth, and dressed all in black. He'd chased after the guy who'd knocked her into the wall, then returned a second later, calling both paramedics and police before checking her over.

She'd asked who he was, and he'd just given her a first name—

Jim. That didn't tell her anything, like where he'd come from or how he'd known she was in trouble. She didn't think she'd screamed during her brief struggle with the assailant, but then, everything was a bit of a blur.

She tugged her phone from her pocket and hovered her finger over Erik's number. She'd meant to call him immediately, but the police had arrived, then the paramedics, and everything had moved too quickly.

She'd just pressed on his name when an engine roared from down the street. She looked up, her breath catching at the sight of Erik's Corvette racing toward them.

He was here…

How?

She hung up the call as Erik pulled to the side of the road. When his gaze hit hers, a full-body shudder coursed down her spine. The anger on his face, the danger radiating off him…it was so dark.

He moved toward her, his gaze running over her body, searching for injuries. Then he was right in front of her, his hands on her hips. His gaze narrowed on the bruise at her temple before shifting back to her eyes. "Are you okay?"

She nodded slowly, her brows pinched. "Just a bump on the head. How did you know?" Suddenly, she glanced back at the man who'd saved her, the pieces falling into place. "Wait…was he—"

"He was watching you, Angel. Protecting you."

Her mouth opened and closed, so many questions bubbling inside her, but she didn't have time to ask any of them because the paramedic returned, as well as two police officers.

"Ms. Jacobs," one of the officers said. "Could you please take us through what happened?"

She thanked the paramedic for the ice pack and pain meds and took a breath before turning toward the officer. She had to be careful with her explanation. If she wasn't, too many questions would be asked…questions she didn't want to answer.

"I went upstairs to turn off the lights and heard something downstairs, but when I went down, I didn't see anyone. I locked and alarmed the house, but when I went to leave, the alarm went off. I went back, re-alarmed and locked, and the same thing happened." She swallowed. "When I went back the second time, the guy grabbed me and shoved me against the wall. He had a knife. That's when the guy who saved me came in and chased the man off."

Every word brought the brief nightmare back to life. Erik was tense beside her, and she could just about feel his anger expanding as she told the story.

The officer looked up from his notes. "Did he say anything?"

She shook her head, not trusting her voice with the lie.

"Do you have any enemies, Ms. Jacobs? Anyone who'd want to hurt you?"

Her skin chilled. She shouldn't. No one should know about what she'd done to Clarence. Not a single living soul. But apparently someone did…not that she'd be sharing that with the police. "No."

The officer closed his notepad. "In that case, it sounds like it was a narrow escape. Possibly a robbery gone wrong. He may have panicked when the alarm kept going off. We'll dust for prints, but if he's not in the system, we likely won't be able to identify him. You're lucky someone was walking past and heard your scream."

Lucky? That was the last thing she felt.

Before leaving, Erik spoke to Jim. She watched the exchange closely. She couldn't hear what either man was saying, but it seemed tense. Both men were so big and muscular, they looked like they were carved from granite.

When Erik returned to her, he cupped her cheek. "I'll drive you home and we'll come back for your car later. Ready to go?"

She nodded, all her energy suddenly gone. He led her to his car before sliding behind the wheel.

She cleared her throat, the question she'd been wanting to ask blurting out. "How long have you had him on me?"

"Since I read the note in your office."

Her brows rose. That was over a month ago. "Why didn't you tell me?"

"I guess a part of me thought you might refuse. We weren't in the best place, and I needed you safe."

On any other day, she'd probably be angry about that. He should have told her. But right now, she was too exhausted by everything that had happened. And a part of her knew he was right, she would have argued about it, and without his foresight, things would have been a lot worse today. Hell, she could be dead. A shudder rolled down her spine.

Erik reached out and slipped his fingers through hers. "I'm sorry I wasn't honest with you."

She sighed and leaned back. "It's okay."

The rest of the trip was silent, though she could almost hear Erik's thoughts. Did he know she hadn't told the whole truth to the police?

When he pulled into the garage, she'd just slipped off her seat belt when he asked, "What else happened today?"

She should have expected that. Erik knew her better than anyone else. He'd probably heard everything she hadn't said.

She wet her lips. "There's something I haven't told you. A part of my past that I've never told anyone but Nico."

There was a small flex of the muscles in his forearm. "What is it, Angel?"

"I told you that when I was sixteen, I did something…something that Nico saved me from." The panic tried to swamp her, the memory of exactly what she'd done stealing her breath.

Erik's hand came over hers. It went a long way toward calming her. "Tell me."

"Remember the story I told you about one of my foster fathers attacking me in bed? He cut my bra off and left that scar in the center of my chest when he tried to…" She couldn't finish the sentence.

She didn't need to. Raw anger darkened Erik's feature. "I remember."

"The bracelet fell off my wrist during the attack. I didn't realize until it was too late and I'd already left." Her gaze shifted to her bracelet, running her finger over the jewelry that used to be her mother's. "A week later, I went back to get it."

His fingers tightened around her forearm. "But the asshole who attacked you was in jail, right?"

Emotion clogged her throat. "I thought he was." God, she'd been counting on him being in jail. "But he wasn't. He'd gotten out on bail, and he found me in my old room."

"Tell me he didn't hurt you, Angel. Tell me the man isn't out there somewhere, because if he is, I *need* to kill him."

Her skin grew clammy. "He didn't hurt me, and he's not out there…because I shot and killed him that night."

A heavy pause followed, and for a moment, she couldn't look up. Because then he'd see everything. The darkness that had been a part of her since that night. The way her actions had affected her on such a deep level.

The man had deserved to die, but taking a life at sixteen…a person didn't come out of that unscathed.

Warm fingers touched her chin and tilted her head up to look at him. Erik's expression wasn't judgmental. Instead, he was frowning like he was trying to understand. "If you shot and killed him, that would have been on the background check I pulled on you. It wasn't."

Her fingers dug into her palms. "Because the police never found out. I panicked. I'd basically broken into the house, going in through a window. And I was scared law enforcement wouldn't believe that I'd acted in self-defense. When I'd told the police he attempted to rape me, some officers had looked at me like I was just another lying, troublemaking foster kid."

She knew the exact moment it clicked for Erik. The frown smoothed out, and his chest rose and fell in one long breath. "Nico covered it up for you."

She nodded, a tear falling down her cheek. "He got rid of the body and cleaned up, so it looked like I was never there. As far as everyone was concerned, Clarence Burns jumped bail to avoid facing trial."

He leaned forward, swiping away a tear. "Angel, I'm so sorry you had to go through that."

She tilted her head, leaning into his warm touch.

"How does that relate to what happened today?"

She swallowed the lump in her throat, forcing the words out. "I've been getting messages for the last month. That one you saw on my desk…and texts. Telling me they know what I did. Then yesterday, someone left a photo of Clarence on my car windshield."

Erik's brows slashed together. "Yesterday?"

"I found it when I left the hospital."

He cursed. "Why didn't you tell me?"

"Because you were already dealing with everything with your dad. I didn't want to add to it."

He leaned his head closer. "Angel…*always* tell me. No matter what else I'm dealing with or where you and I are in our relationship, your safety is my first priority. Always."

She gave one quick nod.

His thumb swiped her cheek. "What else?"

"When I went back into the house the second time today, someone had added Clarence's name on my iPad to the list of people who'd attended the open. And when the guy had me pressed to the wall, he said something."

Erik's jaw clenched. "What did he say?"

"That he was going make me hurt for what I did to Clarence."

If she'd thought she'd seen anger on Erik's face before, that was nothing compared to now. He looked ready to hunt this stalker down and end him.

CHAPTER 23

Hannah read and re-read the same sentence five times. God, she was so tired she couldn't concentrate. Not only that, but she'd been feeling nauseous since the attack.

Days had passed, yet she still didn't feel like herself. She probably wouldn't until she knew exactly who was behind it.

Dread pooled in her belly at the idea that someone in the world apart from her and Erik knew what she'd done. They didn't seem to have evidence...or if they did, they weren't using it.

The nausea in her belly rolled as a knock came at her office door. Her gaze shot up to see Leo standing there, an easy smile on his face. "Hey. I'm just heading out for coffee. Want to join? I can act as your personal bodyguard."

Despite everything, a smile curved her lips. Leo had become a good friend. He was easy to talk to, soft-spoken, and he'd helped her out on so many occasions that she'd be forever indebted to the man. "Thank you, but I'm actually having lunch with my friends today. I haven't had a chance to visit with them since the...incident."

Everyone in the office had received the same version of events as the police. They knew that she'd been attacked but not that Clarence's name had been placed on her iPad. And of course, no one knew what her attacker had said to her.

He cocked his head. "Ah. Well, I hope it goes all right."

"I'm sure it will. They know what happened, they just haven't seen me in person since."

"Have fun." He winked at her before heading to the door.

She was just turning back to her screen when voices sounded from the foyer. She grinned at hearing Henry's laugh as he spoke to Leo.

She opened her bottom door and pulled out her purse but frowned when she looked up. Henry and Owen were in her office doorway…but no Brigid.

"Hey. Brigid didn't come with you?" She glanced at her watch, noticing it was ten past the time they were all supposed to arrive. Brigid was never late.

Henry shook his head. "No. I thought she'd be here already."

Strange. She pulled her cell from her bag and tried Brigid's number, but after five rings, it went to voice mail.

"We could just go get her," Owen suggested. "Her store's only one street over, right?"

Henry nodded. "Good idea. Let's do it."

Hannah rose and walked around her desk, then stopped to place a hand on her stomach. God, she really wasn't feeling well today.

Henry stepped forward, touching her arm. "Hey. You okay?"

"Yeah. I've been taking pain medication for the head injury, and it's making me nauseous."

"How's your blood sugar?"

She tapped her watch, swiping to the monitor reading. "I'm a bit low, but that's not a surprise. It's been all over the place because of stress."

She went back and grabbed a granola bar from her drawer.

When they reached the street, Owen shoved his hands into his pockets, giving her a small smile. "So…how're you doing?"

She lifted a shoulder. "Not too bad, considering. I'd be better if we could find the guy who attacked me." She cast a quick glance around. At least now, the feeling of being watched made sense. The protective detail Erik and Chandler had organized was somewhere, hiding in the shadows.

Was that all it was, though? Were the eyes she felt watching her just from the bodyguard? And if so, and she knew about him, why did the feeling still make her skin crawl?

She forced her gaze back to Owen. "I'm sorry we've had to cancel two of our appointments."

He shook his head. "You don't need to apologize. You've had a lot going on."

"I could take you after lunch?"

Henry grinned. "That's a good idea. It means I can join and give you my very honest opinion."

Hannah's eyes narrowed on her friend. "*How* honest?"

"I'll look at every inch of every wall for cracks. I'll turn on every tap and inspect every air duct."

She wrinkled her nose, not sure she wanted him to join.

Owen chuckled. "It's okay. I need to get to work on a bike I'm fixing up. I'm not in any rush. Just give me a call when you have time."

Yeah, another time sounded good to her too. A time when Henry would be conveniently busy.

When they reached Brigid's lingerie store, Hannah pushed inside to see a handful of customers, all women. Brigid's part-time salesclerk was helping two women on one side of the shop, while Brigid helped a woman on the other side.

Her gaze shot up when they entered, eyes widening like she'd just realized she'd forgotten about their lunch.

"Maybe we should wait outside," Hannah said quietly to the guys.

"*We'll* wait outside," Henry replied. "You stay and make sure the woman doesn't bail on us. But don't take long. I'm hungry."

She smiled. He was always hungry. "Okay."

Hannah moved to the counter, surveying the selection of sexy bras. Every piece of lingerie she owned was from this store, but that wasn't because Brigid was her best friend. She stocked the most beautiful lingerie in town, possibly in the state. And she had something for everyone. All sizes. Modest. Sexy. Even cute pajamas—three sets of which Hannah also owned.

Not that she wore pajamas anymore. Erik's T-shirts had become a bedtime staple for her.

Brigid rushed over. "I'm sorry! I can't do lunch today. We're just too busy." The words came in a rush, her gaze barely meeting Hannah's.

She opened her mouth, but before she could respond, Brigid was already moving toward the back of the store.

Hannah frowned, looking around the shop. There were three customers. She'd hardly call this unmanageable for Brigid's shop assistant.

Carefully, she weaved through the store to find her friend going through boxes in the storage room. She quietly closed the door behind her. "Brigid, is everything okay?"

"Of course." She didn't look up. In fact, she seemed to be doing everything possible to keep her head down.

When she finally turned, lingerie in hand, she tried to pass Hannah, but she blocked her friend's way.

"Brigid—what's going on?"

"Nothing."

She stepped to the side, but Hannah mirrored her, this time wrapping her fingers around her friend's arm. The touch was light, but Brigid immediately recoiled.

Hannah snatched her hand away. "Did I *hurt* you?"

"I'm fine. I did a workout this morning and my muscles are a bit sore."

Her best friend rarely worked out. "Brigid—"

"Hannah, I need to go." Finally, she looked up—and Hannah saw what she'd missed in the store.

"Do you have a black eye?"

Brigid immediately turned her head so Hannah couldn't see that side of her face. But it was too late. Her friend had obviously tried to cover it with makeup, and she'd done a pretty good job, but standing this close, there was no missing the dark bruising.

"Did someone *hit* you?"

Brigid sucked in a deep breath. "It's not what you think. I was in the storage room last night and I pulled a box down from the top shelf. It fell on my face." Brigid's eyes darted around the room, and she touched her cheek.

Hannah's frown intensified. "If that's true, then why are you trying so hard to hide it?"

"Because it's embarrassing." She swallowed. "I've got a customer waiting. I need to go. I'll call you later, okay?"

This time, Hannah didn't block her way. Instead, she watched as she left the room, wondering what the hell was going on...and worrying for her best friend.

* * *

ERIK PULLED into the parking lot at Black Bean. He'd been with his dad all morning and was sick to death of the damn hospital coffee. Why the hell it had to taste like dirt mixed with water, he had no fucking idea.

He climbed out of his car and had only taken a couple steps when his phone rang. He stopped at the sight of Chandler's name on the screen.

"Chandler. Have you got anything on the attack?"

He'd told his friend what had happened years ago between Hannah and Clarence, but only because he knew the information would never go further. He trusted Chandler with his life, and with Hannah's. Now he was looking into Clarence Burns to find out who could've been close enough to the man to know what Hannah had done. It was either that, or Nico had told someone.

"I ran a really thorough background check on Clarence."

A vein in Erik's temple throbbed. "And?"

"I was sure it would be the wife. Hannah said the woman was likely home and passed out. But it can't be."

"Why not?"

"She died a year ago...kidney failure. Probably due to her alcohol abuse."

Erik's hands fisted, anger pumping through his blood. "What about the other foster kids? Hannah said they took in as many as they could for the money. Clarence could have grown close to one of them. Groomed them."

"I'm working on it. Getting the names of the kids who were fosters at the same time as Hannah is hard. CPS records are confidential and never released without a court order. I need to hack into government databases. And I will...I just need more time."

If anyone could do it, it was Chandler. "What about Clarence? He have any close friends?"

"There were a couple guys he seemed to catch up with regularly, but two of them have died, and the other is fighting lung cancer. I'll keep an eye on him though."

Erik ran frustrated fingers through his hair. "Thanks, Chandler."

"You got it."

"You haven't found anything on Nico?"

"Not yet. I'm sorry."

Erik blew out a breath. It wasn't his friend's fault, but it was still damn frustrating. "I need to know if it was actually him who was burned in that apartment. I need to know if the man's alive and out there in the world. Whether he has eyes on Hannah, and if that makes her unsafe."

"You know I'll keep digging. But you also know that if I *don't* find anything, it was likely him in that fire."

"Then I want to find out who set it. I want to know who killed him."

"Got it. I'll let you know what I find. One last thing. On a hunch, I looked into that trafficking ring Nico was part of. It's back up and running."

Erik cursed loudly. "When?"

"Not long after you and the other contractors killed the heads of the organization. Looks like some lower-level members took over. I'm gonna raise it with the boss and see if we can be tasked with taking it down again."

And by taking it down, Chandler meant ending every last member.

"Good. Once you have details of the job, I want to know about it."

Erik hung up, taking a moment to think over everything Chandler had said. He was still leaning against his car when Hannah came into view, Henry and Owen by her side. Immediately, their eyes met.

The smile that stretched across her lips almost made him forget about that damn phone call…almost. He moved toward her. The second his arm was around her, the second he felt her softness and warmth, he was lost. He dipped his head and kissed her, ignoring murmurs from Henry and Owen.

When he lifted his head, he met her gaze. "Hey. I didn't expect to see you here."

"I didn't expect to see you either. It's a nice surprise. You getting lunch?"

"It was just gonna be a coffee, but if you're staying, I'll stay."

Henry clapped his hands excitedly. "Double date!"

Hannah laughed. "I'm staying."

His arm tightened around her waist, and they followed Henry

and Owen into the coffee shop. He'd barely entered when he saw her…

Rachel.

How the hell did she know where to find him?

Then again, he shouldn't be surprised. She was one of his oldest friends. The woman who'd pulled him out of the depths of hell after his final mission and what had happened to Vicky. The last he'd spoken to her, returning her call, he'd told her about his dad being in the hospital.

She met his gaze and rose from her stool at the counter, a huge-ass smile on her face as she crossed the distance toward him.

"What the hell are you doing here?" he asked, the corners of his lips lifting.

"After your text about your dad, I came to town to check on you, of course. I was just stopping for coffee before I went to your place to surprise you. Looks like you've surprised *me*. You gonna give me a hug or what?"

CHAPTER 24

"He sounded exactly like the Count from *Sesame Street*, and he was fucking annoying." Rachel leaned over the table as if to press her point.

Hannah's lips twitched.

"He *did* sound like the Count," Erik said with a grin, the warmth of his side pressing into her.

"And our drill instructor," Rachel continued, "made him get in front of us every fucking day and count every person before we could leave. There were hundreds of us."

The twitch of Hannah's lips turned into a smile. Henry and Owen hadn't stayed for long, but from what she'd seen, they seemed to really like Rachel. And Hannah understood why. She was easy to like, friendly, talkative, and beautiful, but not in an obvious way. She wasn't wearing makeup, her long brown hair was pulled up, and she wore simple jeans and a sweater. She had a natural beauty. Dimples that came alive when she grinned and eyes that warmed when she spoke.

Hannah had never been a jealous person, but there was an intimacy to Erik and Rachel's friendship she couldn't help but envy. A bond between them. Erik hadn't stopped smiling since they'd found Rachel inside the shop, those frown lines that had been carved into his brow gone for the first time in weeks.

You could feel the history between them… So yeah, she felt a bit jealous.

She tapped her phone screen to see if Brigid had replied to the text Hannah had sent twenty minutes ago, asking if they could hang out tonight. She hadn't.

She had a black eye. A black freaking eye. How? Because no way did she believe that falling box story. And if that didn't happen…why wouldn't Brigid tell her the truth?

"Oh my gosh, I'm so sorry, Hannah," Rachel said, her words pulling Hannah out of her thoughts. "You must be finding this so boring."

"No, not at all. I love hearing stories of what you guys went through. If I look like I'm not enjoying it, it's just because I'm tired."

Erik slid an arm around her waist. "Are you okay?"

"Yeah. I should probably be getting back to work though."

He nodded. "I'll walk you."

She shook her head. "You should stay. Catch up more."

His eyes narrowed. "I'm walking you back to your office."

She opened her mouth to object, but Rachel got in first.

"Erik and I will have plenty of time to catch up. We can go now."

He pressed a kiss to Hannah's temple. "I'm just going to pay."

As Erik moved to the counter, she and Rachel rose to their feet. "I'm sorry I just sprang this visit on you," the woman said.

"You don't have to apologize. I'm glad he has you. He's told me so much about you."

She cringed. "Good things, I hope."

"The best. He said you basically saved him eight years ago, when he lost so many loved ones."

The smile slipped, and lines etched into Rachel's brow. "That was the worst. I can't even think about that time without my heart breaking for him all over again." She glanced across the room at Erik. "But he would have been okay without me. He's strong, in so many ways. Sometimes he just needs a reminder."

"He *is* strong." The strongest man she'd ever met.

Rachel looked back at Hannah, the crease in her brow smoothing out and the corners of her lips tugging up again. "You make him happy."

"How can you tell?"

She laughed, a full throw-your-head-back kind of laugh. "I'm sure you know the answer to that. When Erik's *not* happy, the entire fucking world knows about it. He walks around with that I-need-to-kill-someone look on his face."

Hannah chuckled. "Yeah. He's good at that look."

"What look?"

They both glanced at him. Neither had noticed his approach.

"Don't you worry your pretty little head about it," Rachel retorted, following the words with a ruffle of Erik's hair.

Hannah laughed but sobered quickly when they stepped outside and Erik looked both ways, clearly searching for a threat.

Rachel didn't miss it either. "What was that?"

"What?" Erik asked, looking back at her.

"Don't *what* me. Is something going on? Is there something I should be aware of while I'm here?"

He cleared his throat. "How long are you staying?"

Her eyes narrowed. "As long as I need to, to make sure you and your family are okay. Don't change the subject. What's going on?"

A muscle in his jaw clenched.

Rachel stepped closer, her voice low. "Erik Hunter, you tell me right now."

"It's me," Hannah said quickly, knowing he was only trying to protect her privacy. "Someone attacked me a few days ago, so we're being careful."

"Attacked you how?"

"I'm a realtor, and at the end of an open house, a guy with a knife entered and shoved me into a wall. Police haven't caught him."

The woman's eyes narrowed. "Of course they haven't. What can I do?"

"We've got it handled," Erik said, voice gruff.

"Erik—"

"I'll let you know if you can help," he added firmly.

For a moment, Hannah thought Rachel would argue further, but in the end she just sighed. "Fine. I'll let it drop…for now. When am I seeing you next? You said you've been doing a family dinner on Sundays?"

Hannah's spine stiffened. Why, exactly, she wasn't sure. She shouldn't mind that this woman was close to his family. She should be happy about it.

He moved closer to Hannah, an arm slipping around her waist. "Sure. Sunday night."

"Done." Rachel turned toward the parking lot. She got a few steps in before looking back at Erik and Hannah. "Remember, if you need help with anything, I'm a weapon."

He laughed and shook his head. "You like to *think* you're a weapon."

"Hey, I could beat your ass with my eyes closed."

He shook his head with a grin and steered Hannah toward the street. "You wish. See you Sunday night."

And there it was again…the stab of jealousy that the woman could put a smile on his face with such ease.

* * *

ERIK'S GAZE continued to shift around the street as they walked. But that wasn't the only thing stealing his attention. Hannah was too quiet.

He tugged her closer. "Are you okay?"

Her eyes flashed up. "Of course."

He didn't believe her for a second. But he didn't push…not yet.

At her office, she stepped in first. Taylor smiled at them as she walked past.

"Hey, guys. Good lunch?"

"It was great." But even the tone of Hannah's voice wasn't as light as usual.

When they stepped into her office, he closed the door, turning as she went to her desk and put her bag in the bottom drawer.

"Is it your head? Is it hurting?"

She paused at his words, and he wanted to go outside and find the fucker who'd hurt her and tear him apart.

"No. My head's okay."

He studied her, slowly crossing the space between them. "Is your blood sugar okay?"

"It's in range."

When he finally reached her, he gripped her hips, tugging her against him. "You gonna make me guess all day?"

"It's silly." Pink tinged her cheeks. "There's so much going on with this threat and Brigid that this shouldn't even bother me."

Something was going on with Brigid?

Hannah's gaze focused on his chest. "I don't want to tell you."

For some reason, that made him laugh. He lowered his head and kissed a spot behind her ear. "Please?"

She shook her head.

He kissed her again, this time on her cheek. "Is it Rachel?"

Her reaction was subtle. A slight tensing of her muscles. A small shift in breathing.

Bingo.

She gripped his arms. "Did you two ever—"

"No." His answer was swift, interrupting before she could even finish that sentence. "Rachel and I have only ever been friends."

She nodded quickly, but when she still didn't look at him, he gripped her chin and tilted it up. "Hey. It's only you, Angel. It'll only *ever* be you."

Her bottom lip disappeared between her teeth. "I'm embarrassed that I feel jealous. I mean, I'm so glad that you have her. That she's supported you for so long. It's just that…there's so much history between you two. I almost feel like I'm intruding when you're together."

"You're never intruding. You're the most important person in every part of my life. I care about her"—another tensing of her muscles—"but only as a friend. My love for you will *always* trump everything and everyone else."

"Even if I'm not a weapon?"

"*I'll* be your weapon."

Her eyes softened. "I love you."

"I fall in love with you all over again every time I see you."

Her gaze shot up, emotion deepening the blue of her eyes. She cupped his cheeks with warm hands, then rose to her toes and kissed him.

CHAPTER 25

*H*annah pulled over in front of the Hunter family home. Cars filled the driveway and street, including Erik's Corvette. She'd been planning to come with him, but her open house had run late, and then she'd had to go back to the office to do some paperwork for an offer that had been put in on a house.

She leaned her head back against the seat, massaging her temple. A headache had started to ping behind her eyes a short while ago. Not only that, but ever since the attack, she still felt tired and not like herself.

Man, the stress of this guy being out there was kicking her ass. A part of her knew she should slow down to compensate, but she couldn't, not after she'd already taken so much time off. She couldn't keep asking Leo and Taylor to cover for her.

Her watch vibrated. She frowned when she saw her blood sugars were high.

How the hell were they high? She hadn't eaten anything that would spike them, and she'd injected accordingly. She sighed. Stress. It must be the stress. Her numbers had been all over the place for weeks.

Still, she pulled out her lancet and glucometer to double-check. After a strip was in the machine, she pricked her finger and dropped the blood on the end.

Yep. High. Great.

She'd just closed her eyes when a knock came at the window. She jumped, her eyes shooting open to see Erik on the other side of the glass, his brows tugged together, concern on his face.

Crap. How long had he been watching her?

He opened the door and lowered to his haunches. "Hey. You okay?"

"Yeah. My sugars are just a bit high, and I have a small headache." Small, but constant.

His hand went to the back of her neck, and he massaged gently. "You're working too hard."

His touch alone went a long way toward easing the ache in her temple. "I have to. I have so many houses to sell."

By the look on his face, he didn't approve.

She grabbed her bag and climbed from the car. Erik's arm immediately slipped around her waist. She'd always considered herself an independent person. She'd had to be, growing up in foster care. But around Erik, a part of her wanted to just fall into the man and let him carry her anywhere she needed to go.

"Maybe we should skip dinner. Go home so you can rest," he said quietly.

When they stopped at the front door, she looked up at him, her finger slipping around his neck and through his hair. "No, I want to be here. And you *need* to. You've missed too many family dinners. I'm okay."

Because she couldn't stop herself, she reached up and kissed his lips. They were soft and warm as they glided over hers. When the kiss ended, she shifted her mouth to his ear, whispering, "You don't need to worry about me."

"I'll always worry, Angel."

She nibbled her bottom lip. "I've been meaning to ask you, have you found anything on the circumstances of Nico's death?"

"No. Sorry. Chandler's still looking but hasn't found anything yet."

She nodded quickly, hanging on to the *yet* part but well aware they might never get any answers.

He trailed his hand down to hers and turned toward the door, leading her inside his parents' house.

Michael Hunter was sitting in the living room, arm in a cast and sling, a wide smile on his face as he chatted with Rachel, while Andi and Jennifer stood in the kitchen, working at the counter. Nate wasn't here, since he'd had to get back to his team after his short visit.

Everyone stopped what they were doing and smiled when they saw her, and she moved around the room, giving them hugs.

God, she loved this family. They made her feel like she'd always been a part of them.

When she stopped in the kitchen, she gave Erik's mother an apologetic smile. "I'm sorry I'm late."

"Don't be silly. There is no late in this family. When you get here is when you're *supposed* to get here."

Andi touched her arm. "How's your head been?"

"Absolutely fine. I have a headache today, but I think that's because of a slight high in my blood sugars."

Concern washed over the woman's features. "Anything I can do to help?"

"No, but thank you." Her gaze lowered to the salad Andi was putting together. "I'd love to give you a hand with dinner."

Andi passed Hannah a loaf of bread. "We're almost done, but if you could slice this?"

"Sure."

She grabbed a serrated knife and started slicing, her gaze rising to Erik. He'd lowered to the couch opposite his father and Rachel and joined their conversation. A part of her was still feeling just a flicker of jealousy toward Rachel, and she hated that. Neither Rachel nor Erik had given her any reason to feel jealous. They were simply friends. Friends who went back a long way.

Rachel laughed at something Erik said. The rich, feminine tone floated through the room, hitting Hannah in the chest.

She wasn't sure if she made a face or a sound, but she suddenly felt eyes on her.

A second later, Andi stepped back from the counter. "Hannah, can you come help me grab the place mats from the back room?"

Before Hannah could respond, Andi was moving out of the kitchen. Hannah followed, receiving a wink from Erik on the way. They went down the hall to what would've been a small bedroom in any other home.

"My mother calls this space her storage room," Andi said, opening a custom-built cupboard and pulling out a box. "I call it her junk room."

Hannah chuckled. "As long as everything has a place."

"Oh, my mother makes space for everything. She's not one to throw anything out." Andi rummaged around in the box before pulling out some gray linen place mats. "Gotcha."

She closed the box and slotted it back into place before turning to Hannah. "Now, tell me the truth. Are you doing okay?"

Hannah swallowed, considered giving the woman an easy lie, but in the end, she wanted to tell someone how she felt. She'd usually tell Brigid, but ever since Hannah had spotted that bruise, her friend had been avoiding her like the plague. Ignoring calls. Briefly answering texts, when she answered at all. Not making time to catch up.

"I feel jealous of their relationship," she said quietly, as if others would hear her if she spoke too loudly. "I know I shouldn't. Neither of them have given me anything to be jealous about. They're friends. But their relationship just seems so...easy. Whereas he and I haven't had it easy for a second."

Andi nodded. "I can see how you'd feel that way. They're close."

Hannah's belly did a little turn.

"But…" Andi continued, "Erik doesn't want easy. He wants someone who makes him feel alive." She gripped Hannah's arm with her free hand. "He wants *you*. I saw him when he thought he'd lost you, Hannah. He was broken. He will never let anything or anyone get between you again."

Hannah sucked in a shuddering breath, hoping that was true.

"Also, my brother knows hard, and he knows that everything worth having comes *after* the hard stuff. So don't think the fact you haven't had an easy road makes your relationship less important or worthy."

"Thank you."

"Anytime." Andi pulled her into a hug. "And I will forever be grateful that you love my brother so much. So, thank *you*."

They stayed in the hug for long seconds. When they finally returned to the dining room, it was to find people moving toward the table, plates in hand.

Andi put the place mats down as Erik walked toward Hannah. "Everything okay?"

"Of course." She rose to her toes and pressed a quick kiss to his lips.

"Good." He pulled out a chair and she slid into it, then he sat beside her.

"All right, who's ready for some herb-basted salmon?" Jennifer asked as she set a platter onto the table.

The second she lifted the lid, the scent wafted over Hannah. Usually, she loved salmon—but tonight, her belly rolled.

God, what was going *on* with her?

Again, she wasn't sure if she made a face or a sound, but Erik's gaze snapped to her, questioning. Quickly, she pasted a smile on her face and stared across the table. "It looks and smells wonderful, Jennifer."

* * *

Erik kept a hand on Hannah's thigh for most of the dinner. She wasn't eating much, and there was a permanent crease in her brow. Was her headache getting worse?

His fingers tightened around her. He was about to lean down and ask her if she wanted to go when his phone vibrated from his pocket.

Chandler's name was on the screen. He had to take this.

He leaned over and kissed Hannah's head. "It's Chandler. I'll be back in a second."

She nodded, her smile not quite reaching her eyes as she watched him go.

Damn, he needed to find out what was going on with her. Had her head injury been worse than they thought? Did they need Andi to look at it?

He waited until he was outside on the deck to answer the call. "Chandler."

"Hey. Two things. First, I got into the necessary database and found the names of the kids who were in Clarence Burns's care at the same time as Hannah."

"And?"

"There were five of them. Two are dead. One lives in Mexico and hasn't traveled in a year. Another's in a wheelchair and living in Texas. The fifth is a female who's working as a teacher in Tennessee. None of them seem to have traveled to Redwood in the last few months, but I'm keeping an eye on the remaining three for you."

Erik gritted his teeth. If it wasn't any of them, then who the hell was it? "What's the second thing you have for me?"

"We have the all clear to move on this human trafficking organization Nico used to work for, and I need official confirmation that you want in."

The door opened behind him, and he turned to see Rachel stepping outside. "I'm gonna put you on speaker. Rachel's here."

Chandler knew Rachel, not only because Erik was friends with her but because she worked in the same industry.

"Rachel James," Chandler said, humor in his voice. "I heard you were in Redwood, annoying my boy."

"*Your* boy?" Rachel scoffed. "Erik has always been mine, Chandler."

He chuckled.

"So, what's this call about?" she asked, leaning her hip against the railing. "Is there some asshole you two can't handle on your own?"

"A human trafficking ring," Erik explained.

Rachel's eyes hardened, all traces of humor leaving her face. "I want in."

Erik lifted a brow. "You want to work a job with me?"

"You know you need me. I've saved your ass more times than I can count."

"You've saved my ass once or twice, but I think I've saved yours more."

She rolled her eyes. "Keep dreaming. Who's the target, Chandler?"

"The head of the group is a man by the name of Miles Moreno. Mid-thirties. Fit. The trafficking ring is based just outside of Seattle, and he's got a few other associates who help to run things. The FBI have actually had a guy on the inside for a few months, so he can feed us information."

Erik's jaw tensed. So they'd had a guy on the inside but still hadn't been able to shut the organization down? "When?"

"I can probably set it up for a week's time."

Rachel met his gaze, her brow rising. It was Erik who answered. "We'll do it. But if, on the off-chance Nico's alive and working for them again…I'm taking him in."

Rachel frowned, a questioning look in her eyes.

The tapping of keys sounded over the line. "Thought you'd say that. I'll get everything organized and send you the details."

When Erik ended the call, Rachel gave him a look. "Who's Nico?"

"A guy who's supposed to be dead already."

She rolled her eyes. "Aren't they all? So you think you can keep up with me?"

"I think it's you who should be worried."

She shook her head as she headed back to the house. "I never worry about anything."

CHAPTER 26

Hannah walked from her office and into the kitchen. She was working late…again. It was a pattern Erik hated. But houses were closing quickly, and every time she sold one, two more popped up for her to sell. It was amazing, but it was also hard work.

She stepped into the small kitchen and rinsed her mug. She was just setting it on the drying rack when Taylor walked in with a bowl.

Hannah frowned. "Hey. I thought I was the only one still here."

"I'm just leaving now. Elliot's staying at a friend's place tonight, so I can actually work late here instead of bringing stuff home with me."

The smell of tuna permeated the air, making Hannah's stomach roll. She pressed her hand to her belly as Taylor tipped the food into the trash.

The other woman's gaze shifted to Hannah, and she cringed. "Sorry. The smell of old tuna probably sucks. I've just been so busy, I didn't have a chance to clean the bowl earlier." She rinsed the dish in the sink.

"It's fine. Usually tuna doesn't bother me, but lately, all seafood seems to be making me feel sick."

"Ha. That was me when I was pregnant with Elliot. I couldn't stand even *looking* at the stuff, let alone smelling it."

Hannah stilled, a chill slipping over her skin.

Pregnant?

No…she couldn't be.

Her world began to narrow as she tried to count back in her head to her last period. God, when had it been?

Taylor set the clean bowl on the rack before crossing to the door. "I'm heading out now. Don't stay too long."

Hannah just nodded because her mind was moving a million miles a minute. She *couldn't* be pregnant. She was on the pill.

But…there had been days where she'd missed it due to sickness and the attacks.

Oh God.

Quickly, she rushed back to her office and lifted her cell, opening her tracking app.

Her heart stopped.

She was late. Only a couple days, but still, she was *never* late.

Panic swirled in her chest, stealing her remaining calm…her ability to think and breathe.

Maybe she wasn't pregnant. Stress could be messing with her hormones. That could make her late. And her life had been nothing but stress lately.

Various emotions were racing through her, making the panic increase—when the lights in her office suddenly blinked off.

She frowned, her gaze shooting around the dark room, the only light coming from her phone. Even the lights in the foyer had switched off.

Something cold and uncomfortable coiled in her belly. What was going on?

Slowly, she crept to the door and poked her head out of her office. "Taylor? Are you still here?"

Silence. It prickled her skin, causing the fine hairs on her arms to stand on end. She took two steps toward the foyer, intending to lock the door in case Taylor hadn't, when her phone dinged with a message.

Unknown number: Wanna play a game?

Her world slowed, the words dancing in front of her eyes as fear crawled up her spine.

Unknown number: It's called...guess who's gonna die tonight?

She stumbled back a step, her knees almost caving.

What the hell?

Without thinking, she turned and ran, but not to her office. She ran back to the kitchen, where she closed the door and pushed a chair under the knob. Yes, she was closing herself into a small space, but there were knives in here. Knives that could be used as a weapon. And she didn't know if this guy was outside or inside, so running was a risk.

She swiped out of the message, fingers shaking as she called Erik.

He answered on the first ring. "Hey, Angel, are you—"

"He's here."

"What?" The word was an angry bark. He didn't need more explanation—he knew what she meant. Movement sounded over the line. "Where? At your office?"

"Yes." The word was a quiet whisper.

"Find a weapon and hide." An engine roared in the background. "*Now, Hannah.*"

His words pulled her out of her stillness, and she blindly turned toward the drawers near the sink. She briefly used the light from her phone to open the second drawer and grab a knife. The blade was big and felt heavy in her hand.

"Have you got something?"

She nodded, but it took her foggy brain a moment to realize he needed her voice. "Yes. I have a knife."

"Good. I won't be long, but I need to hang up and call your bodyguard. See where he is."

She swallowed, fear trying to engulf her. "Okay."

"Angel—you're going to be okay. You have protection, and I'll be there soon. Do you understand?"

"Yes." But even as the word left her lips, it felt wrong. Everything about this situation felt wrong. Where *was* the bodyguard? Did he see the lights go out in the building? Was he okay?

The call ended, and immediately she wanted to call Erik back. To keep that connection between them alive.

A door opening sounded from somewhere in the office…the front door, maybe? She took an involuntary step back.

Was he here? Or was that Jim, her bodyguard? He *had* to have seen the lights turn off, right? Was he coming to investigate?

Footsteps moved down the hall. They were quick and quiet. Hannah remained so still she didn't even breathe.

Suddenly, a loud thump sounded—like a body hitting the floor. Then more footsteps.

Her hip hit the back counter. There was nowhere to go. Nowhere to run. And the chair against the door would only hold off an intruder for so long.

More footsteps, starting, stopping, then starting again…like perhaps the person was searching for her. When they eventually stopped outside the kitchen door, her pulse sped up, the beats stumbling over each other.

The doorknob rattled.

She lifted the knife, knowing it wouldn't save her from a bullet, but it was all she had.

* * *

ERIK PRESSED his foot to the floor, his Corvette speeding down the streets of Redwood. For once, he wished he lived closer to town because getting to her was taking too fucking long.

Why hadn't he just gone down to her office? He'd known she was working too late.

Fuck.

He'd called the police, but who the hell knew how long they'd take, and Chandler's guard wasn't answering the damn phone.

When he finally made it to the street where her office was located, he saw a car with tinted windows half a block down. That was her bodyguard's vehicle. Was he inside the office? Had he gotten her to safety? He couldn't see through the damn windows, but fuck, he had to hope.

The second he pulled up in front of the building, he flew out of the car, pulling his Glock from his holster. His steps were quiet as he ran toward the door, his gaze shifting down the street.

Before he even stepped inside, he noted all the lights were off, the building dark...but not so dark that he couldn't see. The streetlights offered enough glow through the windows that he could make out where everything was as he surveyed the foyer.

For a moment he was still, listening for any footsteps. Any hint of movement. There was nothing.

He inched farther into the room. He was about to head to her office when he heard the rustle of movement from the back of the building—then the sound of a door.

Erik took off, running down the hall and out the open back door near the kitchen. He quickly glanced around. To his right, he caught the shadow of someone tall running around the corner of the building.

Every part of Erik wanted to chase after him. Catch the fucker. But the person had been alone. Which meant Hannah was probably still inside.

She was his priority.

He went back inside, closing the door and clicking the lock. "Hannah?"

He wasn't trying to silence his movements anymore. He walked back down the hall, passing two empty offices on the way to Hannah's, only steps away when he heard the sound of a chair scraping against flooring. He quickly returned to the end of the hall in time to see the kitchen door open—and there she was, so pale her face was almost ghostly white.

He closed the space between them, cupping her cheek. "Are you okay?"

Her skin was like ice, her eyes wide and frightened, but she nodded. "He tried the knob, then suddenly left."

Police sirens wailed down the street. He ignored them, keeping his entire focus on her. "But you're not hurt?"

"I'm not hurt."

He tugged her into his chest, the thrashing of his heart finally beginning to settle. Slowly, he smoothed his hand down her arm and wrapped his fingers around the knife. She gasped, as if she'd forgotten it was still in her hold.

"There was a thump from somewhere down the hall," she whispered, her fingers uncurling from the knife.

Frowning, he raised his gun as he moved slowly toward her office, ensuring she was behind him the entire time. Just inside the door...

The anger inside him twisted into something deeper. Harder. Acid crawling around his gut.

"Let's get out of here," he said, voice flat as he blocked her view.

She shook her head. "No. I want to see."

"Angel—"

She stepped around him—and her gaze zeroed in on the body of her guard. There was a bullet wound in the back of his head, and blood pooled around him on the floor.

Hannah swayed, and Erik cursed, slipping an arm around her waist and tugging her out of the room. He helped her to the reception couch, lowering to his haunches in front of her.

"Angel...look at me."

She did, but there was only fear in her eyes.

"We're gonna catch this asshole," Erik vowed.

Her phone dinged with a message. With trembling fingers, she unlocked it. He leaned close and read it with her.

Unknown number: Not you. Not tonight. Let this be a little warning...no one can save you. We all pay for our crimes eventually.

CHAPTER 27

*H*annah's feet trod lightly on the stairs as she went down to the kitchen. She'd slept in late, but then, that wasn't a surprise with everything that had happened yesterday. She didn't even know what time they'd gotten home after speaking to the police, but it had been late.

She cringed at the memory of Reuben having to find *another* awful scene at his office. The man was going to fire her, right? He *had* to after all the drama her life was bringing to his business. It was just one thing after another.

The soft rustle of movement sounded from the kitchen moments before she stopped in the doorway. Erik stood at the counter with his back to her. He was shirtless, the corded muscles in his back shifting as he reached into a cabinet.

God, he was beautiful. Most wouldn't give him that label. Rugged and handsome probably fit better. And yeah, he was definitely those things, but he was also the most beautiful man she'd ever laid eyes on. Every inch of him was perfect, from his hazel eyes to his bronzed skin.

A part of her feared how much she loved him. Because what

would happen to her if he ever walked away? If things between them ever shifted, and she lost him?

"You gonna stand there all day, Angel?"

She jolted at his words. Did the man have eyes in the back of his head?

He turned, and his expression punched right through her chest. The impact stole her breath and made her knees weak. Slowly, she moved forward, her feet eating up the space between them until she stood in the circle of his arms.

His eyes darkened, worry swimming in the hazel depths. "How are you this morning?"

She lifted a shoulder. "As good as I *can* be."

The worst part of last night wasn't the fear of what could have been. It was seeing that man dead on the ground, knowing he'd died protecting *her*.

Guilt tugged at her, sending a shudder down her spine. Erik's hands went to her hips and pulled her closer. "I'm sorry, Angel. I'm sorry he got so close to you when he shouldn't have."

She leaned her head against his chest. This was where she felt safest—with Erik. Always with Erik.

Her gaze caught on the Frosted Flakes, and the corners of her mouth twitched. "Cereal?"

"And a lavender oat milk latte."

Her favorites...but not his. She peeked around him to see the pan on the stove. Ah. He was having an omelet, and he'd already drunk half a cup of coffee. Probably *not* a lavender oat milk latte.

He pressed a kiss to her head before straightening. She moved over to the drawer and pulled out a new Omnipod insulin pump. She hadn't been using the pump as much as she should.

As Erik finished making his breakfast, she got the pump ready and set it on her thigh. She waited the five clicks, and it pierced her skin.

Interesting...she didn't flinch this time. Maybe she was getting used to it.

She glanced up to see Erik's eyes on her. "Your blood sugars okay?"

"They've been terrible lately. Very up and down."

His brows slashed together. "Because of everything going on?"

She opened her mouth to tell him it was probably the stress, when suddenly she remembered her conversation with Taylor last night…and the realization that she was late.

The blood drained from her face. With everything that had happened, she'd totally forgotten. God, how could she forget something like that?

"Hannah?"

Her gaze shot up—but then his phone buzzed with the sound it made when someone entered his driveway. He was still frowning when he picked up his cell. "Did you message your friends last night?"

She cringed. "I texted Henry. Why? He's not—"

"They're both here." He set the cereal and milk onto the table before bending down and kissing her head. "Eat. I'll let them in."

She adjusted her pump before pouring herself some cereal and topping it with milk, then she moved into the living room. She'd just sat down on the couch when Henry and Brigid came barreling into the house. Henry lowered in front of her while Brigid sat beside her, arm around her shoulders.

"Are you okay?" Brigid asked.

Henry leaned forward. "Tell us you're okay, Han!"

"I'm okay." She moved her spoon around her bowl. "The guy who was guarding me, however…not so okay."

Brigid squeezed her arm. "Oh, God. I'm so sorry."

"Do they think it's the same person who attacked you at the house?" Henry asked, brows tugged together.

She swallowed. She usually told her friends everything, and so much of her wanted to tell them exactly what had been going on, but that meant revealing her past, and she couldn't burden them with that kind of secret. It wasn't fair to them.

"Probably. Erik and the police are looking into it."

Henry squeezed her thigh. "Well, we're glad you're okay."

Erik took a step into the room. "You guys want anything? Coffee? Omelet?"

Brigid eyed her cereal. "Frosted Flakes, please."

Hannah grinned. Her cereal addiction often rubbed off onto her friends.

"Coffee would be great, thanks," Henry said.

Okay, maybe not all her friends.

Erik dipped his head and disappeared into the kitchen.

Brigid gave her another squeeze. "Tell us what happened."

"The lights switched off in the office. I ran into the kitchen and pushed a chair against the door. While I was in there, the bodyguard was shot in my office, although I didn't hear a bullet, so the guy must have used a silencer or something. Erik saw the back of the killer as he ran away, but he looked for me instead of chasing after the guy."

God, that sounded even worse out loud, and by the horrified looks on her friends' faces, they both felt the same.

Hannah swallowed. "I'm okay though. Tell me how *you* guys have been. Distract me."

Henry moved to the armchair near the couch. "*I've* got information that could distract you. I'm thinking of breaking up with Owen."

Hannah's brows rose. "Really? Why? I thought you really liked each other?"

"We do, but..."

Hannah cocked her head. "But what?"

"I'm kind of liking someone else."

What the heck? Since when did Henry even *look* at another man when he was already dating someone?

"Well, are you gonna tell us who?" Brigid demanded.

Erik returned, handing a bowl of cereal to Brigid and a coffee to Henry. He leaned down and kissed her head. "Eat,

Angel. I'm going to disappear into the office. Call if you need anything."

She watched him leave, her heart thumping with each of his steps.

"See! *That's* what I want." Her gaze flicked back to Henry at his words. "I want to be so utterly obsessed with someone that I can't focus on anything else when they're around."

Well, that was definitely her.

"Tell us who the guy is already," Brigid pushed, spooning Frosted Flakes into her mouth.

He shook his head. "Nope. Can't do that. I need to decide if I want to end things with Owen first and pursue this."

Hannah gave him a small smile. "Whatever you decide, I hope it makes you happy. You deserve all the love, Henry."

She meant it. These two had been her best friends since the day she'd arrived in Redwood, and Henry had been her first protector here.

He winked at her. "Thanks, Han."

She switched her attention to Brigid, her gaze running over her face. Any remnants of the bruise had faded. This was the first time she was seeing her friend since that day. She opened her mouth, but Brigid read her mind and spoke first.

"It's over."

Hannah frowned, and Henry looked just as confused.

Brigid swirled her cereal around the bowl. "I did something dumb. Got close to a guy I shouldn't have. But it's over."

Anger pulsed through Hannah's veins. She *knew* the bruise had looked like the result of someone hitting her, but having it confirmed felt worse.

Brigid lifted a shoulder. "I've just been a bit of a mess since everything happened with James. But I'm trying to get better."

Henry's voice softened. "We all make mistakes when our heart hurts."

Tears gathered in Brigid's eyes, but she blinked them away.

"My heart *has* been hurting. Which is stupid, right? When a man hurts you *and* the people you care about, that love should die immediately."

Hannah shook her head. "It doesn't work like that. Our heart doesn't listen to our head." She wrapped an arm around her best friend's shoulders. "You'll be okay. Because we're going to make sure of it."

Brigid leaned her head against Hannah's. "We came to look after you, not the other way around."

"We look after each other."

* * *

"Fuck. I'm sorry, Hunter."

Erik ran his fingers through his hair, phone pressed to his ear, Rachel on the other end. "She's okay. But I can't leave her until we get this mess sorted out."

Where she went, *he* went. There was no fucking way around it.

Rachel sighed. "I understand. Send me the details of your guy, the one you want detained."

"Will do."

"Guess I'll get to have all the fun myself."

"I'm sure that won't be a problem for you."

She laughed. "Weapon, remember? Slaying the bad guys is what I do."

Erik's lips twitched. How the woman almost got a smile out of him at a time like this, he had no fucking clue.

"Are *you* doing okay?"

Her question caught him off guard, and his frown returned. "No. Nothing in this world scares me except the possibility of losing her. And last night, I came too fucking close."

"But you didn't. And you won't. She's yours, and she'll stay yours."

He forced air into his lungs, wishing he could cement his friend's words as truth.

"I'll let you go," she said. "Let me know if there's anything I can do to help, even if it's just bodyguard duties so you can do a workout."

"Thanks, Rach."

He hung up, his gaze catching on the email from Chandler that had come in yesterday morning. It had all the details of the job he was supposed to do with Rachel, as well as all the current information he could find on the organization. He still couldn't believe the fuckers had resurrected the trafficking ring.

He cursed and clicked into it, reading the intel again. He wanted to do this job. He wanted to kill every one of the bastards. But Hannah was more important to him, and he didn't trust anyone else with her safety.

It was only when he heard Hannah and her friends head to the front door that he finally clicked out. He didn't have to wait long for her to step into the office doorway.

She gave him a small smile. "Hey."

He leaned back in his seat. "Everything okay?"

"Mm-hmm. Are you reading over the job you're doing with Rachel?"

"I'm not doing the job anymore."

Her brows rose. She closed the distance between them. "I'm sure someone else can—"

"No, Angel. I'm not leaving you."

She sat on the edge of the desk, and immediately he tugged her to his lap, her legs straddling him. She still wore his T-shirt that she'd slept in, and it rode up to her hips.

His fingers tightened on her waist. "I can't even comprehend the idea of leaving you alone after last night." He leaned forward and touched a kiss to her cheek, then her neck.

Her breathing stuttered. He lowered his mouth to her breast

to flick his tongue over her nipple through the material of the shirt.

This time her breath stopped. "Erik…"

"You are my entire world. You're the sun. The moon. The stars that shine through the dark night sky." He wrapped his lips around her pebbled bud and sucked.

Hannah whimpered, her chest pushing into him.

After slipping his hands under the shirt, he slid them up her sides until he cupped her breasts, then switched his mouth to her other breast, taking the nipple between his lips, nipping and teasing.

Her breaths quickened and her chest rose beneath his mouth.

He lowered one hand and slid his fingers into her panties, where he stroked her clit. She jolted, her thighs widening. So he did it again.

Her fingers slid into his hair, pulling at the strands.

"You are all I need," he whispered, slipping a finger inside her, loving how wet she was for him already.

Her inhale was loud. "You might start needing more one day."

He pulled his finger out, then pushed it back in, his thumb moving over her clit. "You're all I'll *ever* need, Angel. You and me forever."

When he felt a slight tension in her body, he frowned and lifted his gaze, but before he could ask what was going on in her beautiful head, she leaned in and kissed him, her fingers moving to the waistband of his sweatpants and pulling him out.

Every muscle in his body strained as she glided her fingers over his cock, her mouth nipping and sucking his lips. He growled and tore her delicate panties, ripping them off her—which was becoming a regular habit—before lifting her up, setting his tip to her entrance, and easing her back down.

Her body stretched around him. This was it. This was as close as he'd ever fucking get to redemption. To peace and calm.

He yanked the shirt over her head. Then he palmed her ass

and began to move her up and down. Then he dropped his head, taking one bare nipple between his lips and sucking, rolling the tight bud with his tongue.

She arched, her cries rippling through the room. He kept thrusting. Kept playing with her until she cried out again, louder, her walls pulsing around his cock as she broke.

Fuck, she was beautiful. He wanted to pause time. To freeze this moment with them exactly as they were.

He kept thrusting, kept watching the array of emotions play over her face. But too soon, his own body tensed and then shattered.

This woman was his world. And no one was taking her from him. No one.

CHAPTER 28

"This house is quite a distance away from town, Angel."

Hannah cringed from the passenger seat. "I know. I wasn't even going to show it to Owen because of how big it is, not to mention old. But there's so much land for his bikes, and it's so cheap, he could get a real bargain. I mentioned it, and he seemed interested, probably because of how much space there is."

The place was a huge old mansion. It had been deserted for years, and the family had finally decided to sell. It shouldn't be hard to unload, what with the low price, but it needed a lot of work.

Erik's gaze shifted to the rearview mirror. Henry and Owen were driving behind them. Henry hadn't broken up with Owen, and she wasn't sure where his head was on that. He hadn't mentioned breaking up with him since the morning at Erik's house a few days ago.

"You know you didn't need to come," Hannah said quietly, taking Erik's hand and holding it in her lap. "With both Henry and Owen here, I've got two guys looking out for me."

The muscles in his forearm contracted. "They're not trained. I am."

She nodded. Erik hadn't been more than one room away from her since the attack in her office, and he'd been tense and alert.

She turned her head to look out the window, her mind shifting to the thing she'd been trying not to think about for days. She was *still* late. Every day, she woke expecting to get her period but never did.

She hadn't taken a test yet, partly because Erik was always with her, partly because every time she even considered it, the fear took hold of her body, rendering her frozen. Fear that a positive test would mean the end of her and Erik. Either that or make him resent her.

He didn't want kids. He'd told her that more than once and was so unyielding.

And she understood why. Losing a child before they were born… God, she couldn't even imagine.

She peeked at Erik and chewed on her bottom lip. "Can I ask you something?"

"Anything."

It took her longer than it should have to get the words out. "You thought you'd never heal enough to love another partner."

"That's not a question, Angel." His thumb swiped her thigh. "But you're right, I didn't."

The roof of her mouth was as dry as a desert, and she had to swallow a few times to make the words come out. "Have you ever wondered if maybe you could heal enough to have a child with me?"

His reaction was immediate. The muscles in his arms corded. The softness left his eyes, and his hand tightened on the wheel. "That's never going to happen."

Her stomach dropped. Never. No leeway. Nothing she could do to change his mind. "Erik—"

"I don't have the capacity to take on that kind of responsibility, Hannah." His voice was hard and low as he used her first name. "The sheer thought of having a child to protect scares me to death."

She gripped his hand tighter. "It wouldn't just be *you* protecting the child. I'd be doing it with you."

"No." The word was so hard and final. "I'm sorry. That's not something I can give you."

A sick feeling churned in her belly, and she almost wanted to place a hand over her stomach.

What would happen if it turned out she *was* pregnant? What would he do?

She opened her mouth, not even sure what she might say. Worried the words "I could be pregnant right now" were going to fall from her lips like small explosions.

But Erik pulled into a long drive, and she looked up to see that they had arrived.

She snapped her lips shut and looked up at the big house. It really was huge. Two main floors, with a fully functional attic and a huge basement. There were about eight bedrooms, and every one of them was large.

"I'm sorry, Angel."

Her gaze swung to Erik, and she tried to form a smile, but her lips couldn't make it work. "You can't help how you feel."

A pained look crossed his face, as if he knew exactly what he was asking her to give up yet wasn't capable of changing his mind.

It was only the knock at her window that had her gaze shifting to the side. Henry stood there, tapping his watch.

Her next smile came with more ease. He had a dinner reservation tonight, something he'd told her about very explicitly, giving strict instructions on how long they could stay here.

She climbed out of the car, and Henry was talking before her feet hit the ground. "Remember, Han. Out by—"

"Five. I know. You've told me a million times."

His brows rose. "Well, I'll *keep* telling you, in case you forget. That reservation at Telders was hard to get."

"Leave her alone," Owen said, shoving his hands into his pockets. "She's doing her job by showing me this house."

"Yeah, and she can do me a favor by making sure I'm not late for my dinner reservation."

Hannah shook her head. "Well, come on then."

She was moving toward the door when Erik's fingers wrapped around her wrist, pulling her to a stop. "I'm gonna stay out here and watch the house. Make sure we don't get any visitors."

She looked down the driveway and lowered her voice. "You think we were followed?"

His eyes were unreadable. "No, but you can never be too sure."

She swallowed. "Okay." Rising to her toes, she kissed him, hating the small distance she felt growing between them after their conversation.

Her heart was still heavy as she moved up the steps and to the front door. The second they pushed inside, Henry gasped. "Holy shit, Han. This place is huge!"

It truly was. The ceilings were so high his voice echoed. A chandelier centered the foyer, and the wooden staircase went up, then split off two ways.

She grinned at Henry and Owen. "It's gorgeous, isn't it? Almost a hundred years old, but great bones."

Owen walked over to the staircase and ran his fingers along the balustrade. "I definitely like all the land. But it might be too much house."

Yeah, that had been Hannah's thought, but she figured it was worth a look.

Henry moved behind him. "No such thing as too much house. You can always find stuff to do with space."

Hannah chuckled and gestured to the right. "Okay, first we have the formal living room. Unfortunately, because it's an old house, you don't have an open concept, but walls can always be knocked down."

Henry walked over to a wall and knocked. "Probably load-bearing, but you could get a steel beam put under the ceiling in the form of a bulkhead."

She squeezed Henry's arm. "This is why I need you with me."

They made their way into the kitchen. Again, the space was old and dusty, but Henry moved around the room, explaining to Owen all the renovations that could be made.

Hannah was actually getting invested in the renovation ideas, a part of her even envious that *she* couldn't live here. She knew from experience that Henry was great at renovations. He was in construction, and he'd been the one to basically transform her home.

When they finished downstairs, they were about to move up when Owen turned to Henry. "Can you grab your tape measure? Then we can determine whether some of my stuff will even fit in the rooms."

Henry grinned at Hannah. "The man has a shitload of stuff."

"Lucky there's a shitload of space here."

Henry stepped outside while Hannah moved toward the stairs. "Let me show you upstairs. Although, I should warn you, it's just as grand as downstairs. Plus, there's an attic, which is basically like a third floor."

She moved upstairs and turned left down a long hallway.

"I'll show you the master bedroom first," Hannah said over her shoulder. "It's got a spectacular view."

They stepped into the room. It was huge, with beautiful original colonial windows overlooking the property and an old bed in the middle of the room, although it was covered in a blanket that had its *own* covering of dust.

Owen nodded. "I like it."

The man gave very little away.

When both Hannah and Owen's phones beeped with a text, they each looked down.

Henry: I somehow locked myself out and need someone to come let me in before I make Erik break the door down.

Hannah chuckled. How the man had managed that, she had no idea. She took a step toward the door, but Owen shook his head. "I'll get it."

Owen headed back downstairs just as Hannah's phone beeped again, but this time it was her Dexcom. She wasn't low yet but would be soon. With the nausea, she hadn't been eating as much as she should.

Her mind flicked back to her conversation with Erik in the car. She just needed to take a test and be done with it. Then she'd know for sure.

Even though she was scared the test would be positive, there was another part of her—a part she barely wanted to acknowledge—that was equally scared it would be negative. She loved Erik so much, but all this wondering whether she was pregnant had ignited something inside her. A deep need to have a baby.

When Erik had first told her that he didn't want kids, she'd convinced herself she could give up that part of her life for him. But now, she wondered if that was true.

At the sound of footsteps in the hall, Hannah forced it all to the back of her mind.

Owen stepped back into the room, but he was alone.

Hannah frowned. "Where's Henry?"

"He's measuring the kitchen wall. Probably a bunch of others too."

She grinned. "He's probably knocking on a bunch of walls, as well. Come on, let me show you the bathroom." She headed to the attached bath. "There are many in this house and they're all quite old, but nothing some renovations can't fix."

Owen nodded as he moved around the small space. "There's a lot of potential here."

"There definitely is. Did you own your own home in Georgia?"

He shook his head. "No. I've never owned my own home. I've never had much at all. Growing up, I had a single mother and a lot of siblings."

Her brows furrowed. "I'm sorry to hear that. Henry may have told you that I grew up in foster care, so I understand not having much."

He ran a finger over the vanity. "My mother always had different boyfriends. Every one of them was an asshole. For most of my childhood, all I wanted was to get out of that house. And I almost did."

Hannah studied him, surprised Owen was sharing something so personal with her. "Almost?" she asked.

They both moved back into the bedroom as Owen continued. "I was close to my uncle. He was actually the closest thing to a father I'd ever known. He told me I could move in with him and my aunt."

"Why didn't you move in with him?"

"He died." There was a new hardness to his voice. "And my auntie was an alcoholic, so I was stuck in a house where stepfathers beat the shit out of me, and my mother didn't give a fuck."

Hannah frowned, a dread she didn't understand unraveling in her belly. "How did he die?"

Something flashed in Owen's eyes—an emotion she couldn't quite place. "Well, the official story is that he just disappeared. Of course, the police barely looked into it because he was out of jail on bail, so they just assumed he ran to avoid the trial."

Her vision grew fuzzy at the edges, nails digging into her palms, almost breaking skin.

"But…" Owen continued, taking a step toward her, "my auntie was quite the drunken rambler. One of the last times I saw her after he disappeared, she told me a story. About this foster kid they took in, who broke into her house and shot him. She heard the gunshot and went to the room, peeked in to see this girl standing over the body of my uncle, a gun in her hand. My aunt ran and hid. Probably passed out. And when she woke up, the body of my uncle was just…gone. Now, I know that she was a raging drunk—but she was never a liar."

For a moment, Hannah couldn't breathe. The air literally wasn't making it into her lungs. "You…you're Clarence Burns's nephew."

A cruel smile spread across his lips. "I am."

"And you're the person who's been harassing me."

He pulled out a knife from somewhere behind him. It was so big, her skin crawled. "I was the only one who seemed to care about what my aunt was saying. She told me your name. That you'd wrongly accused him of attempting to rape you before going back to their house and killing him."

She fisted her hands to stop the tremble. "It wasn't wrong. He *did* try to rape me. And I only broke into the house to get my bracelet. Your uncle tried to attack me again. Shooting him was self-defense."

Owen laughed, but the sound was eerie. "You expect me to believe that? If it was self-defense, you would have called the goddamn police, who would have called an *ambulance* and given my uncle a chance to live!"

Tears pressed at her eyes. "It was a shot to the heart. He was dead. And I was young and scared."

"You're a liar," he growled. "Because of *you*, I had to grow up in a hellhole with a host of stepfathers who treated me like the dirt on the bottom of their shoes."

"Owen—"

"Imagine my surprise years later when I see a news reports of a woman named Hannah Jacobs from Redwood, who was involved in a shootout at a bar in Seattle."

She stumbled back another step. *That* was how he'd found her? "So why haven't you just killed me already?"

"Because I wanted to scare you first. Ruin your life for a while before I killed you, just like you ruined my uncle's life before you killed *him*." He cocked his head. "Notes and texts to scare you. Henry told me you couldn't swim, so shoving you into the pool was a bit of fun. Oh, and I put sleeping pills mixed with clozapine in your juice the morning we had breakfast together."

Her mouth dropped open. It wasn't a virus…he'd drugged her.

"Did you really think you could kill a man and just get away with it?" he asked.

"He deserved to die."

Anger distorted his features. "My uncle *did not* deserve to die! *You* deserve to die!" He lifted the knife and angled it toward her. "Getting you alone proved a challenge these last few weeks. I almost thought I'd missed my chance. But this works. I can gut you instead of shooting you so lover boy outside doesn't hear. But don't worry. I have a bullet ready for both him and Henry when I'm finished with you."

Oh God…Henry. Where was he?

On her next step back, her hip hit the dresser…a dresser that had an old lamp on top.

Owen closed more of the distance between them. "You want to beg for absolution before I kill you?"

She reached behind her and wrapped her fingers around the lamp. "No. Because I don't regret killing Clarence Burns. He was a rapist—and I'm glad he's dead. I'd kill him a second time if I could."

The rage that crossed Owen's face was like nothing she'd ever seen. He lunged.

Hannah ripped the lamp from the dresser and swung it at his head.

rik returned to the front of the house, his gaze moving to the long driveway. He hated being out here. It was too isolated. If something happened and he needed to call in backup, it would take too fucking long for help to arrive.

He'd watched his tail the entire drive. They hadn't been followed. No one should know they were here. So why did something feel off? Why was acid crawling around his gut, making him feel sick?

He shot a look to his watch. He'd give them another ten minutes, then they were leaving. He didn't care if they weren't done—Hannah's safety came first.

He moved toward the house but stopped when his phone rang, Chandler's name flashing on the screen. "Chandler. Did Rachel get the job done last night?"

He needed his friend to say yes. That this human trafficking ring was taken down once and for all. "Actually, no. They heard rumors of a mole, but they don't know who, so the agent's cover is holding. But the scumbags scrambled to move their operation at the last minute. We're already trying to find them, but obviously the job was postponed."

Erik cursed. The fuckers would live another day, but Chandler would find them. He always did. Although he hoped it was sooner rather than later so that no more innocents got hurt.

"But that's not why I'm calling." There was the usual tapping of keys over the line. "I found something on Clarence Burns."

Erik straightened. "Tell me."

"He had a lot of nieces and nephews because both he and his wife had a few siblings. I didn't think anything of it, until I looked into Anne Burns's hospital records. She had a fair few because of her alcohol addiction. And one of her nephews visited her a lot, particularly during a hospital stay shortly after Clarence died."

"Hannah mentioned she thought her foster mother was home that night but was probably passed out. Though she could have seen what Hannah did and told her nephew."

"That's what I'm thinking. I'm sure that, because she was a drunk, law enforcement wouldn't have believed anything she said. But if this kid cared enough about his aunt to visit her in the hospital—"

"He might have believed her."

"Yep."

"Who?"

"His name is Oden Menzes. He's a mechanic from Everett."

Erik's entire world slowed, a darkness slipping over his vision. "A mechanic?"

"Yeah, I have a photo." More typing sounded. "It's old. He's probably eighteen here, but it's the best I could find."

Erik pulse beat so fucking fast it was all he could feel as he pulled the phone from his ear and clicked into the image Chandler had texted.

Fear, panic, and fury rivaled inside him.

"Owen..." he whispered.

"What? Who's Owen?"

The guy in the photo was younger, but it was Owen. Same eyes. Same shaggy brown hair.

"Call the police, Chandler." His friend had a tracking device on Erik's phone, so he would know where to send the cops. "Oden's here with us right now!"

Then he was running, a million emotions spreading through his limbs, threatening to consume him as he pulled his Glock from its holster.

* * *

HANNAH'S BREATHS sawed hard and fast through her lungs as she ran down the hall. Fear tried to choke her. To buckle her knees and pull her to the floor. But she refused to let it.

Survive. That's what she had to do. Survive long enough to get to Erik. He was armed. Trained.

And Henry—God, she needed to find Henry! There was no way he was measuring walls downstairs. Owen had done something to him, she knew it.

A sob tried to break free from her lips, but she choked it down.

She opened her mouth to call to Henry when an angry growl ripped through the air from behind. She shot a look over her shoulder, and her heart nearly stopped.

Owen ran toward her, knife in hand. Blood dripped down the left side of his head, and he staggered into the wall to his left, unsteady on his feet.

She instinctively screamed, "Help!"

But she knew it wasn't loud enough for Erik to hear. The house was too big, and she was on the second floor. She had to get downstairs. Without stopping, she pulled out her phone to call Erik.

She reached the top of the stairs, her thumb hovering over his name, when Owen's body slammed into hers from behind, sending her to the floor.

The impact stole her breath and had the cell flying from her fingers and tumbling down the stairs.

Before she could recover, he flipped her to her back. She started to scream before fingers wrapped around her throat.

Quickly, she grabbed one of his fingers, just like Erik had taught her, and pulled.

Owen cursed, wrenching his hand away. She bucked her hips, and the second she had a bit of space, she rolled to the side, away from the edge of the steps. She attempted to get up, but fingers wrapped around her ankle in a punishing grip and pulled her back. When he lifted the knife, her heart jumped into her throat.

She kicked at his hand, sending the weapon flying to the floor. Then again—this time, the heel of her shoe connecting with his face, the momentum shoving Owen backward.

He cried out and tumbled down several steps before grabbing a baluster and stopping his descent. He grabbed his nose, blood pouring down his face.

Hannah was already on her feet. Getting to Erik wasn't an option with Owen blocking the stairs. Instead, she turned right, running down the hall and passing half a dozen doors.

All the doors were open. She quickly and quietly pulled half of them closed as she moved, hoping Owen would have to stop and check each one.

At the end of the hall, she slipped through the last door leading to the attic, soundlessly shutting it behind her.

Her heart beat so hard against her ribs it was as if her fear was trying to break right out of her. Slow and silent, she sneaked up the stairs. At the top, she surveyed the cavernous space. It was filled with the owner's possessions. There were boxes and dressers and chairs and a million other household items, all piled everywhere.

A bullet sounded from somewhere below, and she jumped. What was that? Had Owen shot at someone? It sounded like it had come from the first floor. Had Erik realized what was going on and attacked Owen?

God, please be the latter.

She lifted her Apple watch to message Erik, dismay filling her when she saw the cracked screen. Shit! It must have broken when Owen tackled her to the floor.

Her gaze shot up. There was a small window in the attic, but it was too high. There was no way she'd be able to reach it. Which meant, without her phone, she had no way of connecting with Erik or calling police.

A weapon…she had to find a weapon. And she had to do it quickly and quietly.

She'd taken a few steps when suddenly her vision narrowed and her knees trembled, threatening to give out on her. She grabbed a wall to steady herself. She was low…God, this was the worst timing.

Slow and steady, Hannah. You've got this.

With those whispered words in her head, she crept around the space, looking in open boxes, lightly moving things around. She opened drawers and looked under chairs. Long minutes passed, and she found nothing.

A sob tried to escape her throat, but she swallowed it. After looking under a table, she climbed to her feet—and the world spun around her. This time she couldn't save herself. She fell to her knees.

She was just about to get up again when her gaze caught on something on the floor. A toolbox. Quickly, she crawled over to it and opened the lid. The hammer was the first thing she saw. It wasn't as good as a gun, but it could be used as a weapon none-theless.

She lifted it, her muscles trembling even from that slight weight. Once it was in her grasp, she moved to one side of the attic stairs, found a large box to hide behind, and waited.

CHAPTER 30

*F*uck. The front door was locked.

He stepped back and fired, not caring about the noise the shot made. He needed to get to Hannah, and he needed to get to her *now*.

One shot was all it took. He ran into the house, Glock aimed and ready.

Silence. It fucking surrounded him. There were no voices or footsteps. No rustling of movement.

Had Owen already attacked Hannah and Henry? The thought made bile crawl up his throat.

"Hannah?" He didn't shout her name but said it loud enough so that anyone close by might hear.

Slowly, he moved into the living area, always keeping his back to the wall. He walked through quickly, checking every inch of the room. Then he went to the kitchen. That was empty too.

He returned to the stairs and tried the door to what he assumed was a den or study. He cursed at what he saw on the other side—Henry, on the floor, blood dripping from his skull. Someone had hit him.

Erik reached down to search for a pulse at his neck. It was there. Thank God.

But where was Hannah?

He scanned the room. Other than Henry, it was empty. The rage and fear inside him coiled, but he shut it all down. Those emotions weren't useful right now. He needed to focus on finding her and ending Owen.

Keeping his gun drawn, he pulled his phone from his pocket and dialed her number. The vibration of a phone sounded from the stairs.

He left the office and moved toward the stairs. He was halfway up when he saw her cell. He hung up, but the phone kept flashing with a notification.

Her Dexcom…she was low. *Really* low.

Fuck.

At the top of the stairs, there were long halls to the left and right. He tried to listen for movement, but again there was nothing. The quiet crawled over his skin, cutting into his flesh. Had he silenced her? Hurt her? Killed her?

No. He had to believe she'd gotten away. That she was hiding.

Something inside Erik told him to go right. As he moved, he kept his Glock at the ready, quickly clearing every room in the hall. When he reached the last door, he tried the handle. Unlocked, like all the others. He opened it to find stairs. An attic?

He moved up the steps quietly and had just opened the door at the top when a hammer flew toward his head.

He ducked and grabbed the wrist before the hammer could finish its swing.

His gaze hit Hannah's just as a single word left her lips. "Erik…"

He slid the hammer from her fingers and pulled her against his chest. She trembled hard, and he wasn't sure if that was from fear or low blood sugar…maybe both. "Are you okay?"

"Yes…I'm really low though. I can't stop shaking."

Shit.

"Owen's Clarence's nephew!"

He tightened his hold on her. "I know. Chandler called."

He didn't want to release her, but he had to get them out of here, and he had to find that asshole Owen or Oden, whatever the fuck his name was. He stepped back, cupping her cheek. "I'd leave you here while I find the asshole, but I saw on your phone how low you are. We need to get you to the car, where there's food. And I don't want him to slip past me and find you."

She nodded quickly.

"Stay behind me, okay? I'm gonna cover you as much as I can."

"Okay." She eyed the stairs. "Did you see Henry on your way up here?"

"Yeah, Angel, I did. He's unconscious but alive."

The air stuttered out of her. "Alive! Thank God!"

He pushed some hair behind her ear. "You're okay to walk?"

Even though she nodded, the expression on her face was less confident. And fuck, she was pale.

With gritted teeth, he took her hand and turned toward the stairs. She stumbled twice on the way down, and each time, his heart stopped. When they reached the bottom, he kept her behind him as he stepped into the hall, gun raised.

Every step was as silent as the last. They passed the same half a dozen rooms in the hall, and each of them still appeared empty. Where the hell had this fucker gone? Had he left? Erik hadn't heard a car engine, and the house was big enough that there were plenty of places to hide.

They made it to the end of the hall. This was the part Erik had been dreading. The staircase wasn't against a wall, which meant gunfire could come from any direction, and there was no way for him to have eyes everywhere.

Hannah stumbled behind him, and he grabbed her arm and righted her before she could fall. "Stay with me, Angel."

She nodded, but her eyes were unfocused and, if possible, she'd lost even more color from her face.

He bit back a curse as they moved down the stairs, his Glock continually shifting above and below, searching for the enemy.

They'd just reached the bottom when a flash of movement came from the study. At first, he thought it was Henry. Then light glinted off metal—and he threw himself over Hannah's body, shoving her to the floor.

A bullet nicked his side, but he ignored the pain, swiftly lifting his own pistol and firing at the doorway.

The asshole had already moved behind the wall. Erik rolled Hannah to the opposite side of the staircase.

"You guys are the perfect fucking couple, aren't you?" Oden yelled. "Murderers who think you can kill whoever you damn well please and there won't be consequences!"

Erik could have laughed. "And what are you doing right now...*Oden*?"

The man paused, probably surprised at hearing his real name. "There's purpose behind what I'm doing. She *deserves* it."

"And her bodyguard? Did he deserve it too?"

Bullets peppered the staircase. Erik gritted his teeth, remaining on the floor. Hannah whimpered, and fear gripped him. He kissed her temple. Her skin was damp. "Five minutes, Angel, and I'll get us out."

A scuffle sounded from the study. Erik turned his head to see Henry moving slightly on the floor, waking up, and Owen's arm inching around the wall, weapon raised.

Erik fired, getting the asshole in the arm. He cried out and dropped the gun.

Erik moved around the staircase, but Oden had already rolled and grabbed Henry, tugging him practically into his lap and using him as a shield as he put a knife to the man's neck.

"Let him go, Oden," Erik said, voice low and hard. "It's over."

Oden growled. "No. It's *not* fucking over! I want her *dead*! I want—"

Henry flung his head to the side, heedless of the knife—and Erik fired, getting Oden right between the eyes.

CHAPTER 31

Hannah watched the flurry of movement around the front of the house. It was hard to focus on any one thing because of the exhaustion. It tugged at her limbs, making her feel like she was weighted to the ground.

She sipped her juice, wishing it would give her just a bit of life.

A big part of her exhaustion was the low. If Erik hadn't gotten her to the car when he had so she could eat something... God, she couldn't even think about it.

That wasn't the only reason she was so tired, though. It was also the crash of adrenaline.

Owen—no, *Oden*—was Clarence's nephew. It still seemed crazy to her. He'd come to Redwood, started dating Henry, just to get close to *her*. To torment her before he killed her.

A shudder coursed down her spine.

She wasn't sure if Erik saw the shudder, but he stopped his conversation with the police officer and moved straight over to her before slipping an arm around her back. "Are you doing okay?"

She opened her mouth, but before any words could come out,

the front door of the house opened and paramedics stepped outside with a gurney, a sheet over Oden's body.

"This whole time it was him," she whispered, trailing the paramedics with her eyes. "I can barely believe it."

Erik stepped in front of her, blocking her view. "But he's gone now. And he won't bother you ever again."

She lay her head on Erik's chest, closing her eyes and letting the thuds of his heart sink inside and calm her.

They'd told the police that Oden blamed her for his uncle's disappearance. That he'd accused her of lying about the attack. It was as close to the truth as they could get.

It was only the sight of Henry, getting out of the other ambulance and moving toward her, that had her head shooting up.

She started to stand, but Erik grabbed her arm. "Hey. Slow."

When Henry was close enough, she wrapped her arms around his waist. "Are you okay?"

She immediately wanted to take back her words. What a stupid question. Of *course* he wasn't okay. His boyfriend had turned out to be a psychopath. He'd attacked Henry. Planned to kill him to protect his identity.

She pulled back. "I'm sorry, I shouldn't have—"

"I'm okay. And *I'm* so damn sorry that I didn't see the signs. That I let him get close to you."

She cupped his cheek. "No. I'm sorry that he got close to *you* because of me. He was good at playing his role."

"He was." Henry's eyes shifted between hers. "Are you all right?"

She swallowed and stepped back, Erik's arm immediately sliding around her waist again. "Physically, yes. But my head's a mess."

Henry's brows tugged together. "So, he was your foster father's nephew? The foster father who attacked you when you were sixteen?"

She hated not telling him the entire truth. "Yeah. And he

blamed me for his uncle's disappearance after he got let out on bail."

Henry scowled. "The scumbag."

That seemed too kind a word for Clarence *and* Oden.

When the police came over to ask more questions, the little energy Hannah had fizzled out, and she leaned heavily on Erik.

His chest rumbled as he tugged her into him. "That's enough. She needs rest. You have more questions, you can call us tomorrow. We're going home."

She opened her mouth to say it was okay, but before the words could come out, Erik lifted her against his chest and carried her toward his car, Henry not far behind.

And then Hannah just…couldn't. His heart beating against her cheek felt too good.

This was just one of the reasons she loved him so much. Because he was, and forever would be, her greatest protector.

CHAPTER 32

*E*rik stroked a hand down Hannah's back as she slept. He should get up. But even though days had passed since the attack, he still felt physically sick at the very thought of being away from her. How could he not? He'd been in the same damn place, at the same *house,* and yet she'd *still* been attacked and could have been seriously hurt…or worse.

His gut coiled, and he tightened his arm around her as if he needed the closeness to remind himself that she was here with him and safe.

The only thing keeping him sane was the fact that the asshole was dead.

She still wasn't back to herself. She'd been quieter. Smiled less. But then, of *course* she had. She'd almost been killed by a person she'd trusted.

There was also something else. Every so often, he caught her staring at him in a way he'd never seen before. In those moments, she looked nervous. But that didn't make sense.

He stroked a finger down her arm.

He needed to get to the bottom of that, and soon, because he wanted nothing between them. He wanted all of her, and that included all of her secrets.

When her thumb grazed his chest, his skin tingled. How was it that still, months after meeting her, her touch affected him so damn much? He had no clue, but he knew it was something that would continue to happen, no matter *how* long they were together.

A low, feminine hum sounded from her throat before she lifted her head, and her gaze collided with his. The slow smile that spread across her lips gutted him. She wasn't just beautiful. She was more than that. Magnificent in every way.

Her head tilted. "When you look at me like that, I want to hide from you."

"There is nowhere you could hide that I wouldn't find you."

"Well, look too long, and you'll see every flaw."

"Someone once told me that the flaws are what make us beautiful. That they should be celebrated."

Emotion crept over her face. "It's true…when it comes to you. Mine, on the other hand—"

He rolled them and kissed her before she could finish that sentence. When he lifted his head, he brushed some hair from her face. "Your flaws are as beautiful as you are."

Not that the woman *had* any damn flaws. Each part of her was as perfect as the next.

The corners of her lips lifted. "We can agree to disagree."

"Luckily, I have a lifetime to convince you."

And there it was again. The small hesitation in her expression. The ghost in her eyes.

He leaned back a bit. "Hey. Are you okay?"

Her eyes widened just a fraction, but it was enough for his heart to slam against his ribs. No. Everything wasn't okay.

"Angel, if something's wrong, you need to tell me."

Fear flashed in her eyes, and it made his entire body ice.

"Hannah—"

The ringing of his phone cut off his words.

"Get it," she whispered.

"No. Tell me what's going on."

"Erik, it can wait. Answer the call."

He remained exactly where he was, waiting for the ringing to end. It did. But immediately started back up again.

Goddammit. He rolled to his side and put the phone to his ear. "What, Chandler?"

"Damn, someone woke up on the wrong side of the bed."

He took a moment to breathe through his frustration. "I'm sorry. What is it?"

"We have a location for the trafficking group, and I need to know if you want in. Rachel stayed in town for this, so she's going, but she could use a second person."

Erik ran a hand through his hair. He knew Rachel had stayed for the job. When she started something, she always saw it through. It almost became an obsession for her. "When?"

"That's the thing…it's tonight. My source says they'll be moving again tomorrow. If you say yes, I'll send the information so you can go through everything before you leave."

Something hard and uncomfortable slammed into his gut. Oden was gone, but he still didn't want Hannah out of his sight. He wasn't sure when he would.

"It's too soon, Chandler. I need to be with Hannah."

Smooth, warm hands touched his back. He turned to see Hannah beside him, shaking her head.

"I'm fine," she said quietly. "Take the job."

"Hannah—"

"It's been days. My physical health is fine. My mental health is fine. I'm not in danger. You go. I need to spend time with Brigid anyway."

He wanted to growl—because *he* was the one who wouldn't be fine. But how did he tell her that?

"So…" Chandler said softly. "You in?"

Hannah mouthed, "Go."

He *did* want to nail these assholes, and she probably knew it. He bit back a curse. "I'm in."

"Great." Chandler's typing sounded over the call. "Sending over the job details now. I'll let Rachel know."

The call ended and Hannah scooted toward the side of the bed, but before she could stand, he grabbed her wrist and tugged her back to him. "You trying to get rid of me?"

Her lips hovered over his. "If there are bad people who need to be eliminated, you should be the one to do it. After all, you're the best."

Finally, she kissed him. And fuck, he got so lost in that kiss, he turned and pulled her beneath him, forgetting every fucking thing that came before this moment.

* * *

Hannah watched through the window as Erik's Corvette pulled out of the garage. Every second that ticked by had more nerves trickling down her spine.

She stood in the living room, fingers shaking as she held on to the window frame. Even after the Corvette disappeared, she didn't move right away. Something stopped her. A fear that sat so deep in her belly it felt unmovable.

It took her several deep breaths before she could stand. Then another to head down the hall and lift the keys to her house and step outside. The wind was cold against her skin, every hair on her body standing on end. But that chill wasn't only from the weather. It was from what she was about to do.

The uneven ground crunched beneath her feet, the distant sound of birds barely reaching her ears.

It was early evening, and fortunately, Erik had spent the

entire day prepping for his job, so he hadn't asked what was bothering her again.

God, she could kick herself for not hiding it better. She should have known he'd see it all over her face. He saw everything. Certainly more than she wished he did.

Her fingers trembled as she slotted the key into her front door and slipped inside. Her small home always felt even smaller after spending so much time in Erik's house. And today, it was cold too. But again, maybe that was just her.

She toed off her shoes and moved down the hall. She didn't stop to turn on the heat. A part of her was scared that if she paused to do anything else, she might lose her courage again. She couldn't do that. She had to be strong. She had to know, one way or the other.

She slipped into her old bedroom and straight into the walk-in closet. At the open cubicles, she rose to her toes, reaching into the top one. Her finger reached beneath clothes, feeling the hard edge of the box. She pulled it down.

For a moment, she just looked at the thing.

Breathe, Hannah. Just breathe.

She forced her legs to move. Once she reached the bathroom, she tore open the box and took out the stick. With one final breath of courage, she turned toward the toilet.

Once she was done, she shoved the stick back into the packet and dropped it to the counter like it was a bomb about to detonate. So many thoughts and emotions rolled through her mind. If the test was positive, what would Erik do? She'd brought up the possibility of kids more than once…would he think she'd done this on purpose? Would he leave her? If he stayed, would he resent her *and* their child?

A panicked sob bubbled inside her. It was so consuming, she almost grabbed her chest and keeled over. Erik had become her entire world. Her heart couldn't take it if he started hating her.

She didn't think he'd leave, but then…she also didn't think he had a lot of control over the fear inside him at the prospect of being a father.

Of course, the test could always be negative.

But the thought didn't bring her peace. Instead, it made an ache cut into her heart. She pressed a hand there. The idea of not being pregnant hurt just as much. Because she wanted to be a mother. She hadn't realized how much until that option had been taken away from her.

Tears gathered in her eyes. Either way, she lost something. There was no way for her to come out of this unscathed.

When it was finally time, her fingers trembled so badly that it took her three goes to pick up the packet without dropping it, then another few tries to get the stick out. She started to turn it over, but hesitated, courage faltering.

Just do it, Hannah. Turn it over. Read the stick.

She turned it over—and her world stopped.

A wave of emotion passed through every limb, crumpling her to the floor.

Pregnant…she was pregnant with Erik's baby. A tear trickled down her cheek.

She was going to be a *mother*. She didn't know the first thing about being a mother, but God, in this moment, she wanted to give this child the world. She wanted to give it every ounce of love. Every bit of comfort and safety that she'd been denied as a child.

She pressed a hand to her belly, taking a deep breath. "We're going to be okay."

There were moments in her life when she'd wondered how she'd survive to the next day. But this wasn't one of them. There was no doubt, only determination. She would be okay for her baby.

With shaking fingers, she pulled her phone from her jeans pocket.

Hannah: Brigid…I need you.

She watched the screen like it was a lifeline. Like it was the only thing keeping her here and whole. The three dots popped up.

Brigid: I'm home. Come over.

$\mathcal{E}$rik moved quickly and quietly around the side of the nightclub. The club itself was closed tonight, so there wasn't a soul in sight, but that didn't mean the place was empty. Conversely, he knew one section of the club was full of the scum of the Earth…the basement. They'd already done a quick check of the club itself via its own indoor security cameras, confirming the place was empty.

"I'm on the east side of the building," Rachel said through the earpiece. "All clear."

"West side." Erik pulled a gun from his holster. He had another on his other side, as well as knives strapped to his legs. "All clear here too."

Chandler's voice sounded next. "Good. Remember, I have no cameras down there, so you'll be going in blind. But I've hacked the FBI system, which tells me their guy is there."

The agent had been undercover for a while, still failing to get the evidence necessary to shut down the organization. That told Erik the man wasn't fully trusted, wasn't privy to the ring's secrets.

Hence he and Rachel were here. Official channels took too damn long.

Miles Moreno was the new leader of the organization. Back when Erik had shot Nico, and other members were taken out by additional contract players, Moreno had been a low-level grunt. Not anymore. He was their first priority. There were six other men in his inner circle. They also needed to die tonight. But of course, there'd be security to get through as well.

Rachel cleared her throat. "Once you've finished whatever meditation calming ritual you're doing over there, Hunter, I'm ready to go."

Erik's lips twitched. "I was waiting on you. Ladies first. But if you're scared and need me to lead—"

Rachel scoffed. "Pull up your panties and let's go."

Erik shook his head. He'd done a few jobs with Rachel when he'd first started this work. He'd almost forgotten how much she made him smile, even in situations where smiling should be the last thing he did.

He strode boldly around the corner, gun at the ready, spotting three security guys by the door.

Their heads swiveled toward Erik, but before they could reach for weapons, he shot two men in the temple while Rachel took out the third. The silencers on their guns meant no one else was alerted.

He continued forward. All signs of humor were gone from Rachel's face, but that didn't surprise him. She could joke one second and be as deadly as they came the next. When it was go-time, she was ready. And you wanted her on your side...always.

"Just disabled the cameras at the entrance," Chandler said. "Good luck."

Erik and Rachel moved inside, making quick work of confirming the place was empty, then down the stairs to the basement. Without pause, they fired at the knob on a sturdy-looking door before Erik kicked it open. The second they were inside, men fell off chairs, some dropping glasses of whiskey, all of them reaching for weapons.

Erik didn't give them the chance. Just like with the security outside, he shot three men before they could so much as touch their guns, and another just as he'd wrapped his fingers around his pistol. Rachel was even better—five kill shots to the forehead in a matter of seconds.

Then there was stillness, everyone in the room on the floor. But Erik and Rachel didn't pause. They kept their weapons drawn as they moved down the hall to the left.

"Nine dead," Rachel said under her breath so Chandler could hear. "Miles Moreno and three of his guys missing."

Erik stopped at a closed door in the hall, while Rachel went to another. They moved at the same time. Erik fired at the first door handle before pushing into the room, then cursed at what he saw inside.

Women. Four of them. All looking terrified, probably because they knew they were on the verge of being sold.

Fuck. He wanted to go back and kill the assholes a second time, drawing their deaths out.

"You're safe," he said as softly as he could manage. "The assholes are dead and help is coming." He turned back to the hall, speaking quietly into the earpiece. "I have four women who need assistance."

Rachel stepped out of her empty room, her gaze moving to the women, fury in her eyes before she glanced up at him. "Let's keep going."

There were two more doors. A part of him hoped the remaining assholes were inside, but another part knew they weren't. They would have heard their men shouting, falling to the floor—and come out to do something about it, guns blazing.

Still, Erik moved forward and shouldered the door.

Another empty room. He turned to see Rachel's was the same. He cursed. "They're not here, Chandler."

"Shit! The agent told his team everyone would be in tonight."

"Well, they aren't," Rachel said through gritted teeth. "Find them. I want them dead. *All* of them."

* * *

HANNAH KEYED in the code for Brigid's apartment building before stepping inside. The foyer was warm, but it did nothing to heat her skin. She would have called Henry over too—God knows, she needed all the support she could get—but she couldn't dump this on him. He was still recovering from what had happened with Owen.

She jogged up the stairs, toward Brigid's apartment on the top floor. The building wasn't old, but it wasn't new. The elevator worked just fine, but she needed to work off some of her nervous energy.

A part of her felt guilty for telling Brigid before she told Erik, but she needed someone to assure her this would all be okay. Promise her that she'd get through this—with or without Erik.

When she reached the fourth floor, it was an effort to walk and not run. She wanted to spill her news as quickly as possible. In her head, she told herself to chill, to tell her friend calmly…but could she?

Probably not.

She knocked on Brigid's door. As she waited, she began to run her finger over the angel charm that Erik himself had put back on her bracelet. It went a little way toward calming her, but not nearly enough.

When Brigid didn't answer, she frowned and was about to knock again, but at the last second, she tried the door handle instead. Unlocked.

That was odd. Brigid rarely left her door unlocked. If anything, she was ridiculously paranoid, always claiming her nosy neighbors might just barge in if she didn't keep them locked out.

She stepped inside, immediately noticing how cold it was. God, why was it freezing in here? And not only that, it was dark. Why were all the lights off? Was she not home?

She closed the door quietly and flicked the light switch on the wall. She took two slow steps into the room…when suddenly a bare foot behind the couch came into view.

A loud gasp tore from her chest. Her purse slipped from her fingers, and she ran toward her friend, dropping to the floor beside her.

Oh Jesus…there was so much blood pooled around her head!

"Brigid?" She wanted to touch her, but what if she hurt her worse? "Brigid, can you hear me?"

She didn't even stir.

With shaking hands, Hannah felt for a pulse. It was there. Faint, but there.

Paramedics. She needed to call the paramedics and get help for her friend!

She rose and rushed toward her bag but stopped at a noise behind her. A figure stepped out of the bedroom. Her breath caught in her throat, blood roaring between her ears.

No…it couldn't be.

"Hello, Hannah."

James's deep voice turned her blood to ice. He had a gun in his hand pointed directly at her chest.

She shook her head, stumbling back a step. "*No.* You're supposed to be in jail for attempted murder."

"Bail."

Bail? Who the hell would give an attempted murderer *bail*? Her vision almost blackened at the sheer irony that two men who'd wanted to hurt her, years apart, had both managed to get bail.

"But you don't have money," she finally whispered.

"You're right. I don't. But someone came to visit me…several times. And I told her how much it would mean to me if she helped me get out." His gaze shifted to Brigid, and Hannah's heart stopped.

No. She wouldn't have.

Brigid's drunk rambling came back to her…about doing something stupid. When Hannah had pushed about it the next day, her friend had refused to tell her what it was.

This…*this* was the stupid thing.

"She did," James said, as if reading her thoughts. "I've thought long and hard about how to make you pay for what you did to me. You *destroyed* my life!"

"No, James, *you* destroyed it. By getting into drugs. By stealing something that wasn't yours."

"It all would have worked out if you hadn't ruined everything."

"James—"

"You can't talk your way out of this one, Hannah." He took a step forward, the gun never wavering.

"The police will find you and arrest you again."

"I'm not going back there. I'm not wasting my life rotting in a goddamn cell."

"How will you disappear without money?" Hannah whispered. "If Brigid bailed you out, she can't have much left."

The smile that crept across his face made bile crawl up her throat. "That's where you come in. This is kind of a two-birds-with-one-stone thing. I get money so I can disappear. And I get my revenge on you at the same time."

Her breath stuttered. "How?"

"I've made some new…connections. There are people who are willing to pay a pretty penny for a woman who looks like you."

Her skin became clammy, little black dots dancing in her vision. "No…"

"If you scream or call for help, I shoot Brigid. Got it?"

Hannah had to remind herself to breathe. To suck in one shallow breath after the next.

James pulled a phone from his pocket, then hit something on the screen before pressing it to his ear. "I've got her."

Hannah scrambled for a way out of this. She couldn't do anything in here, not when James clearly had no problem shooting Brigid. But when they left, she could fight. She *would* fight. She'd do whatever was necessary to get away.

James hung up, an evil smile playing on his face. "They're in the alley behind the building, ready to pick you up." He reached into a huge black bag by the door and pulled out masking tape. "Now, I'm gonna tape your mouth, hands, and feet—and carry you out of the building in that bag."

"No!" The word was out of her mouth before she could stop it.

"Yes. And remember, make a sound and I kill her."

"You're a monster."

"Maybe." He grinned again. "She was so excited to have me back…as if I'd completely forget that she helped you set me up," James said, walking toward her. "But then I guess she saw the red flags. I stole some of her money. Got a bit angry once or twice and may have hit her."

Fury raced through Hannah's veins. "That was you?"

"Yep. She kicked me out after that. Changed the locks. It was naive of her to think I wouldn't be back. She was part of my downfall, so it's only fair she helps me rise again."

The asshole! God, she wished she had a gun right now.

He cocked his head, his expression almost one of excitement. "You should have seen the fear on her face when she found me in her apartment today."

"Did you *ever* love her?" Hannah whispered, terrified for her friend.

"When you've been through what I have, you learn there are things a lot stronger than love. Like survival instincts. When it comes down to it, we all do whatever it takes to survive. Now, masking tape? Or should I knock you out?"

"James—"

He lunged, grabbing her and spinning her around.

She fought him, hitting and kicking, struggling with everything she had, but he was too big. With one hand, he grabbed her wrists as his mouth went to her ear. "Stop or I kill her."

Her gaze fell on Brigid… God, she was so still.

Rage raced through her blood as James pulled tape across her lips. As he bound her wrists, she fisted her hands, making her wrists as thick as possible, hoping it would help her get out later.

When he shoved her to the couch and got to work on her ankles, something stabbed the back of her thigh. She eased her hand under her…it felt like one of Brigid's bobby pins. Quickly, she snatched it into her palm just before James yanked her up.

"Let's go."

CHAPTER 34

"This doesn't feel right," Erik said quietly from behind the wheel.

They were almost back in Redwood, but no part of him had wanted to leave Seattle. Chandler had organized for the women to go into protective custody, but that wasn't enough. They weren't safe until these assholes were gone.

"I feel it too, my friend," Rachel said quietly from the passenger seat. She'd been silent on this drive, which was nothing like her.

They were leaving their job unfinished. It felt wrong.

"You know what this means though, right?" Rachel's lips twitched. "That you won't be rid of me just yet."

"So you're staying?"

"Hell yes, I'm staying. These assholes deserve a special place in hell, and *I* intend to make sure they get there. Especially this asshole Moreno."

There was that don't-mess-with-me best friend of his. "Chandler will find them. He's never let me down before."

"Even if it takes him a while…I don't mind. I've been getting a bit bored of Arkansas."

He chuckled. "No one gets bored of Arkansas."

She lifted a shoulder. "You know me. Not much can keep me occupied for long."

Yeah, he knew that.

"I came here for *you*," she continued quietly. "To make sure you were okay after your dad's fall. When you told me what happened, I was worried. But what I found was even more shocking."

He scowled. "What?"

"You're not okay, Erik. You're so much fucking *better* than that. I'm happy that you've found Hannah."

"She's my world, Rach. Before her, I was barely surviving. Trying to live within the fucking prison that I called my life. But she's made me want more. She's made me believe I *deserve* more."

Rachel gripped his arm. "Erik…that's beautiful. Tell her every day how important she is. Don't let her slip away."

"Every damn day."

He'd just crossed over the border into Redwood when his phone rang. He used the car Bluetooth to answer. "Chandler, you find anything?"

"The agent just reported to his supervisor that they're making a last-minute pickup tonight. That's why they weren't at the club. They just reached the location."

Erik's knuckles whitened on the wheel. Pickup meaning they were grabbing a damn woman. "We're back in Redwood. Even if we drove to the location now, we wouldn't—"

"They're *in* Redwood."

Rachel was already reaching into her bag for weapons.

"Where?" Erik asked through gritted teeth.

"Waiting in an alley at the back of an apartment building. Twelve Brentwoode Drive."

Erik actually flinched, which caused Rachel to look up from her task of reloading a gun. "What? You know the place?"

"Are you certain he's there?" Erik growled.

"Yes, why?"

"That's behind where Hannah's best friend lives—and she mentioned possibly visiting her tonight."

He pressed his foot harder on the gas. It might be nothing. But something in his gut told him to get there fast.

"I'll call her," Rachel said, pulling her phone out and putting it on speaker.

It went to voice mail. *Fuck.*

"I need to try her number, Chandler." He ended that call and tried dialing Hannah on his own cell. When she didn't answer, he cursed and tried her again. Then he tried Brigid's number. Same fucking thing.

He slammed a fist against the wheel, ignoring every fucking traffic law as he sped toward the location, praying that his gut was wrong and Hannah had nothing to do with this.

* * *

CLAUSTROPHOBIA CRAWLED over Hannah's body, making her brain foggy and her limbs shake. Darkness. It surrounded her. There was no space to move, barely any air to breathe. And the tape around her mouth just made everything worse.

James had shoved her into a gym bag, then swung her over his shoulder. She closed her eyes and breathed through her nose, forcing herself to stay calm. She'd been in bad situations before, and she'd gotten out of them. She could do it again.

Opening her eyes, she tugged at her wrists. The tape was a tiny bit loose, thanks to her making her wrists as big as possible when James had bound her. And she still had the bobby pin in her palm.

First, she attempted to use the bobby pin to prick the tape, but it was too awkward. Then she started to tug at her wrists. She twisted them back and forth, feeling the burn of her skin, the pulling and yanking on her arms.

Almost…there…

When one hand finally pulled out, the relief was so swift, her heart thumped hard in her chest. Quickly, she reached up and tore the tape from her mouth, finally sucking in a deep breath.

The ankles were the hardest part. She had to separate her thighs as much as possible and reach between them for her ankles.

Suddenly, she slammed into something hard. Her head rebounded off some kind of surface, shooting pain through her skull.

"Stop fucking moving," James growled. "Or I'll slam you against the wall so hard next time, I'll knock you out."

Her body bounced as James moved down the stairs, aggravating the pain in her skull. She took one deep breath to ward off the dizziness, then tore off the last of the tape.

If the asshole thought she was going to go down without a fight, he was dead wrong.

The second her feet were free, she pulled the rubber off the pin and shoved one end through the bottom of the bag, piercing the material.

She did it again and again, all in the same area, until she could push a finger through. She tugged at the hole, making it a bit bigger. The larger the hole grew, the easier it was to tug apart.

She forced herself to go as slow as possible, not wanting the sounds to alert James to what she was doing. The hole was just big enough for her hand to fit through when she saw the ground beneath the bag shift from stairs to flat flooring.

She'd lost track of the stories. Was there another set of stairs or—

The creak of a door sounded, then cool air came up through the hole in the bag.

Shit. They were outside.

She didn't try to silence herself anymore. She pulled at the bag with one huge, frantic tug, tearing the hole until it was large enough to fall right through. She hit the ground at James's feet.

"What the fuck?" His words were loud and angry.

He lunged for her, but she kicked him in the shin, hard enough that he cried out and hunched over, grabbing at his leg.

She jumped to her feet and raced back toward the building, realizing they'd exited through the doors facing the apartment parking lot on the west side. She barely got the code punched in before she was falling through one of the doors, into the hall.

James would have the code as well.

Spying a broom beside the door, she slipped it through the handles. It wouldn't keep him out for long—the wood was thin and old—but it might buy her enough time to find help.

She spared one glance over her shoulder to see James through the window, running toward the door, before she turned and ran. Instead of heading up the stairs, she ran down the hall and banged on the first door she came across.

"Help!" she screamed. Her fists hit the door so hard that her hands ached.

No one answered.

She moved to the next one. Same thing.

Shit.

Panic crawled in her belly, but she kept banging on wood and frantically turning knobs. Was *no one* in the damn building home?

It was at the fourth door when she turned the handle—and it opened. Just as James stepped into the hall. She gasped and entered the apartment, then turned the lock.

Would he shoot at the door? Surely not. It would alert other residents, probably cause a few people to call the police. But it would also be the fastest way to gain entry. She turned and sprinted to the small kitchen to the left. The apartment was a mess, with dirty dishes all over the place, but there was a knife block on the counter. She pulled out the biggest knife before returning to stand beside the door.

If he came in, she'd stab him. The idea made her stomach rebel, but what other choice did she have? She couldn't let him take her.

A shudder rolled down her spine.

The door handle jiggled, and Hannah lifted the knife. It kept moving for another two seconds before stopping.

She froze. Was he going to shoot now?

Second after second ticked by.

Nothing. Nothing but utter silence.

Was it possible he was leaving? She almost didn't want to hope in case it wasn't true.

Slowly, she inched forward, trying to keep her body away from the dead bolt on the chance it was met with a bullet.

Rising to her toes, she peeked out into the hall through the peephole.

It was empty. He was gone.

Hope rattled her heart. All she wanted to do was run out of this apartment and upstairs to help Brigid. But that would be a risk. There was every chance he was waiting for her to do just that.

Instead, she ran toward the kitchen counter, pushing and shoving through the mess.

Phone...she needed a phone. A landline. A cell someone left on the counter. Anything to call for help. Brigid needed an ambulance, and she needed the police and Erik.

Oh God, Erik... He'd lose his mind.

When she found nothing, she checked the first bedroom, her gaze shifting over the drawers, then the side tables. Still no phone.

She moved out of the bedroom and into a small home office. That's when she saw it—a landline.

She'd just taken a step toward it when a high-pitched squealing sound came from the living room. Tentatively, she peeked out to see James had shoved open the ground-floor window—and was already halfway through.

Her heart stopped, and for a moment, she considered sprinting across the room to the front door, but it was too late. He was in. And he had a gun.

She slammed the office door closed and slipped the lock before grabbing the phone.

"Nine-one-one, what's your emergency?"

"There's a man trying to hurt me! I need police assistance *now*. And my friend's in another apartment. She needs an ambulance!" Hannah quickly rattled off the address of the building as a body hit the door—hard. She cried out and dropped the phone.

James rammed the door again, and her breath stopped. The cheapy, flimsy lock wouldn't hold. He was going to get in.

With a straightening of her spine, Hannah lifted the knife.

The lock broke, then James was in front of her, less than an arm's length away.

His chest moved up and down with his fast breaths, his face contorted in anger. "You fucking bitch! You think you can get away from me again?"

"I *know* I can." Her voice was firm this time, any tremble gone. "And I'm going to make sure you go back to jail and stay there for the rest of your worthless life."

Anger reddened his cheeks. "I should just fucking kill you."

She swallowed, trying not to focus on the gun pointed at her. "But then how would you get your money?"

He stepped forward, looking angrier than she'd ever seen him. "Put down the knife, Hannah."

"No."

He lunged—and she swung the knife, slashing at his chest.

He growled as blood bloomed across his shirt, but he didn't stop, grabbing her wrist and sending them both to the floor. Her head hit the corner of the desk on the way down, pain shooting through her skull and her vision blurring.

It was enough to give him the upper hand. He took the knife

from her fingers and pressed it to her throat. "Now, this is what's going to happen. We're going to go meet my friends, and you're not gonna make a fucking sound. Because if I feel threatened in any way, I *will* just fucking kill you and run."

The car had barely stopped before Erik was out and running toward the side of the building.

"Erik. *Fuck*. Wait!"

He ignored Rachel's call and kept moving. He was almost around the corner when fingers wrapped tightly around his arm, yanking him back.

"*Stop*," Rachel growled. "You're gonna get a bullet to the fucking head. We have to be smart and work together."

"I need to know she's safe!"

"Yeah. But if she isn't, if they have her, she needs you to be *alive* to get her out. Understand?" When he didn't answer, she rolled her eyes. "We need to enter the alley together and cover each other's asses."

He took a deep breath. "Fine. But we go *now*."

They moved quickly and quietly along the side of the building, toward the alley. Erik's muscles twitched with the need to move faster. To kill every asshole involved. They'd seen an image of the undercover FBI agent. He was the only man who wouldn't die tonight.

When they reached the alley, Rachel held up her hand to signal that she was ready.

The second she dropped it, they both swung around the corner, briefly taking in the handful of men who stood several yards away before firing.

The agent immediately dropped to the ground, making him easy to miss.

A man in black lifted his weapon, but Erik fired first, getting him between the eyes.

It wasn't until every man was down, bar the agent, that Erik's heart slowed. Hannah wasn't here.

But neither was Moreno.

Erik moved forward as the agent rose to his feet. "We're government contractors. Not a threat. Where's the woman they were picking up?"

"I don't know. A guy was supposed to bring her, but he hasn't arrived. They were supposed to be here ten minutes ago. He even called to confirm he was coming down."

Erik's muscles tightened. "So you're telling me there's some asshole with a hostage somewhere?"

The agent squirmed. "Most likely. From what I was told, he's out on bail for attempted murder. Probably wants the money to disappear."

Erik's eyes narrowed. Out on bail for attempted murder? "Who is he?"

"I just got a first name. James."

The name hit like a physical blow. The same James who'd framed Hannah a few months ago? The same James who'd then tried to *murder* her?

"Do you know the name of the girl?" Erik asked through gritted teeth.

"Hannah."

Ice filled his veins. He turned and ran back around the building, feet pounding against the pavement. He ignored the calls from Rachel and the agent. Nothing would stop him now.

When he got to the side door, he keyed in the code, still remembering it from the day he'd brought Hannah to see Brigid. He was about to race to the stairwell when voices sounded from down the hall. He turned to see several people standing around a door, looking nervous.

Erik ran down the hall. "What's going on?"

An older guy answered. "This woman was running down the hall, banging on doors and screaming for help. We think she's in Terry's apartment. He isn't home and tends to leave his door unlocked. We just heard some noise in the room."

Erik shoved through the neighbors to the door. He tried the handle, not surprised to find it locked. Quickly, he aimed a boot right beneath the door knob and broke it open.

The crowd gasped, but he ignored them. His gaze whipped around the small space until he heard the rustle of movement. He crossed the apartment to the doorway of an office.

The scene in front of him made his blood boil.

James, on his feet, holding Hannah against him with a knife to her neck. The guy's hair was shorter, but other than that, he looked like the same scumbag Erik remembered.

Erik's gun was at the ready as he scanned Hannah's face, silently thanking God that she was alive. He shifted his attention to James. "Let her go. You're done."

"What the fuck are *you* doing here?" he seethed.

"You know those assholes you were planning on selling her to? They're dead. The deal's off."

Moreno wasn't, but that was a detail Erik wouldn't be sharing.

"No…" Real panic widened the guy's eyes. "No! They can't be! They're my fucking ticket out of here!"

"Not anymore." He took a small step forward. "Put the knife down, James."

His eyes were wild, filled with pure rage and panic. "No!"

James's knuckles whitened on the knife, his grip tightening.

And Erik didn't hesitate.

He fired, sending a bullet through James's head, ending him as quickly as he'd ended Oden.

The man dropped, and Erik lunged forward to catch Hannah before she could hit the floor.

"Erik!" She grabbed his shirt, burying her face against him. "You're here! I can't believe you're here!"

He held her so tightly he was scared he'd cut off her air. But he couldn't release her. "Tell me you're okay, Angel."

"I'm okay! My head hurts, but I'm okay." She looked up, tears in her eyes. "Brigid bailed him out of jail. We need to check on her! He hit her and she wasn't moving."

Sirens wailed in the distance. When footsteps sounded behind him, he turned to see Rachel. She stopped and blew out a long breath when she saw them together.

He turned back to Hannah, taking his first easy breath since the agent spoke her name.

CHAPTER 36

"*E*rik, I'm *fine*." Hannah smoothed her hands down his chest, wishing he wasn't so tense. "I spent the entire night here with doctors and nurses keeping an eye on me. They've confirmed multiple times that I'm okay."

Erik's eyes narrowed. "You could probably be bleeding out and still tell everyone you're okay. Does your head hurt?"

She rolled her eyes, although he wasn't far off the truth. She'd needed a few stitches in her head, and she would have fought to go home last night if Erik hadn't looked so on edge. "My head's fine. I have a dull ache, but that's all. Now, I need to go find out which room Brigid's in."

"You need to wait for your discharge papers."

Oh, this man…he was wonderful, but sometimes just a tad overbearing. He'd stayed with her all night and had barely let her out of bed, insisting he get her everything she needed. He'd also carried her to the bathroom every time she needed to go.

There'd been just one time he'd left her room last night to go down and get a coffee, and in those few minutes, she'd quickly beeped the nurse to ask for a blood test to confirm that she was pregnant. She'd told her she didn't want anyone else knowing, so of course she'd yet to get the results because Erik never left her side again.

Yes, the home pregnancy test had been positive, but she needed to hear the words from a nurse or a doctor.

Her smile wobbled, and Erik noticed immediately. "You're in pain."

"No," she replied. "Look, why don't you go get a coffee while I change into my clothes."

"Hannah—"

"Please, Erik? You need caffeine so you're not a grouch, and I need a second to breathe."

Some of the hardness in his eyes softened. "Fine. But call if you need—"

"Anything. I know."

He lowered his head and kissed her, and she felt that kiss everywhere. In her skin, her bones. Deep in her chest.

Seconds after he left, she pressed the call button. This was her only chance to talk to someone alone. She wasn't sure *why* she needed that blood test confirmation so much. Maybe to confirm that she really had seen those lines on the home test. Maybe because hearing the words out of a medical professional's mouth would make it more real.

When the door opened, she looked up, expecting to see the nurse. Instead, Brigid stepped in wearing jeans and a sweater, Henry behind her. She had a bandage around her head, but other than that, she looked okay.

Tears immediately gathered in Brigid's eyes, threatening to spill over as she stopped beside the bed. "I am so sorry, Han."

She pulled the woman into her arms. "You made a mistake."

Brigid dug her head into Hannah's neck. "A huge, could-have-cost-both-of-us-our-lives mistake."

Sobs began to rattle her friend's chest, and Hannah held her tighter, trying to keep her friend in one piece. "James is the mistake you were talking about at Andi's party, wasn't he?"

Brigid pulled back, cheeks wet, face red. "Yes. I don't know why it was so hard to let him go," she said, her voice small. "I just felt…hollow without him, and I wanted the pain to end! So I went to visit him in prison a couple of times, hoping it would give me closure. And he was like the old James. He said he loved me, and he made me feel *whole* again. He kept telling me how sorry he was. How much he regretted what he'd done. He told me if I bailed him out, we could have some time together, begin to mend things before he went to prison."

She shook her head. "I was such an idiot. I fell for his act because I desperately *wanted* it to be true. I wanted him to be the same man I fell in love with."

"I know all about heartache," Hannah told her. "I know how much it can affect every decision."

Henry wrapped an arm around her shoulders. "We'll all get through this. Because we have each other."

"You're both too good to me." Brigid sniffed. "I hate myself for what I did, for what could have happened."

"Don't," Hannah pressed. She tilted her head. "What *did* happen between you two after he got out?"

Brigid sucked in a long breath as she looked down at her hands. "I had this pit in my belly the whole time. It was like the second he was out, I knew I'd made a mistake, but it was too late. I couldn't stop thinking about what he'd done to you. About the reasons why he was in jail. Then I caught him stealing my bank card. We had a huge fight, and I told him to get the hell out. That's when he hit me."

Henry growled, while Hannah clenched her friend's forearm. "I'm sorry."

She lifted a shoulder. "I got back that night after work, and his things were gone. I figured he'd found somewhere to live until he was due back in court. Then, last night, I got home and he was there with a gun. He asked for my phone. When I refused, he hit me with the butt of the gun and…and that's the last thing I remember."

Henry scowled. "I almost wish he was alive so I could murder him myself."

"Me too," Brigid said quietly, looking back to Hannah. "I was so scared you'd never forgive me."

"I love you," Hannah whispered, wiping a tear from her face. "Of course I forgive you."

Brigid leaned into Hannah's shoulder. "Thank you."

Hannah shifted her gaze to Henry. "How are you doing after the Owen-Oden nightmare?"

"Okay, actually."

Brigid frowned. "Why do you have your I-did-something-dirty look on your face?"

He laughed. "Not dirty, *per se*, but I was texting that guy I like last night, and he may have come over to…console me."

"You're shitting me?" Brigid gasped.

"Nope."

Hannah's brows shot up. "Do we finally get a name for this secret man?"

"Leo."

Hannah almost choked on her tongue. "Leo, as in—"

"Leo, who you work with. Yeah, him."

Brigid straightened. "I didn't know—"

"He was into hot, ruggedly handsome men like me? I know. Luckily, I did."

Hannah reached out and squeezed his hand. "I am so freaking happy for you. Leo's an amazing person."

"Yeah, well, I'm just hoping he's not secretly a psychopath."

Hannah swallowed. "Yeah, we've had enough of them to last us a lifetime."

"Miss Jacobs?"

They all looked up to see a doctor stepping into the room.

Brigid rose. "That's our cue to leave." She gave Hannah one more hug, and Henry did the same.

When the doctor closed the door after them, her pulse sped up.

"Just tell me," she whispered.

He nodded. "You're pregnant. About seven weeks."

The breath that slipped out of her lungs seemed to leave her in slow motion. Her second confirmation, and still, it didn't feel real.

The doctor pushed his glasses up his nose. "You may have a good endocrinologist, but you might want to switch to one who specializes in pregnancy. We have one here at the hospital if you'd like a referral. Women with type 1 can have a healthy and safe pregnancy, but it's important to monitor things like blood pressure, vision, and kidneys."

The doctor kept talking, but Hannah barely heard a word. She wanted to be happy. She wanted to cry tears of joy. But one question kept rolling around in her head—in gaining a child, would she lose the man she loved?

The ring sat in Erik's palm, the afternoon light reflecting off the diamonds. It was perfect. The slim band, the oval-cut white diamond.

All he wanted to do was get it on her finger now. Today. But Hannah deserved the moment to be special. She deserved candles and romance and magic. And damn, he wanted to give that to her.

At the sound of footsteps on the stairs, he dropped the ring into his pocket and turned to see Hannah stepping into the kitchen.

Her eyes immediately closed, a groan slipping from her lips. "Mm, something smells amazing." She moved straight over, rose to her toes, and kissed him. "Are you making me dinner, Mr. Hunter?"

"Chicken cordon bleu skillet."

She sighed. "Don't tease me. Really?"

"I would never tease." He nipped her lip before lifting a glass of red wine and passing it to her.

For a moment, she hesitated, some emotion he couldn't identify flashing across her face, but then she slipped the glass from his fingers. "I shouldn't. I need to drop some keys to my safe at work before dinner."

His brows flickered. "Is that all?"

She nodded quickly. Too quickly? "Yeah. And I'm also tired." She set the wine on the counter. "How are you feeling about Rachel leaving this weekend?"

He lifted a shoulder. "She'll be back soon, so I don't mind."

The woman had given them notice that she was moving to Redwood…for a while, at least. She certainly wasn't leaving until they located Moreno and ended him.

Erik wasn't dumb enough to assume she'd be here long-term. She had too much of a restless soul to stay in one place for long. But having her here, even just for a couple months, would be nice. "Are you okay with her being here?"

"Of course. I *do* like her, Erik. And she's been so great since everything happened. We had lunch together the other day, and she was pretty protective of me the entire time."

That was the Rachel he knew. A badass on the outside, but a softie at heart. "Everything at work okay?"

"Yeah. With Leo and Henry dating, I've been seeing a lot more of Henry at the office, which is nice."

He stirred the pasta. "So, the problem isn't work. It's not Rachel. Is it money or your diabetes?"

She swallowed, looking nervous.

Yeah, something was definitely going on.

Her chest rose on a deep inhale. Then she looked at him—and *now* she seemed almost scared. "I'd like to talk to you again about us having kids."

The panic was instant. It seized his chest, catapulting his heart into a dangerously fast rhythm. Because all he could think about was the past. The loss.

He had so many fucking memories of Vicky's pregnancy. Her

beautiful round stomach. The appointments. Seeing sonograms and hearing the heartbeat. Fuck, he could still hear that heartbeat in his head…and he'd sworn to protect them.

Their deaths had nearly killed him.

"I'm not open to talking about that, Hannah. I'm sorry, but you know where I stand on the matter."

"What happened to Vicky was a tragedy. And I'm so sorry for what you lost. But it won't be the same with us."

His heart tore in two. What had happened was worse than a tragedy. It was a nightmare he still couldn't wake up from some days. A devastation that repeated in his head more often than Hannah knew. And the idea of *her* stomach swelling with his child, then something happening… It made a fear like nothing he'd ever felt seize everything in him. Choke him.

"I can't."

Hannah took a small step forward. "I know you're still healing. But eventually, you need to *live*. Creating a family together doesn't have to be painful. It can be so many wonderful things. Beautiful and peaceful, bringing so much love to our world—"

"Hannah, stop!"

She flinched, and he instantly regretted the hardness in his voice.

He tried to force his tone to gentle. "I'm sorry. So fucking sorry that I actually hate myself for saying this…but I will *never* want to father another child. And I will *never* change my mind. I can't be a father, Hannah. We will not be having kids. Ever."

Tears gathered in her eyes, but she blinked them away. "You can't just make that call for us."

Yeah, he knew he was a selfish bastard. "It's already done."

"What if I said what you're *already* saying, just without the words? What if I said it's us *and* kids…or there's no us at all?"

The panic inside him turned wild. "Don't do this, Hannah."

If she did…if she told him to choose, it would be an impossible choice.

Hurt whispered across her face, her hand pressing to her stomach as she said quietly, "I want to be a mother."

"I *can't* be a father."

The tears finally fell from her beautiful blue eyes. He took a step toward her, but she stepped away.

"I need to go to work and drop off those keys. Then I need time to think."

Instant fear. It damn near crippled him. "About us?"

"About everything."

"Hannah—"

He reached for her, but again she stepped back. "I have to go, Erik."

When she turned and walked toward the door, it took everything in him not to call her back. Not to chase after her and beg her to stay.

Because what could he say?

Nothing would change his mind on this. Vicky had been six months pregnant when she'd been killed. He'd never been able to hold their child in his arms. Hear them laugh or cry.

When his phone rang, he almost let it go to voice mail. But it was Chandler.

"What?" Erik rasped, the air almost nonexistent in his lungs.

"I found something on Nicholas Spalder. It's big."

* * *

HANNAH SCRUBBED the tears from her eyes as she ran to her old Honda, which Erik had repaired—again. Pain lanced her chest, cutting so deeply she wanted to drop to her knees and wrap her arms around herself. Stem the blood that felt like it was flowing out of her.

She slid into her car and started the engine, then went down the long drive and out onto the road.

I will never want to father another child. And I will never change my mind.

Every one of his words had hit harder than the last. Never... he'd *never* want to be a father. What did that mean for them? What did it mean for the baby growing in her stomach?

Her breaths became shorter and faster as she hyperventilated, air barely making it to her lungs. She took a left, driving aimlessly, forgetting all about her office.

She hadn't been behind the wheel for long when a car came up behind her. It got so close, so fast, that she instantly slowed down so they could pass her. But they didn't.

The high beams flashed on, blinding her.

She cursed and tilted her rearview mirror away, but the light was still hitting her from the side mirrors.

She pressed her foot harder to the gas, speeding up. What the hell were they doing?

When they continued to tail her closely, their lights blinding her, her heart began to pound, sweat beading her forehead. God, what could *possibly* be happening to her now? And why the hell hadn't she taken the G70? It was faster and took the turns better.

She was slowing down for a stop sign when the car suddenly hit her, sending her vehicle into a skid. She barely got it under control.

Her fingers tightened on the wheel, fear overtaking her mind.

From the side mirrors, she noticed a second vehicle closing in on the car behind her. Were they together?

She blew through the stop sign and sped up, but this time the car behind her didn't give chase. Were they leaving her alone? Was she safe?

She slowed again, deciding to take the next turn, hoping they wouldn't follow.

The car suddenly accelerated, smashing into her Honda so hard there was no regaining control. She cried out, her tires squealing.

The car sped away. She vaguely noted the second vehicle stopping on the road as her Honda spun in a circle before smashing into a tree.

Her entire body flew forward, the seat belt cutting into her chest. Her knee hit something below the wheel and her head collided with the side window, causing her vision to darken.

Then, there was stillness.

Everything hurt. Her chest. Her knee. And her head ached with such intensity that she didn't want to open her eyes. She peeled one open anyway—only to see a wisp of flame dancing from beneath the hood.

She had to get out!

Even though the words screamed in her head, she couldn't move. Could barely breathe.

Darkness tried to close in on her again, slipping through her vision, tugging her eyes closed. She was seconds from fainting when she heard the sound of breaking glass. A hand reached across her body, sliding the seat belt off.

Was this the person who'd been driving the car behind the one that hit her?

She cried out as strong arms maneuvered her out the window, every pain in her body screaming to life...but then...a scent cut through the pain.

It was familiar. So strangely familiar.

She forced her eyes open. The man was a blur.

She blinked once. Twice. But he was just lines...lines that she couldn't pull together to form a person.

He lay her on the ground several yards from her car, and she whimpered again. Then a voice—one that she still heard in her dreams. One she'd recognize *anywhere*.

"You're safe, Cloud."

Nico.

Order the final book in the Beautiful Pieces trilogy, ERIK'S REFUGE, now!

Declan

Cole

Ryker

BEAUTIFUL PIECES

Erik's Salvation

Erik's Redemption

Erik's Refuge

SHORT CHRISTMAS STORY

Hidden Shadows

RECKLESS SERIES

(series ongoing)

Reckless Hope

Reckless Trust

JOIN my newsletter and be the first to find out about sales and new releases!

~https://www.nyssakathryn.com/vip-newsletter~

ABOUT THE AUTHOR

Nyssa Kathryn is a romantic suspense author. She lives in South Australia with her daughter and hubby and takes every chance she can to be plotting and writing. Always an avid reader of romance novels, she considers alpha males and happily-ever-afters to be her jam.

Don't forget to follow Nyssa and never miss another release.

Facebook | Instagram | Amazon | Goodreads